THE CASTLE ON WASSAW SOUND

THE SAINTS OF SAVANNAH SERIES

LEIGH EBBERWEIN

Old Fort Press
Savannah, Georgia

The Castle on Wassaw Sound

Copyright © 2023 by Leigh Ebberwein

Library of Congress Control Number: 2023904881

ISBN: 978-1-7376152-5-5 (Paperback)

ISBN: 978-1-7376152-6-2 (E-book)

CONTENTS

1

—————

FOUNDATIONS

"A foundation made of sand can never be built upon." That sentence still haunted Stephanie. The last words from a mother's mouth are never forgotten, even if her leaving had been by choice. It was strange that she could still feel the sting behind her eyes after so many years when she thought about that moment. But crucial scenes from your past shape you into the person you become, whether they're good or bad.

She could almost remember it in sequence now. It was the first day of the summer, and not just any summer, the summer before she started high school. She was riding the school bus home after the last day of eighth grade. The bus moved slowly, curving respectfully around the old oaks that were part of the island long before the road. Stephanie knew the giant oaks well; her driveway was the first one past the most enormous remaining oak on the island.

As she stepped off the bus, the other children stuck their heads out the window, yelling promises of hanging out over the summer. They all shared a common bond: they lived on "the island." She knew she would see them all soon, probably that very night in someone's backyard playing kick the can. But right now, she only wanted to be out of her school uniform, the dreaded hand-me-down of her older sister, held together with safety pins.

She turned and saluted the driver and then broke into a run down her dirt driveway. She ran as fast as she could, the smell of the marsh pulling her along. She tripped getting through the gate, straightened, then sprinted down the dock as fast as her feet would carry her. When she reached the end, she jumped right into the Wilmington River, clothes and all. "Summer," she murmured into the wind, then raised her voice. "It's summer!"

Little did she know that summer would change her life forever. Her mom had begun to drop hints that a fourteen-year-old girl could never have understood. "You're starting high school next year. You don't need your mama anymore," was the one that laid the groundwork, the one that forced Stephanie to feel guilty for getting older. But no one prepared her for that day in August.

The Savannah heat is a strange thing. It can make the sanest of people do crazy things. When the temperature sits at a hundred degrees day after day, it causes your mind to play tricks on you. Or, it makes you jump out of things you no longer have the patience to continue. She witnessed that firsthand with her mother.

Just as the sun rose early that morning, her mom had woken them. She gathered them on the front porch as they each rubbed the sleep from their eyes. Standing before them, she proclaimed, "A foundation made of sand can never be built upon." Confused by her statement, they began questioning her. She repeated, "A foundation made of sand can never be built upon," as if this line was the only explanation her children needed. She added a couple of random thoughts in an attempt to explain things further, blaming her failing marriage for her poor parenting. But in the end, she drove away without looking back.

Stephanie had learned a valuable lesson that summer: to only lean on sturdy things. She found one such sturdy thing at the end of the month when she sat at the lunch table with five other freshmen at Saint Vincent's Academy. They became her tribe. But more than that, they were her rock, the best type of foundation.

Her mom's final declaration at her leaving became why Stephanie was drawn to structural engineering: she wanted to find her perfect footing. She wasn't like the other engineers who tried to work with every historic building to make it unshakable. No, Stephanie knew it was all just putting Band-Aid upon Band-Aid on the unstoppable. Time takes its toll on everything, living and nonliving, and Savannah's salt air and humidity multiplied the inevitable. She knew what lay beneath the beautiful Savannah streets and its borders: sand. It was the haunting lousy luck of any building project in the Savannah area. Many people had tried to sway her, saying they could add extra steel beams or dig more footers, but time after time, the answer was the same: they were irreparable.

She had condemned more old buildings than she cared to admit and became the Savannah historic district's worst nightmare. They fought to keep all of the homes built before 1950. Handmade craftsmanship pulls on the heart. But underneath the beautiful staircases and arched entryways lie uneven floors, doors that will no longer shut, and moisture damage. It becomes a constant battle for its existence, with replacement parts costing an arm and a leg. Why wouldn't they tear it all down and build something new that appears to be the same? There was a reason all the materials had been improved: to make things stronger and, therefore, better.

Knowing her record, she was surprised to get a call from the state of Georgia to hire her company as one of the structural engineering firms for Savannah. She had placed bids on jobs and was turned down year after year, but now they had come to her.

Within a week, Mr. Henry Lane hired her sight unseen. He explained her first job was an old building on a secluded island. He didn't tell her it was a castle built on a land grant from King George II in the 1700s.

Stephanie had never worked on a case like this. There were so many documents and paperwork to go over, most dating back over two hundred years. *Why am I wasting my time?* she thought. *I should go ahead and stamp this project "CONDEMNED." This building is almost 250 years old. There's no way it's still standing.* But something made her stop, probably because this was her first job working with the government. She had to cross all her t's and dot all her i's.

She had tried to contact the architect, Mr. Philip McLaughlin. She had called and emailed him numerous times, but he had not replied. She knew the city was watching her closely and didn't want to seem indecisive, so she decided to ride to the castle to locate the man. If she failed to find him, she would be forced to shut the project down until she had further information. She dug through her work bag, pulled out the roll of red plastic tape that read "STOP WORK," and headed towards the door.

After driving for an eternity, she finally found the dirt road at the tip of Skidaway Island. A small chain had been loosely stretched across the entrance, but Stephanie unhooked it, laid it on the ground, and proceeded. The road was narrow and very overgrown. Still, she proceeded with a fire in her belly to finish this job. Each never-ending pothole fueled her fire as she continued moving forward. She stopped when she came to a makeshift bridge, contemplating whether to continue, but then she saw the castle. "Oh, wow!" she said out loud. It was unlike anything she'd ever seen, at least in the States. She knew she must get closer. She inched the car slowly across the bridge of death as the forest opened up to the bluff of Wassaw Sound.

She sat in her car for the longest time, taking in each inch of the property. "He's really got something here," she mumbled. She searched for him, but the place was deserted. So, she did the only thing she could do. She walked straight to the entrance, pulled the red tape across the walkway, hurried back to her car, and retraced her path home.

"He'll have to come to me now. I can wait," she mumbled. But waiting wasn't something she did well. Luckily, she didn't have to wait long.

2

TRADITIONS

Savannahians are known for their traditions. They hold their customs close, like priceless treasures, pulling them out as much as possible to adore them, then tucking them away in secrecy until they are needed again. Others may regard them with a mixture of envy and amusement, while wondering how these rituals continue. But when you're raised in Savannah, it becomes a way of life. The Heritage Ball was one of those traditions.

Every spring, the Savannah Society put on the Heritage Ball to raise funds to keep the neighborhood parks beautiful. The tickets were usually gone within the first hour of sale, and the event grew larger and larger every year. The tribe made it a point to attend. It became a tradition to say farewell to winter and welcome the bloom of the azaleas that lined Victory Drive.

Strolling into the Victory Drive mansion, Stephanie scanned the crowd. She made her way through the sea of hoop skirts and crinolines to where she spotted the tribe huddling in the corner. "Glory be, don't y'all look fetching in your liveries," she exclaimed.

The group looked up in surprise, then welcomed her with hugs that made the back of their hoops swing towards the ceiling.

Ball gowns didn't come cheap, so every year the ladies would meet and swap out dresses. Some required being taken in or let out, but not having to purchase one yearly was terrific. They studied each other appreciatively, each spinning to show off their dress, but their attention focused on Stephanie.

"Do you like the new dress?" she asked.

"I call dibs on it next year," Jan said quickly before anyone else, clapping her hands excitedly.

"So, you couldn't get the chocolate stains out of the other one?" Latrice asked.

Kathleen held up her champagne with appreciation. "We should thank that broken fondue fountain. We all got a new dress out of it. It really is beautiful."

Stephanie's dress was emerald green with a plunging neckline that sat perfectly on her shoulders. After years of leaning over a drafting table, she constantly reminded herself to stand up straight and pull her shoulders back. She was glad the stays sewn into the dress seemed to do that for her. "I can't wait for each of you to wear it." She looked around. "So, where are our gentlemen friends?"

"They were lured onto the portico by cigars and brandy when we walked in. That doesn't usually happen at the ball until much later," Agnes explained while motioning towards the glass door.

"Jack wanted to introduce himself to the newcomer, Philip McLaughlin, so he followed along," Kathleen added.

Stephanie squinted her eyes to peer out the glass panel door and spotted him immediately. His red plaid kilt stood apart from the wall of morning jackets and dark pants. "Damn," she said under her breath. She grabbed a Champagne flute from a passing silver tray, cleared her throat, and announced. "Come on, ladies. This isn't an awkward middle school dance with the boys on one side and the girls on the other. Follow me." Usually, she was very self-conscious; her costume gave her courage. She tossed back her drink and flung the veranda doors open with such thrust that they banged loudly against the doorjamb. All heads turned to watch them cross the gender border. All except one: Philip McLaughlin.

Her friends moved toward their dates, but Stephanie had come alone this year. After a string of "unsteady" boyfriends, she was on a dating hiatus. Men who acted like Philip helped reinforce that decision.

She walked straight up to the Scot, who was conversing deeply with an elderly gentleman, and said, "Hi, I'm Stephanie."

Philip nodded but didn't say a word. He turned his attention back to the man to finish their conversation, explaining how he doesn't ever dance and stays on the porch not to be embarrassed. He spoke as if she wasn't there at all.

Mortified, Stephanie spun on her heels. Her eyes locked with Kathleen, who had witnessed the whole thing. A flush of embarrassment stung her cheeks as she walked over to her and leaned in to whisper, "Well, I never."

"And you probably never will, with that one anyway," Kathleen answered, causing them to giggle.

"Who does he think he is, anyway? He's on my turf," Stephanie murmured.

"Who the hell is he?"

"He's that big shot architect from Edinburgh that I told y'all about at lunch last Wednesday."

"Oh, the one that's restoring the old Wassaw castle?"

"That's the one. I keep calling and e-mailing him because he needs the approval to work on the historic structure, but he keeps ghosting me."

"And it looks like his ignoring streak continues," Kathleen said sympathetically.

"See! This is why I'm taking a dating hiatus. Men!" Stephanie groaned and left the room in search of another drink. Her friends slowly made their way back into the party while she spent time visiting with all the women around the rooms. She told each one that the handsome Scot on the porch had requested a dance with them once the music began.

As the president of the Savannah Society welcomed its guests, he explained that the ball had begun when General Oglethorpe settled Savannah. It was a necessary means to raise money to keep the neighborhoods beautiful. The ball stopped running during the Civil War and eventually stopped altogether. But in the 1900s, the city reincarnated the ball to preserve tradition and raise funds for the city. It was renamed The Heritage Ball.

As the dance began, Stephanie watched as Philip was surrounded by tons of women requesting a dance. *Well, that should ruffle his kilt a bit,* she thought with a smile. Philip turned under the weight of her stare. Their eyes locked, and she felt the question in his gaze. *Did you do this?* Like a deer in headlights, she couldn't break his stare. Finally, she shook off the trance, held up her Champagne for a fake toast, and watched as he realized he had been duped. Turning away, she searched the room for her friends, only to find them all on the dance floor.

Someone tapped her exposed shoulder, and as she turned, she was met by the stern face of Philip McLaughlin. She felt the hot stares from the gang of women he left in the lurch and began searching for her exit strategy. She turned to leave, but Philip grasped her wrist.

"Oh no, you don't, lassie. You want me to dance? Then you'll get your wish, but it's you that I'll be dancing with." He slid his other arm around her waist and pulled her into him.

She contemplated her options. The dress wouldn't allow a quick getaway. And even if it did, a gang of angry women would give her the tongue-lashing she deserved. So, she stood tall and played along.

They didn't say a word to one another; they just danced. And, actually, they danced well together, almost anticipating each other's steps. It surprised Stephanie, and she almost forgot how much she disliked him. Almost. Once he opened his mouth, she instantly remembered.

"I don't know how you do it here. But where I come from, you say what you mean and don't play games."

Stephanie stopped dancing and looked him square in the eyes. "I shut down your project on Wassaw because you ignored me. It will stay shut down until you comply. Is that clear enough?"

Recognition played across his face but was quickly

replaced by anger. He opened his mouth to lash out at the same time the song ended. Philip was instantly surrounded by a throng of waiting women who pushed to be near him. As he tried to explain himself over the commotion, Stephanie slipped into the crowd to find the only people she could ever count on: her tribe.

3

RED TAPE

Philip rolled down the window as he drove to the island that morning. He felt the warmth of the sun on his left arm and was happy to be enjoying the much-needed spring. He let his mind play out the day ahead. As he crossed the small bridge, he noticed the red tape stretched across the front door and began cursing under his breath.

He had applied a few weeks back to begin renovations to the castle, only to find that he couldn't get a building permit until the requirements for a remodel had been accepted. They told him to contact an S. Normand to perform an archaeological investigation on the property and gave him a business card with the point of contact. However, Philip decided it would be best to finish the initial clean-up portion of the project first, getting rid of the rubble and under-growth, where the inspector could see the castle was still in good condition. If only he had returned those emails to explain himself.

Philip dug through his wallet, pulled out the card, and called the number.

"Hello," said the female voice.

"Who in the bloody hell do you think you are? You can't shut my project down."

"Who am I speaking to?" she asked, knowing full well he was the only person she knew with a Scottish accent.

"You know damn well who this is. Or do you go around shutting people's projects down every day?" When she didn't respond, he calmed his voice as much as he could. "I would like to speak with you about the castle. Are you at your office?"

Stephanie noticed she had wandered to the middle of one of the many soccer fields at Daffin Park while talking on the phone. She smiled and said, "I'm in the field now."

"What time will you be in?"

"I'm swinging by Aggies for breakfast, so I'll be in about 9:00." She cursed after it popped out her mouth, knowing she had said too much.

"That's two hours away. What should I do for two hours?"

"Goodbye, Mr. McLaughlin," was all Stephanie said, then ended the call. Looking down at Cooper, she unhooked his leash, pulled out a ball, and threw it as hard as possible. As always, the small Scotty took off after it. He could do this all day long. But unfortunately, she didn't have all day. After the tenth throw, she hid the ball in her pocket, fastened his leash, and made her way home.

After showering, she got dressed and walked to Aggies. It was still early, so there were only two tables taken. Stephanie walked behind the serving counter, slid a mug from the rack, and poured herself a coffee. Agnes had only opened the cafe a year ago, but Stephanie couldn't remember where she had eaten breakfast before Aggies. It sat just past the intersection of Waters Drive and Washington Avenue. It stayed busy from seven a.m. until they closed at four.

While Stephanie stirred sugar into her coffee, she heard the bell on the front door. She turned just in time to see Philip walking in. He scanned the restaurant and walked to the counter. She quickly turned her back to him.

"I'll have a large coffee, black," he demanded.

She stood motionless. If she made him a cup of coffee, she would appear to be serving him, and she couldn't give him that satisfaction. But if she refused, she would seem bothered by him. It was a no-win situation, so she quietly began pouring.

He noticed the waitress' hesitation and apologized. "Oh, I'm sorry if I seem abrupt, coming in here demanding coffee before saying hello. It's just this woman inspector is making me crazy. You might know her. Her name is . . ."

"Stephanie Normand! I see you've helped yourself to some coffee again," Agnes chided as she walked out of the kitchen and kissed Stephanie on the cheek. Agnes then noticed the waiting customer. "Good morning, sir. What can I get you?"

Philip stared past Agnes at Stephanie, who slowly turned and met his stare. She forced herself not to break his gaze. The smirk across his face was unreadable. She wished she could wipe it right off. Finally, she shrugged, snagged two gooey cinnamon rolls from the glass-domed display case, and walked to a table.

Philip turned back to Agnes. Reading her nametag, he

answered, "Good morning, Agnes. I'd love a cup of black coffee, please."

Agnes pushed the mug of steaming coffee that Stephanie had been pouring across to Philip, then turned to help another guest.

Philip carried his cup to Stephanie's table and slid into the opposite bench seat. "You're S. Normand? Now it all makes sense. The statement you made at the Heritage Ball confused me. I searched for you when I finally came up for air so you could explain further, but you had disappeared. But the biggest surprise was finding you this morning, serving coffee."

"Life has many surprises, doesn't it?" she answered.

"In Savannah, more than you know." He plopped a folder directly in front of her. "You should have everything you need right here. Can you please pull the 'stop work' contingency off my job?"

Stephanie slid the folder to the side and set the plate of cinnamon rolls in front of her. She slowly took a bite and sighed at its warm, buttery flavor. "I'll be in the office at nine. I've emailed you and driven out to the castle. You have no respect for my time. Now, you will have to wait on me. And right now, I'm going to enjoy my breakfast." She held up her coffee in a mock toast.

"I don't have any emails from you," he lied in an attempt to save face, "and I only missed one call."

"Where I come from, you say what you mean and don't play games," Stephanie answered.

"I truly don't have any emails that I know of." He bobbed his head, "I did, however, ignore the call. I wanted to clean up the site before setting up a time for the inspection. Sorry."

Stephanie nodded with justification, but then he continued.

"At the Heritage Ball, you told all those women I wanted to dance with them. Do you know how long it took me to leave that night?"

Stephanie shrugged, then waved to a lady coming through the door.

Philip was not amused. "Are you always this infuriating?"

"No, right now, I'm being nice." She stood from the table and brushed the crumbs off her lap as a teenage boy passed her table. Smiling, she addressed him, "Hi, Jacob."

"Good morning, Miss Normand," he answered.

"Miss?" Philip asked. "Well, there's a shocker."

Stephanie glared at him. "I've got to get going. Some of us must work today." She carried her plate behind the counter and placed it in the large industrial sink. She kissed Agnes' cheek and waved back over her shoulder as the tiny hanging bell on the door announced her exit.

4

WASHINGTON AVENUE

Philip stood on the pavement before Aggies, pondering his next move. He had absolutely nothing to do for the day. Others might relish lazy days, but they unnerved Philip. Since he couldn't change the fact that his job site was closed, he would find other ways to occupy his time. One option was to hide in his extended-stay hotel room on Abercorn and binge-watch a series, but he longed to be outside. So, he began to walk.

He felt a twinge of excitement as he turned down the street marked Washington Avenue. Just when he thought he'd witnessed all of Savannah's charm, it surprised him once again. The oak-lined road was beautiful. He knew this type of architecture well. It was called Federalist Style and was found in nearly every eastern seaport town. The architects had been early colonists influenced by Great Britain's famous architects.

A Federal-style house was usually a two-story rectangular box that sat two rooms deep. In Southern states, the houses were typically made of brick. The roofs were often capped by a low protective wall along their edge called a parapet.

It was no surprise that the houses reminded him of the castle. The house on Wassaw Sound wasn't technically a castle. Castles were built in Medieval times and were used for protection. His castle wasn't either of those. His castle? That still felt weird to say, but it was true. The lawyer was surprised that he didn't know it was part of his inheritance. His father had only focused on the castle at hand; he never mentioned the one near Savannah, Georgia, belonged to his family. Why put all his time and effort into the estate house in Beauly? Several of these similar properties seemed to be competing for the same tourists. Why not put that effort into the castle on Wassaw Sound? It had no competition, and the best part was he could leave Scotland.

What he didn't know was the building restrictions were much more problematic. The Scots were a more rugged lot. They didn't always cross their t's and dot their i's as long as the building was sturdy. These Americans worried about everything. They worried about problems before they were even problems. They had been building houses for two hundred years, whereas Scotland had been building for two hundred decades. Shaking his head, Philip ran his fingers through his hair as he continued to walk. He chose to leave Scotland for a reason. And in all honesty, he loved Savannah. He just wished he could resume work.

He traveled across Paulson Street and straight to the front of Savannah Arts Academy. Standing on the sidewalk, he took in every inch of the building. He thought he had seen it all, but as he spun to leave, he noticed the long promenade that ran down Atlantic Avenue. "Wow," he whispered and began the walk toward Victory Drive. Halfway down, he saw the "For Rent" sign for what he hoped would become his new Savannah home.

———

Stephanie parked her car in one of her two private spots behind her downtown office. She was happy that her sister sold real estate. When she had moved back home after working with an architect in Atlanta for three years, her sister had convinced Stephanie to spend some of the money she had been saving and invest in the street-side level of a three-story building on Bull Street, just off Liberty. The building needed a lot of upkeep, but it had a strong foundation. She knew this because that's what she did for a living.

She used the two-bedroom apartment as a two-room office and rented out the second office to a draftsman named Chris. Every time she got paid by a client, she would spend half of her paycheck updating the small but sturdy office. Over the last five years, the property had risen significantly in value and had become an excellent investment in the heart of the historic district.

She walked down the small lane and onto Bull Street. The smell of coffee wafted onto the sidewalk from Gallery Espresso on the corner. It mingled with the scent of fresh-cut grass coming from Chippewa Square. The phone rang as she unlocked the door, so she hurriedly threw her bag on the desk and answered. She didn't even hear him come in behind her and felt his presence before she saw him.

When she answered the phone, Philip sat down in one of the high back wing chairs in her office.

"What kind of bones?" she asked the caller and plopped down into her office chair in despair. "Well, what do we do now?" Stephanie ended the call with exasperation. She shook her head and glanced at Philip, who had propped his feet on the sofa table.

"Looks like we're both shut down for the day," he said.

She wanted to strangle him and the annoyingly handsome smile that he wore so well. Instead, she answered, "At least my 'stop work' wasn't because I didn't file paperwork." She knocked his feet down, grabbed her bag, and went to the door. She assumed he was following, but when she looked back, he was still planted in the chair and had propped his feet back onto the table.

"I've got to go meet the police. Come on. Up and out," she said while shooing him with her hand.

He leaned further into the chair and placed his hands behind his head. "Oh no, we have an appointment. You made it yourself. You may disregard such things in the States, but when you make an appointment in Scotland, you keep it."

She closed her eyes and inhaled slowly. She couldn't let this man get under her skin. She plastered on a fake smile and steadied her voice. "Would you have the time to drive around the corner with me? We can talk on the way."

He quickly jumped to his feet. "Until you lift my shutdown, lassie, I've all the time in the world."

5

———

LUNCH WITH THE TRIBE

"Watch where you're going, Stephanie." She could still hear her mother's voice when she stumbled on the uneven bricks of Bull Street. People thought her clumsy when actually she was just too busy concentrating on other things to bother watching where she was going. She had learned, over time, that it was better to stop walking altogether. So, she pulled herself out of the flow of the street traffic to stare at the clock tower of The Independent Presbyterian Church.

Stephanie counted the Roman numerals of the clock. "One, two, three," she murmured to herself. "Wait a minute, one, two, three," she said again and burst out laughing. "Will you look at that? The Roman numeral four is written with four lines instead of a line followed by a V," she said aloud, wanting to share her discovery. But everyone was busily going about their day, walking with a purpose. They didn't seem to notice the amazing things around them. Or, at least, that's how it appeared.

She looked back at the clock tower one last time, trying to picture it being built in the late 1700s. She imagined the scaffolding with ropes and makeshift ladders propped against the outside walls. *The Roman numerals on the church were probably the last thing on the person's mind when they were suspended so high from the ground,* she thought. She couldn't wait to share her new find with her friends at lunch.

Stephanie continued traveling down the red brick sidewalk. As she crossed beautiful Oglethorpe Street, her eyes traveled down its median. The magnificent oak trees stretched out their branches protectively over both sides of the street like a parent extending their arms lovingly to their children. She thought about how they say oaks live for three hundred years. The first hundred they grow toward the heavens, the second hundred they hold steady, and the last hundred they slowly die away. Eventually, they would lay down, showing their roots which directly mirrored their branches. But for now, the trees offered much-needed shade to anyone traveling along the path. She never gave much thought to greenspace and usually viewed it as a nuisance to maintain, but she always appreciated the grand oaks. They had a purpose.

Opening the glass door to Collins Quarter, she saw her friends perched in a line at the bar. They sat on the corner, three on one side and two on the other, with an open seat for her.

"I just knew you'd get here before us and save a seat for our late asses. Sorry, we have to sit at the bar," Jan said apologetically. The restaurant had been Jan's pick, and she regretted not getting there earlier. She patted the barstool next to her, and Stephanie settled in.

Stephanie looked sheepishly at the group. "I was early," she said and cleared her throat. "But then I discovered something on the way."

"Oh, Lordy. Another crack creeping up the first-floor wall of a historic house?" Latrice asked.

"Or was there something that needed to be tightened before someone got hurt?" Agnes said with a wink. "Thank you for catching that loose stool at the shop, by the way," she added under her breath.

"No, no. This is really cool." Stephanie looked at their faces and paused. She knew how much they loved her, but she spoke a different language than most people. She rerouted her conversation and focused on her phone call the day before. "They found bones on my Daffin Park job."

They all stopped talking and listened intently.

"The phone was ringing when I walked into my office yesterday. My crew at Daffin found bones when they were digging, and the county manager had to shut us down while they investigate. Philip and I went straight over and waited for the coroner to come and remove them."

"Wait. You were with Philip? I thought he drove you crazy," Kathleen said.

Stephanie cursed herself for letting that slip. "I just told you we found bones in Savannah, and you're asking me about a man? And yes, he irritates the crap out of me. He just happened to be in my office when I got the call."

Agnes piped in, "Yeah after you had breakfast together at my restaurant."

All eyes went to Stephanie, waiting for her to continue her story, but she was interrupted by the waiter. "Thank heavens," she muttered quietly.

"Hello, ladies, are you ready to order?" the attractive waiter who resembled Thor asked the group.

Stephanie looked at her friends sitting around the corner of the bar. They had been friends since their first day at Saint Vincent's Academy, the all-girl Catholic high school in Savannah. They called themselves "the tribe," a name that had stuck. But they were more like her family.

The group met every Wednesday for lunch, and during their meals, everyone would catch up on what each other was up to. They each took turns choosing the restaurant and always enjoyed a game they would play of rating the waiter.

Stephanie could tell by the look on Jan's face that mini-Thor would be getting a very high rating from her. Jan was batting her eyes at him while she ordered the fried green tomato sandwich and thanked Thor at least three times. She caught Stephanie's gaze, placed her fingers behind her ears, and made her glasses rise and fall as she wagged her eyebrows. This had always been Jan's way of saying, "Hubba, hubba." Being an artist, her taste in men had always been much different than the rest of the group. Stephanie giggled and focused her attention on the next person ordering.

Latrice ordered the power green salad with fresh salmon and, as usual, asked for Hidden Valley Ranch dressing. She was a sauce snob and never accepted off-brands. After ordering, she quickly glanced at her watch. She worked for the city of Savannah and was always on a tight schedule.

Maggie, tanned from being outdoors with her Kayak Adventure Company, was the only one that seemed comfortable sitting at the bar. She ordered the one-pound burger with a turmeric latte. The group cringed at her choice of drink.

Kathleen asked if they had any specials and quickly grabbed the B.L.A.T, asking for extra avocado. She lived just a short distance away, on Jones Street, and loved when the group chose a place within walking distance.

Agnes ordered next. "I've served everyone else breakfast all morning but never stopped to eat myself," she explained to the group. "I'll have the bacon, egg, and cheese sandwich."

"No one does breakfast like you," Stephanie told Agnes, ordering the short ribs hash. As the waiter nodded and walked away, she asked the group, "So, what's new, ladies?"

"Good try, but we are waiting for you to explain Philip," Latrice said.

Stephanie shook her head. "Philip needs me to sign off on him rebuilding the castle, which I can't do. But I think he's going to bug the hell out of me until I do." Turning to Maggie, she asked, "Hey Maggie, could you run me out in Wassaw Sound one day next week? I want to see it from the water."

"Sure, just name the time."

"The problem is that a house built on sand can never survive," Stephanie blurted out.

"Are you still saying that? I thought you had decided that statement was bogus," Kathleen retorted.

"I don't know. It might apply in this instance," Stephanie answered.

"Well, I'll tell you what I do know. That man looks good in a skirt," Latrice teased.

"Yeah, he does. And those hairy knees between his knee-high socks and kilt makes you wonder," Agnes added, making the whole table laugh.

"No way!" Stephanie exclaimed.

"Way!" they shouted back and giggled when they all answered together.

The patrons around the bar and at neighboring tables turned toward the outburst. This was a trick they learned over time to end a conversation and still include everyone. Stephanie knew that her friends were only teasing and would do anything in the world for her because they were always there for each other through the good and the bad.

6

DAFFIN PARK

Stephanie walked Cooper once around the outskirts of Daffin Park, then cut in towards the work site. Once he was away from others, she pulled off his leash like always. She loved Daffin Park and its history. Her father had told her stories of him and his siblings swimming in the lake every summer. Its dirt bottom and fresh water had been a welcome change to the saltwater that surrounded the city. In the 1920s, the man-made lake was created in the shape of the United States, all forty-eight of them. Since then, the lake had been converted into a cemented pond with beautiful water features. But over the last few years, the bottom had settled so much that the concrete bottom had many cracks. The city wasn't able to refill it as quickly as it emptied. They thought about draining and patching but decided to completely rework the space.

It was Stephanie's job to make the park blend with the beauty of Savannah yet have it be enjoyable for its residents.

She was only three months into a two-year project. The old pond had been completely drained, and its concrete bottom was in the final stage of being removed. That's when they found the bones. The police knew the concrete had been poured in 1943. The area underneath would have been leveled before that. So, they could reason the body was buried during that time.

Stephanie walked toward the tractor left on the spot of its last dig. She stood on the side and gazed into the hole. Large pieces of concrete created a makeshift stairway to the bottom. She was so deep in thought she didn't notice Cooper had climbed halfway into the hole. "Cooper!" she yelled out in despair. Catching herself, she forced a smile and tried to take all the worry out of her voice. "Come here, boy. Wanna walk some more?"

He looked up at her and immediately started whimpering. "It's always easier going down, isn't it, boy?" Cooper's short Scottish terrier legs couldn't climb out of this jagged concrete hole of doom. She cursed under her breath, "I have a good mind to leave your hairy ass down there."

After surveying the hole for the best exit point, she realized there wasn't a best exit point, so she began to climb in. As angry as she was, his whining made her soften. "It's okay, boy. I'm coming. Just hold on." She reached him quickly, rubbed his head, and hoisted him onto the side, where he scampered out. He peered down at her anxiously, whining even louder than before.

She tried to climb to the top, but the large concrete chunks teetered when she put her weight on them. As she leaned on one of the sides, the concrete gave a bit, and she saw something mixed in with the dirt. "What is that?" she murmured, praying it wasn't more bones. She slid her hand between two smaller chunks of concrete to where her fingertips could graze the object. *That looks like a leather strap. I should call the authorities. I have a stop work notice on this project,* she thought, and stopped in mid-reach.

As she stood motionless, she realized Cooper's whining had stopped, and the absence of the noise was as deafening as his whimpers. She looked up in the open hole and began calling for the dog. "Cooper? Cooper, are you there, boy?" Frustrated, she yelled, "Where are you, you worthless mongrel?"

The head that peeped over the side of the hole wasn't Cooper's; it was Philip's.

"That's no way to speak to a Scot," he teased and rubbed the terrier's head. "Good morning, lass," he said as casually as if she wasn't in a ten-foot hole.

"What the hell are you doing here?" she spit out.

"That's funny. I was wondering the same about you. Do you need help out?"

"No," she said a little too quickly, then cut her eyes up to him and begrudgingly added, "Thank you." Glancing at the strap, she wondered if she should tell him what she had found. As always, she quickly began to run through the scenarios in her mind with the possible outcomes. So far, everything had happened by accident. But once she crawled out of the hole, she would need to call the authorities to tell them what she found. However, if she pulled this item free right now, she could just give it to them, and there would be no waiting on someone else. That could get her back on her job faster. She glanced back up at Philip. Could she trust him? She took a chance. "Could you pop down here for a second?"

"Sure," he answered excitedly and jumped right into the hole. The force of his jump knocked her off balance, and she began to fall backward. He grabbed her shoulders to steady her while her hands went to his chest. She hadn't anticipated they would be face to face, and the smell of his shampoo filled the air around her. Nervous excitement ran through her. Judging from his smug grin, he felt it, too. "How can I help?"

"I don't need your help."

Disappointment played across his face. "Then why did you call me down here?"

"I wanted to show you something." She pointed to the strap. He ran his fingers under the cement and pulled the strap out further. "It looks like a satchel of some kind," he announced.

She tried to hide her excitement, but it rushed out, "That's what I thought, too. We need to move these cement pieces to get to it."

"So, you do need my help?"

She cursed under her breath. She always prided herself on being independent. It physically hurt her to ask for help. But it was true: she needed his help. "Could you please help me dislodge this?"

A smile spread across his razor-stubbled, irritatingly handsome face. "I'd love to."

They worked slowly, moving the concrete piece by piece, and finally, the object dislodged. It was a brown leather satchel. Although the strap had nearly deteriorated, the folded leather was still holding. She carefully lifted it from the ground. "We did it," she called out happily and smiled at Philip over their discovery.

"Yes, we did," he answered while holding her stare. "Now, let's get out of this hole."

With the concrete removed, they were able to climb up the side. They found Cooper stretched out asleep in the sun. "Some guard dog you are," she told him as she gently set the bag on the ground. She brushed the dirt from her hands, scratched behind Cooper's ear, and then clicked his leash into place. As she gently picked up the bag, she motioned toward her house to Philip.

"I'm this way," he pointed across Waters Avenue to the numbered streets of Ardsley Park.

"You parked over there?"

"No, I rented a house. Moved in yesterday. I had been living out of a suitcase, which is not my style. Then one day, I ate breakfast at this cute little place called Aggies. I had some time to kill afterward, so I went for a walk and found a nice two-bedroom house for rent. So, I guess we're sort-of neighbors."

She stood motionless and said nothing but cursed her luck. It irritated her that he was encroaching into her life.

He glanced over at the open hole, nodded, and said, "I guess our work here is done. I better be on my way," as he walked off toward his house.

"Thanks again," she called out and was rewarded with a wave over his shoulder.

She continued to stand in place and watched him walk away. She couldn't get a read on this man. She was surprised that he didn't ask questions about the bag and had no interest in anything else about her day. He just turned and walked away. She watched him a second longer as he picked up a piece of trash and then tipped his hat at two elderly walkers. "Have a great day, Mr. McLaughlin," she murmured, then turned toward home.

7

———

THE AFTERNOON CRUISE

Stephanie slowly turned into Maggie's driveway, anticipating the crackling of her tires compressing the crush-and-run shells. *What are they all doing here?* she wondered when she saw the familiar cars. She maneuvered into an empty spot under the sizeable Japanese plum tree.

Walking in Maggie's front door, Stephanie followed the familiar voices of the tribe straight back to the kitchen.

Kathleen was the first to notice her arrival. She smiled and said, "Maggie didn't want to bother you at work, but we decided to pack a cooler and make an afternoon of it."

Stephanie kissed her cheek with a hello. "You always bring tomato sandwiches when you go out in the boat. Where are they?"

Kathleen pointed toward the large cooler.

"Hello, ladies," Stephanie called out as she moved around the packed containers in the cooler until she spotted the sandwiches. Sheepishly, she pulled out a tomato sandwich and took a hearty bite. "Yum! I don't know how you do it, Kathleen. I've followed your simple recipe a thousand times, and they never taste the same."

"You're just hungry," Kathleen answered.

"No. It's more than that. You're holding out one of the ingredients from me."

"I've told you a thousand times, it's just Duke's mayonnaise, fresh tomatoes that are salt-and-peppered, and plain ol' white bread," Kathleen explained but added, "and a lot of TLC."

Stephanie laughed, "Then that's where you got me. There is never tender loving care in my kitchen. It's survival skills only." She winked at Kathleen, and Kathleen air-kissed her back.

Stephanie turned to the group, who had plopped themselves around the kitchen island. She and Maggie wore gym shorts and tank tops with their hair pulled back in a ponytail, but the rest of the group wore their best nautical wear. "What time is Skipper picking us up for the yacht party?" she asked teasingly. Everyone looked down at their outfits and then over to Stephanie and Maggie.

"Maybe we should have asked what type of boat trip we were going on before crashing it," Latrice said.

"No worries," Maggie answered. "We're not planning on getting out. Just doing a little recon ride-by to a Castle at sea. Right, Stephanie?"

"Aye-aye, Captain," she responded.

They all piled into the 18' Scout and slowly made their way out of Chimney Creek. As they turned into the Back

River, Maggie yelled over the motor, "Hold on to your hats," and pushed the speed until the boat got up on a plane. With hair flying in every direction, Stephanie caught Maggie's gaze and offered her a knowing smile. They were the only ones dressed appropriately.

Maggie slowed as they came upon Little Tybee. The boat rose and fell as the waves from the Atlantic Ocean hit the beach.

"Ugh, why is it so rough today?" Agnes asked.

"Once we get around this corner, it will be fine," Maggie announced.

As soon as the boat ran parallel to the beach, Maggie could speed up and level things out. She looked to Agnes, who gave a thumbs-up sign.

"Did you take your Dramamine?" Stephanie asked Agnes.

"You know I can't drink when I take that medicine. I'll be fine," Agnes answered, defending herself.

Jan and Latrice, sitting next to her, mentally planned their escape if she got seasick. They had witnessed it before. One summer in high school, the group had crabbed in Maggie's little trawler. The motion of the water while waiting for a nibble on her line had caused her to yak off the side of the boat. It was awful to watch but even worse to see how crabs had been drawn to it. Disgusted by the experience, everyone tossed their lines over the side of the boat and into the mud with the chicken necks still attached. Everyone knew crabs were bottom dwellers but seeing it firsthand was unforgettable. The incident had been one that no one wished to experience again.

As they sped along, the movement of the boat with the roar of the motor was almost hypnotic. They were each lost in their own thoughts. Kathleen had leaned over onto Jan and closed her eyes while Stephanie sat in the front, watching for anything that might be floating in their path.

As they turned into Wassaw Sound, Maggie slowed the boat, and they all began to chatter again. Everyone except Kathleen, who was fully asleep now on Jan's lap.

"The castle is just up here on the right," Maggie announced. "It's tucked away perfectly on an inlet that protects it from storms. That's probably how it survived so many years."

The castle couldn't be seen from the ocean, but as soon as they turned into the cove, it slowly appeared surrounded by large oaks and pines. It sat high and proud, looking over the water, like a father puffed up with pride over his child's accomplishments. All the chatter in the boat ceased as they approached. Stephanie stood to get a better look.

"Stephanie, can you pull the anchor out from the front and throw it in?" Maggie asked.

Stephanie pushed, "I need to get closer, Maggie. We are so far from shore. Can we go in further?"

"Let me check." Maggie flipped on the depth finder, but only a blank screen appeared. "Ah, hell. The depth finder is on the blink again. Everything breaks so fast living on the salt water." She looked to Stephanie, who waited for an answer. "I haven't ever been farther than this. It will be risky, at best."

"I'm up for the risk," Stephanie said quickly, then looked to her friends. Everyone nodded in agreement except for Kathleen, who was now openly snoring.

"Alrighty. But know that we are literally in unchartered waters. If we start kicking up sand, we're outta here." Maggie raised the motor and proceeded slowly. They began to get close to the castle. They could now see two of the three exposed sides, but Maggie was leery. "I think this is as close as we can get."

"Don't you own an adventure company?" Stephanie teased, egging her on.

"Yes. For kayaks. They require one inch of water."

"Can we just go a tiny bit further so I can see the third side of the building?"

Maggie nodded and crept further. That's when they heard the scraping of sand on the bottom. Maggie knew the moment it happened. They were stuck. Each of her friends looked at her while she started barking orders. "Pull out the oars and push from each side. Throw the anchor from the back and try to pull us off. I'm going to try to back us off quickly."

They all worked hard, but within five minutes, it was clear they weren't going anywhere.

Kathleen finally woke up startled. "Where are we?" she asked, then looked at the castle. "Oh, it's beautiful, isn't it? You can't tear this down, Stephanie."

The exhaustion from getting the boat back to water overwhelmed the group, and they each plopped down.

Kathleen looked from one to the other. "What's going on?"

"We're stuck," Agnes said.

"For how long?"

They all turned to Maggie for an answer.

"It's 7:30 now. High tide was at five. This boat is stuck

until at least four or five in the morning." She watched the fear wash across each of their faces and quickly added, "But we're safe. We will be fine."

"What do we do until then?" Stephanie asked.

Maggie pointed to the castle. "We're going ashore."

8

TRESPASSING

The boat listed to starboard as the water quickly ran out of the cove. Maggie was excited about their adventure to shore and immediately took the lead. Everyone was busy inside the boat with their assigned task. She knew that her employee, Mack, always kept his radio close by, so she reached out and arranged for him to meet them at four a.m. to help tow them out of the sand.

Turning to Stephanie, Maggie asked, "Is there an address or directions we could give Jack for him to come get us?"

Slowly shaking her head, Stephanie answered, "No. There is a map at my office, but it's locked. Sorry!"

Maggie reached out one last time to Mack and had him contact Kathleen's husband. Jack was close to Kathleen's friends, so he knew who to contact to inform them of the ladies' safety.

The tribe waded through the sand and mud, sinking in several spots and dropping items in two feet of water while going to the shore. Once on land, they trudged through the overgrowth and brambles as they clambered the incline of the bluff. Once at the top, they stopped walking to enjoy the magnificent view of the castle.

"Well, that's a sight to behold," Latrice blurted out while the others agreed.

As her friends continued to walk toward the building, Stephanie remained planted in place, lost in thought. *Did it appear this way 250 years ago? Was this planned? What type of architect could envision this before beginning construction?* Her mind took her back to the tools and practices in the 1700s, and a deep appreciation set in. She turned, looked over the bluff, and noticed a new Adirondack chair. Making her way towards it, she was aware of its direction. Instead of facing the beautiful waterway, it faced the castle. She knew immediately to whom the chair belonged: Philip.

Stephanie rushed to catch up with her friends just as they stepped onto the stone that encircled the house. The only thing on the outside that brought the scene into the 21st century was the large contractor's dumpster sitting on the side. They pushed through a heavy wooden door that led directly into a massive empty room.

"Welcome home, ladies," Jan said as they sat their heavy bags of food and drinks on the concrete floor. "How is it so clean in here?"

"They had preliminarily started cleanup before construction so they could assess the structure," Stephanie explained. Looking around the room, she noticed the scaffolding was in place around the perimeter. Two large brooms were propped against the wall, and an industrial trashcan sat beside them.

Stephanie had seen the proposed plans, which would be

done in stages, beginning with the castle itself, then adding an adjoining luxury hotel and guest cottages. But, without the castle, the whole project would die. She applauded Philip for this original idea. How many castles were there in the United States? Locals would love to see this addition to their history-laden city, and tourists would visit from all corners of the nation. But was it safe? She had yet to be convinced of that.

She thought back to the floor plans and began to walk around as her friends followed. "This would be the great hall. It runs nearly the full expanse of the building across the marsh, except for this." She motioned to a doorway at the end that led to a primitive round staircase.

"Where does that lead?" Maggie asked.

"That's the tower that looks out over the Atlantic Ocean."

Maggie asked excitedly if they could climb to the top but then looked up the stone spiral steps. "These remind me of the stairs inside Cockspur Lighthouse, except these are still intact." Glancing towards the light at the top, she backed down. "Maybe we better wait until Stephanie runs the structural report."

The group continued to walk behind Stephanie as she explained each area, "Kitchen, dining room or library, entrance hall, and main staircase. If I remember correctly, the upstairs holds two large bed chambers and a chapel." She continued walking and circled back around to where they began. The shadows began to fall upon the walls as the sun made its final descent into the marsh.

Stephanie looked back towards the inner staircase and decided to see the whole castle. "I really want to go up and check things out. You guys start arranging our bags in the great hall. I'll be right back." She took the stairs slowly, ensuring the granite on each step remained intact. When she made it to the top, she wandered into a large room that was completely bare and then over to its twin across the hall. It wasn't until she stepped foot inside the back room that she was shaken to her core. The small chapel was anything but typical. The walls and floor were stone, and a small altar was just off the back wall. Behind the altar was a window set back into the eight-foot wall. The window itself was missing many of the stained-glass panels. Its brokenness made it appear ominous. Her eyes traveled around the room and focused on a primitive, life-size statue on the left side. It was of a woman, that much was for sure, but who she was remained to be seen. Being raised Catholic, her obvious choice would have been the Virgin Mary. But this statue, while wearing a crown, wore braids and appeared to be from the Middle Ages. Somehow, the figure made her very uncomfortable. She noticed the arched alcove where it had been placed and tentatively walked towards it but was overcome with fear. Without knowing why, she mumbled, "Fight or flight," and was surprised when her body responded with flight.

The ladies had situated themselves along the wall, and each had pulled the snacks and drinks from the cooler and bags. "This is probably the first cucumber sandwich to be eaten here," Latrice stated, and they all laughed in agreement. They were shocked when Stephanie came running into the room.

"What's wrong?" Agnes asked.

"I'm not sure," Stephanie exclaimed, trying to catch her breath. She made herself pause. What was upsetting her so much? Was the castle haunted? Turning to Kathleen, she asked, "Can you come to take a look at something?"

"Oh, no! Not again," Agnes snapped. "You know I don't do ghosts; you just went to the one person who talks to them." Agnes stood up and moved into the corner behind Jan.

"I'm sure it's nothing," Kathleen said reassuringly.

The room was nearly dark, so Kathleen picked up one of the flashlights and walked with Stephanie toward the stairs. This time, with only the flashlight leading the way, it looked entirely different to Stephanie. When they reached the landing at the top, Stephanie pointed Kathleen towards the chapel and noticed when the flashlight bounced upon the arch of the ceiling.

Kathleen slowly swept the room with a glow of light and walked towards the alcove holding the statue. She bowed her head towards it as she approached, then stopped before it. Glancing at Stephanie, she whispered, "I see what you mean, but it's not a ghostlike feeling." She closed her eyes and stood motionless for what seemed like forever. "There is something different in here. I can't quite put my finger on it. Could this alcove have been where the chapel's tabernacle was located? We could be feeling the lingering effect of it holding consecrated hosts." She turned and let her eyes sweep the room one last time. "I'm really not sure, Stephanie. But it's not an unsettling feeling; it's calming." Kathleen reached over and gave Stephanie's hand a slight squeeze. "I'm sure you'll figure it out over time."

Stephanie squeezed her hand back in response, grateful for her friend's love. Then they made their way downstairs and joined the group. The contents of the coolers had been spread across the floor while everyone was nibbling finger sandwiches and wine. They even lured Agnes out of the corner once Kathleen explained that the castle wasn't haunted. Time passed quickly, as it always did when they were together, and before they knew it, both the food and the drinks were almost gone. It wasn't until someone had to go to the restroom that they noticed it was pitch black outside.

"I'm not going out there," Kathleen said. "It's safe inside. No animals and no ghosts."

The animals they could handle, but the ghosts always seemed to seek Kathleen out. She had good reason to stay where it appeared to be safe. However, there weren't bathrooms inside.

"Well, you can't use the floor. It's going to be a long night for you," Jan announced.

"Oh, all right. But we all go together."

"Why?" Jan asked.

"Have you never watched a horror movie? They are always picked off one by one. You should always stay together."

Everyone agreed, so they grabbed the lantern and exited the main door. "Let's go quickly as soon as we are off the stones. No dilly-dallying," Latrice ordered. They walked a bit further until Jan said, "Okay, go," and they each began to squat.

Agnes was the first to scream, followed by Latrice, then Kathleen. Each of their faces were illuminated by light.

"What in the bloody hell are you women doing out here?"

Stephanie cringed at the Scottish brogue, then scurried

to pull up her shorts as the cell phone light scanned each woman's face, coming to a stop on hers just as she zipped. "Hello, Mr. McLaughlin."

"I'll ask you again, lass. What are you doing out here?"

Stephanie didn't like being reprimanded and barked back at him. "I could ask you the same thing. I put a stop work on this site. You are not legally allowed to be on the premises."

He narrowed his gaze. "Really?"

She knew she was in the wrong and admitted it. "No, not really." She glanced at her friends, trying to straighten themselves up, so she asked, "Can we go inside and give these ladies a little privacy?"

His look said it all. Still, he motioned his arm for her to take the lead, then followed behind. Stephanie began explaining the situation. The more she explained, his angry mood lightened until the scowl-induced crease between his eyes softened. When she painted a vivid picture of the boat listing and the group trudging through the water, a smile spread across his face as he said, "You ladies have had quite an adventure today. How about I get you all home before the midges come out."

"Midges?"

"You know. The little bugs that live in the sand and bite like fire."

"Sand gnats?"

"Midges or sand gnats, they both are evil."

Philip helped them carry the coolers and bags to his truck. He held the door open as each lady piled in, then waited for Stephanie to hop in the front. He offered his hand to help her while asking, "You know what puzzles me? Why were you all the way out here in the boat? Were you spying on me?"

Stephanie shrugged and then struggled to climb into the front seat most ungracefully. Once she was settled, he leaned on the open door waiting for an answer.

She decided to be honest. "It really is a beautiful castle."

Her honesty disarmed him, causing his lips to curve into an easy grin. "She is quite lovely, isn't she?" Leaning in further, he studied her face before continuing. "Do you really think so? Did you get to look around?"

"Just a bit."

Disappointment played upon his face. "I would love to show you everything before the hearing. Would you be available next week?"

Glancing down, she realized she was still holding his hand, so she slowly let it go. She didn't want to give him false hopes about the property, but the castle and the grounds were gorgeous. It would be a shame for the building to be destroyed. However, she had ordered many buildings to be destroyed because they were unsafe. This was the oldest one she had ever viewed. She had a lot of homework to do.

She told him she would ride back out with him for the castle's sake. And told herself it had absolutely nothing to do with the fact that she already missed the warmth of his large hand.

9

SUNDAYS

Stephanie shuffled slowly towards the kitchen. "Coffee!" she cried out to the empty house and got excited when Cooper came running around the corner. He whined when he saw her and moved quickly towards the door to be let out. She groaned, trying to keep up to avoid a mess. Opening the door, he quickly shot into the backyard.

She poured her first cup of liquid sunshine and took a long hot gulp. Her eyes traveled to the end of the counter where the leather bag sat. She had examined its contents the day she and Philip had unearthed it, but little was inside. There was a small leather-bound journal whose pages had turned to dust, two pins that appeared to be military style, and a metal cigar tube with random numbers etched on the outside. Setting the empty journal to the side, she carefully wrapped the other items in tissue paper and placed them in a plastic storage bag. She could hardly wait to show them to her family at lunch.

Rolling her eyes, she checked the time. It would be so much easier just not to go to church today, but her dad had chastised her at lunch last week saying, "If you can make lunch, then you can make Mass. I really hope you try harder next week." Shaking her head, she hurriedly got dressed and rushed out the door.

She entered Saint Peter the Apostle Church, on Wilmington Island, with not a minute to spare and raced down the side aisle until she saw her dad's full head of white hair. She never remembered it not being gray, even when he was a young man. She secretly prayed she wouldn't inherit that trait. He looked over while she was genuflecting and shook his head for her not to enter the pew. Following the nod of his head, she followed his eyes to the woman walking behind her, Mrs. Wilmot. She was a striking older woman who was always impeccably dressed. *Not a chance, Pop*, she thought but humored him just the same by entering the pew in front of him.

Sure enough, Mrs. Wilmot genuflected and entered the row where her father sat. She patted Stephanie's shoulder, sidestepped into the pew, and sat beside her father. Stephanie glanced back at him, and he wagged his eyebrows at her. *Peter, you old dog*, she thought and knelt. This was when she should say her prayers, but they were hard to conjure up in the last couple of years. She looked around the room at the throngs of faith-filled people eagerly anticipating the Mass ahead. Some were deep in prayer, while others prepared for the hour ahead by locating the readings in the missal or finding the hymns. Why couldn't she be more like them?

As the entrance hymn began, Stephanie considered how

long her dad had been seeing Mrs. Wilmot? How many Sundays had she missed Mass? When Stephanie turned at the sign of peace, she witnessed their hug, and her heart melted. He deserved a little happiness. He had been lonely for a long time and carried it without complaint. When her eyes met her dad's, he nodded, and she blew him a kiss. He beamed in return.

As Mass ended, Stephanie scanned the crowd for her sister. As usual, she sat with her husband and their two children in the cry room while her brother sat in the back left pew. He was habitually late and barely reached the back bench before the priest processed in. Stephanie wondered where she would be sitting from here on out. She and her father always sat on the right side towards the middle. Would she now sit there with her dad and Mrs. Wilmot?

She hated feeling left out but had been struggling to attend church for a long time. This might just be her out. Her Saturday morning was always full of events she wanted to do. Sunday morning was her only day to rest and stay in her PJs until lunch. Now, she could do that and meet them at her dad's house for lunch. She could still have great family time without getting dressed for church. Surely, she was old enough to make a decision like that without the Catholic guilt that came with it.

After Mass, they went to her father's house for dinner and were surprised to find Mrs. Wilmot helping him in the kitchen.

"I brought ham and mac and cheese," Mrs. Wilmot told the group. "Your father was in charge of the green beans and rolls."

"Heck yeah," her brother called out. "I was waiting on

the 'CC Special' again."

"What's the 'CC Special?'" Mrs. Wilmot asked.

"My dad's combo dinner. He orders Chinese rice and fried chicken. He gets the fried rice from a Chinese takeout place and the chicken from KFC. He's been ordering that for years. It's good, but ham and mac and cheese is a welcome change."

They talked comfortably through dinner, with several interruptions from her nieces that kept the conversation from running too deep. As Cathy cut the praline cake she had bought for dessert, Stephanie decided to pull out what she had found on her jobsite.

"So, I found a buried bag at my jobsite at Daffin Park," she told the group. The idle table conversation halted as she piqued everyone's curiosity. Even the children wanted to hear more once they heard the word "buried." Stephanie unwrapped the items from the plastic bag, explaining she had left the journal shell at home, and placed each on the table. "I believe these are military-style pins and a cigar tube."

Keith came around the table and picked up the pins one by one. "This is an old brass Benedictine Military pin, I'm sure. Those are crossed rifles and the letters BMS." He set it aside and picked up the second pin. "And this is a JROTC pin. I had to wear the same one when I was at BC. Where did you say you found them?"

"At my jobsite in Daffin," Stephanie answered, which wasn't a lie but wasn't the whole truth. She purposefully omitted the fact they had laid beside a dead man's body. It wasn't until that moment that she was sure she must tell the authorities.

While speaking to Keith, Mrs. Wilmot picked up and inspected the cigar tube. "Do you know what these etched numbers are?" Stephanie shook her head, so Mrs. Wilmot explained. "They are nautical courses. There appear to be two separate routes."

"How do you know this?" Stephanie asked.

"My husband was a seaman," she answered.

Keith snickered, so Cathy popped him on the back of the head. "What are you, in middle school?" she asked in her typical mother voice, then turned her full attention back to Mrs. Wilmot.

"Mr. Wilmot was a Navy man. Once he retired, he bought a sailboat and traveled the world. Sometimes, I would go with him, but most of the time, I did not. When he chartered his course, the numbers read like this."

They passed the cigar tube around the table.

"I wonder where these would take us?" Stephanie's dad asked. "Wouldn't it be fun to find out?"

The table shook as Mrs. Wilmot slammed her hands hard on the table and stood up. "No, it would not, Peter. The sea became the woman I couldn't compete with in my first marriage, and she finally had her way and took him from me. I will not have another man I love go after her."

The table was silent as Mrs. Wilmot slowly sat back down and straightened the linen napkin in her lap. The siblings looked at one another, trying to hold back laughter but unsure why.

Peter stood up, smiling like a cat who swallowed a canary, shocked by Mrs. Wilmot's declaration of love. "Well, you got a landlubber here. And believe you me, there is no competition for my affection. I'm all yours!"

10

THE ABANDONED CASTLE

As his truck began its descent down the steep Skidaway Island Bridge, Philip was able to catch quick glimpses of the water. The high tide covered the mud, causing the salt water to mingle with the marsh grass. The reflection of the setting sun made it appear to be ablaze.

Philip pulled off towards Butter Bean Beach to get a better view. He parked his truck in the lot, let down the tailgate, and enjoyed the drop of the sun.

The afternoon had been confusing, and he tried to put the pieces into place in his mind. When Philip wore his kilt to the Heritage Ball a couple of weeks ago, he had drawn the attention of the president of the Saint Andrew's Society. The president assumed since Philip was Scottish, he understood that the society had originated to celebrate people of Scottish descent. He explained there were several chapters all over the U.S. Still, Savannah's chapter dated back to the time when General Oglethorpe settled Savannah. The group had been meeting since before the Revolution.

Philip was surprised when the president called to ask him to speak at the next meeting. When Philip asked for the topic, the man told him to talk about what they had discussed at the Heritage Ball. Philip couldn't remember anything more than idle chitchat in their conversation and had thrown together a talk about Scottish heritage. But as he watched the men pile into the banquet room, he began questioning why he had agreed to speak at all. He enjoyed talking to groups but couldn't get a read on the American Scots. He decided to just be himself. What did he have to lose?

They had placed him at the head table, where he got to know the men around him while they were served dinner and drinks. As soon as the desserts were passed, the president introduced Philip.

"Last week, I walked into the Heritage Ball, and a kilt immediately caught my eye. Mr. Philip McLaughlin sure can make a great impression, especially to the ladies." The president chuckled while the men around the room let out small cheers. "Mr. McLaughlin is an architect who comes to us from Edinburgh to restore the castle on Wassaw Sound. Gentlemen, join me to welcome our speaker."

Philip rose to a round of polite claps as he began his speech. "I'll start where my father always started. General Oglethorpe was of Scottish descent, just like you and me. His parents were Scottish and were loyal Jacobite supporters. The good General did many things, one of them was beginning this chapter of Saint Andrew's Society." Philip held up his glass in a toast, and everyone followed. He continued, "When Oglethorpe discovered Savannah, he brought 170

Scotsmen with him. After a couple of years, he asked for more men from Scotland to come and make a settlement on the city's outskirts to protect them from the Spaniards in Florida. These people were my family.

"I recently learned this information when my father passed away. The land obtained from a grant almost 250 years ago belongs to my family. It is the land of my forefathers. The property sits on Wassaw Sound, and the original castle the Scots built still sits upon it. And aye, she's a beauty. Some of you may know of it firsthand, and some may have heard about it. I have plans to renovate the castle and open it up to the public. We've uncovered a bit of Savannah's history that showcases the people of Scottish descent who made Savannah the unique city it is today. I invite you to celebrate with me when this land is reopened." He scanned the room, smiled, and added, "Thank you!"

The room erupted in applause as the president returned to the microphone. "Thank you, sir, and God bless your family for all they did for our fair city." The room began to clap again as Philip sat down, then the president announced that the bar was reopened, and people began to move about. Several men passed by and shook Philip's hand, some even asked questions, but they all left by the night's end, except Tommy Morgan.

Tommy pulled up a chair directly across from Philip. "So, you say this land has sat in your name for almost 250 years?"

Philip answered, "Yes, for the most part."

"And now you are just going to come back because some relative from your far past has your same bloodline?"

Philip looked the man over. There seemed to be much

more to his story, and Philip was out of the loop. "Have I offended you in some way?" Philip asked.

Tommy stood abruptly. "I hope that you get everything that you deserve, Mr. McLaughlin," he blurted out before walking off and leaving Philip sitting at the table alone.

———

Skidaway Island had been the playing ground for the Morgan boys for years. Their papa had taught them how to fish and hunt on the island just like his papa before had taught him. They didn't own the land; they had leased it from the government twenty years ago. They opened a makeshift lodge and turned a steep profit by offering their services as hunting guides. They also began to bring cows to the island. Over time, the island was stocked with over three hundred of them.

They were surprised when the U.S. Government came knocking, asking them if they were interested in buying the property for $50,000. They laughed in the solicitor's face when he told them he was giving them the first right of refusal. Why would anyone want to buy an island when the only way to it was by boat? But they weren't laughing when they were notified to vacate the property.

They had sixty days to round up hundreds of cows. They didn't anticipate how difficult it would be, but cows that live in the wild become fast like deer. Most of them were unapproachable. They almost decided to leave them, but there was no way the cows would become someone else's feast. So, they called in all their old buddies for one last hunt.

In the meantime, the new landowners had placed stakes

around the property to mark their borders. As the hunters chased the cows to the southern portion of Skidaway Island, they noticed the stakes had stopped, and a sign had been hung by the State of Georgia marking off the tip of the island. "This land is not for sale."

All this time they had been renting the land, they weren't aware that the island's prettiest, most fertile, and highest point hadn't been included. A large castle-like building stood upon the property, but it had long been abandoned. Although it was old, it was still very sturdy. They had spent many nights hiding from a stray storm or lousy weather inside but had never questioned its origins. They had grown up with it always there, so it just belonged.

The Morgans rounded up the cows and scared them onto this small, attached island. They took down the makeshift bridge, the only way on and off the island without swimming, and left the cows until they could come back for them. But their curiosity about who owned the island got the best of them, and they began to look for answers.

They eventually found that the land had been a grant by the King of England in the 1700s and had been continually renewed. They also found out that land grants expired after 250 years. The Morgans had marked off the date and knew it well.

Over time, the brothers passed away, one by one, leaving only the baby in the family, Bobby. When Bobby met his maker, or most likely his tormentor, he passed the watch down to his son, Tommy, to do his bidding.

Tommy was mean as a snake and slippery as one, too. He had anticipated the day for as long as he could remember. He had plans for the property. Big plans. The island's special zoning could be used for a casino. And not just any casino, the cream of the crop. He had the plans ready and the contractors sitting on go. The wait had been long, but it would be over by the year's end. Everything was going according to plan, or so he thought, until that very minute sitting in the Saint Andrew's Society meeting.

11

PAYING RESPECT

They met in the Fox & Weeks Funeral Home parking lot, all dressed in their version of what was appropriate for a visitation: black or navy-blue slacks or dress. And then there was Jan, who thought a fuchsia bubble jumpsuit was suitable.

The sun was still unbearable at five p.m. as they made their way to the building, so they walked quickly.

"I can't believe she passed away. She was such a hard-ass teacher. I'm surprised she didn't run the angel of death right out of her classroom," Latrice noted.

Agnes shushed her. "Don't disrespect the dead. I loved Mrs. J."

"So did I, but we all were thinking it; I just said it," she countered as she held the door open for the group.

Each of them sighed from the welcoming cool of the air conditioning and made their way to the sign-in book. They nodded at the many familiar faces spotted around the room as they got in line to greet the family. After giving their condolences, they proceeded to the front of the chapel to the long kneeler that ran alongside the open coffin. Mrs. Jenkins had been an exceptional math teacher, and they each greatly respected her.

A small tear escaped Kathleen's eye. As she wiped it away, Stephanie turned to her to smile, but her eyes widened in shock. Stephanie turned away from Kathleen and whispered something in Agnes' ear; she, in turn, whispered to Maggie, then Latrice, and lastly, Jan. They each began giggling uncontrollably.

Kathleen squeezed Stephanie's hand hard until she met her eyes. "What's going on?" she asked between clenched teeth.

Leaning over, Stephanie whispered, "You are wearing the same shirt as Mrs. Jenkins." Kathleen looked down at the corpse to verify and uttered a horrified cry. The congregation behind them mistook it for an emotional goodbye. At the same time, all the ladies' backs shook with what appeared to be grief.

Finally, Father Sullivan, who had been the rector at St. Vincent's when they attended, approached the ladies. "I'm sure she feels your love from heaven above. God bless you for coming," and he gently escorted them away from the front so other mourners could pay their respect.

They hid their faces as they quickly exited, but they burst out laughing once outside.

Kathleen wrapped it all up by saying, "Mrs. J always did have great taste. The last one to Spanky's bar has to buy the first drink. Go!"

The tribe sang the SVA fight song as they walked down the lane behind Kathleen's home on Jones Street. As they approached her house, Kathleen began to hush the group. "Shhh. Jack and the children are asleep," she warned. "I don't want to wake them."

They opened her backyard garden gate and quietly walked around the fountain and herb garden. They attempted to enter through the kitchen door and were as quiet as a band of Navy Seals making an attack, or so they thought.

Kathleen's husband, Jack, slowly opened the door. As he took in the sight, he ushered them inside. Then his eyes focused on his wife. She was holding her heeled shoes in her hand and was only wearing her camisole. He looked at her questioningly and opened his mouth to ask her what had happened when she cut him off.

"I know this looks bad, Jack, but we're in mourning," she hurriedly explained. The group of ladies behind her all began to explain, too. They sounded like teenagers who were late for curfew.

Shaking his head, Jack held up his hands and hushed them. "Have a seat, and I'll put on a pot of coffee."

Kathleen had made monkey bread that morning for her children, so Jack brought the glass cake tray and set it in the center of their long farmhouse table. The ladies were finally quiet as they devoured the cinnamon and sugar pull-apart loaf, each one fighting for the glazed pecans on top. When Jack brought the coffee to the table, Kathleen began to tell him about their evening.

"To begin with, the visitation was very nice. But, while we were all kneeling by the casket, my caring friends pointed out that I was wearing the exact same top as Mrs. Jenkins." Jack winced. "I know, right? Well, we went to Spanky's afterward, and others from SVA had stopped by, too. Many toasts were made to Mrs. Jenkins, and we might have been overserved. For as long as we can remember, Mrs. J. would always say she wouldn't leave SVA until she was buried and gone. She just loved the school that much. Somehow, we thought going inside Saint Vincent's would be a good idea. You know, in remembrance." Jack began to shake his head while Kathleen continued her story. "So, we jumped the fence and went to her classroom. Somehow, I was coaxed to leave my shirt in the classroom, so all of Saint Vincent's wouldn't forget Mrs. J. And let me tell you, I was happy to get out of the shirt whose twin was in that coffin. Anyway, we hung it up and wrote 'Rest in Peace, Mrs. Jenkins' on the board."

Everyone began to add parts to the story, explaining why they had to break into the school, but Jack interrupted. "That's trespassing. You all swore not to do anything that could land you in jail. What if you got caught?"

Kathleen answered, "Well, that's where I need your help. Sister Mary Michael saw the light from the convent, and she caught us in the classroom." Kathleen took a deep breath and spat out the ending. "So, I made a small contribution to the renovation campaign. We have the sisters coming over for a steak dinner on Friday night. Sister Mary Michael said to let you know she takes hers medium-rare."

12

THE REVIEW

Philip walked into Stephanie's office, swinging a letter angrily in the air. "A personal courier just delivered this. What are you trying to pull?"

"Hello, Philip. Nice to see you," she answered, pulling the matching letter out of her top drawer. "I was delivered the same letter by courier this morning."

Philip plopped down in the chair across from her. "So, you don't have anything to do with this?"

He looked so deflated that Stephanie wasn't sure how to proceed. "This is my first job for the City of Savannah, so I wasn't sure if sending a letter by courier was the standard, but I thought it was odd. Why would they move up the hearing by a full month?"

"I don't know. The receptionist at the city's office couldn't tell me, either," he answered.

"Usually, hearings are moved up because of deadlines or time constraints with the project. I didn't notice anything like that with your case."

"I wish there were someone I could ask, but the Scot in me has difficulty trusting people." He contemplated his following words. "You promised you would walk the castle with me before the hearing, and now that it's moved up, we don't have much time." He paused and looked her over. "You wouldn't happen to be free tonight, would you?"

Her stomach did somersaults from how he looked at her, but she hid them well. "I do not have plans this evening. But I want you to understand my decisions for the castle will be based on the facts. I am not for you or against you; I am just doing my job for the safety of the many people coming to your beautiful resort."

He smiled. "So, you've reviewed my plans and proposal, I take it?"

She nodded, "Yes, it will be spectacular if the building is structurally sound."

"Good. I can accept that," he answered. "Can I pick you up at five?"

"I'll just meet you there."

"That's a wasted ride. We're practically neighbors."

She cringed. She always liked having her car; it kept her in control of when she could leave. Still, she agreed. As she watched him walk out the door, she wondered how he could simultaneously be so irritating yet so handsome.

She went about her day, working on other projects that required her attention, yet the hearing being moved up an entire month was nagging at her. Pulling out the case file, she began doing some research. One click led to one hundred; time had gotten away from her before she knew it. When she glanced at the clock that read 4:30, she snatched up her purse, grabbed the file, and ran out the door.

Pulling into her driveway at the same time Philip pulled in, she motioned for him to give her a minute and ran inside.

Philip let himself in behind her and began playing with Cooper. "Hey, would you like me to let Cooper out?"

"That would be great. I'll only be a minute," she answered and smiled that he had remembered the dog's name.

They chatted easily on the drive to the castle. Stephanie had so many things she wanted to tell him from her research, but she kept them under wraps until she had seen the castle closely. Everything might be a moot point if she found the building in ruins.

He parked in the front, and they entered the building through the main doors. They were heavy dark wood, which had aged over time, leaving a rustic grey appearance. This time when she entered, she was standing in the entrance hall.

"Let's walk around downstairs and then go up," he suggested, and she followed. They walked through the library and dining room, but they were just large open rooms with nothing significant. The kitchen was also just a large room but did have the remnant of what appeared to be a sink. She remembered the great hall well because that is where she and her friends had gathered when they had run aground. It ran entirely along the waterfront side of the building and circled back to the entrance hall. They climbed the staircase upstairs, which held two large bed chambers that exited into a foyer area and a chapel with the altar still remaining.

"What faith were these Scottish people?"

"They were Catholic for hundreds of years, but when the

British took control of Scotland, most became Protestant." He motioned to the large stone box behind the altar. "Most, but not all."

When they walked back downstairs, Philip cut immediately to the tower door.

When he began walking up the stairs, she stopped him. "Is this safe?"

"I go up there every time I ride out. It is as safe as can be."

She eyed him warily and didn't move forward. "Are you sure?"

"Do as you must," he answered. "But you'll miss an incredible view."

She followed tentatively, testing each stone step as she followed slowly behind him. She was amazed that she didn't notice a shift in any stairs. When she finally reached the top, she was rewarded with a beautiful view of Wassaw Sound and the Atlantic Ocean behind it. She closed her eyes and breathed in the saltwater air. When she opened them, she sighed, "It's beautiful."

Philip beamed with pride. "It's amazing, for sure." Moving closer to where she leaned along the parapet, he explained, "From what I've read, there was always a lookout stationed where we are standing."

Stephanie knew a lot about Savannah's history but predominantly the history of the various buildings downtown. She asked, "What were they looking out for?"

"They were watching for enemy ships on the ocean." He looked at her questioningly and asked, "This is Savannah's history. Do you want to know more?" After she nodded, he explained further. "The treetops camouflage the tower from the ships on the ocean. King George II granted this land to the Scots. General Oglethorpe asked for the grant to bring in Scottish Highlander settlers and position them between Savannah and the Spanish who had settled in Florida. His one condition on the land was that they have a lookout tower."

Stephanie looked past the marsh and out to sea. She hesitated at first but decided to proceed. "What do you know about this land grant and how it works?"

"Not very much. Only the records on the land from my dad. Is there something I need to know?"

Stephanie hated to be the bearer of bad news, but she knew she must inform Philip. "Land grants given to colonists last for 250 years. I looked up your information today. It's up at the end of this year."

Philip let this news register. "Then what?"

"At that time, if the land is prosperous and residents dwell upon it, it is reevaluated, and the landowner begins paying taxes at the new level. If the land is not bringing in a profit or there is no building, it will be auctioned to the highest bidder." She questioned herself about revealing too much information but decided to finish telling him everything. "There is already someone who has placed a bid."

Philip's eyes scanned across Wassaw Sound, then turned to Stephanie. "Let me guess, Tommy Morgan?" Her face verified his answer as his jaw clenched in response. He then added, "Let him try!"

13

THE HEADMASTER

Stephanie and her brother walked around the outskirts of Benedictine Military School. The school had only been in session for two weeks, and the young cadets had already begun marching in regiment around the plaza. She stopped to watch as the upperclassmen officers gave commands that the newbie grunts tried to follow.

"It's always like this at the beginning of the school year. There's a lot to learn in JROTC," Keith said with pride. "Every graduate remembers when they learned how to walk in formation and being punished by doing JUGS if you took too long to master it." He laughed, then pulled her along. "We better get going. Father Gerald keeps a pretty tight schedule."

As they made it halfway around the plaza, the overhead bell rang to announce the lunch period. Everyone stopped to say the prayer. Thirty seconds later, the doors to every school wing flew open as the young men raced for their place in the lunch line.

"Good gosh," Stephanie exclaimed and cleared out of the way. Yet, in under two minutes, the plaza was nearly clear of students, and they could continue to the headmaster's office.

Father Gerald was excited to see Keith and stood to greet him with a handshake and pat on the shoulder. He then welcomed Stephanie to his office. "What can I do for you?" he inquired.

Keith motioned to Stephanie, who began explaining. "I came across these buttons at one of my jobsites. When I asked Keith about them, he thought they might be old military buttons. Could you take a look at them, please?"

He agreed, so she handed him the pins wrapped in tissue paper. The headmaster unwrapped each pin reverently, appreciating their age and respecting the person who once wore them. Looking at Stephanie, he asked, "Were all three of these found together?"

"Yes, they had been buried in a leather pouch of sorts. Why?"

"The first one is the standard issue JROTC pin from the mid-1900s. The second is a Benedictine pin with crossed rifles and BMS. This last one with the eagle and flags appears to be from an Army officer's uniform. Putting them together would make this person one of Benedictine's JROTC officers." He placed the pins back in the tissue and asked them to follow him to Alumni Hall.

Once there, they slowly inspected each old black-and-white military picture.

"We are in luck," Father Gerald exclaimed. "Benedictine had a full military program until 1968, so military uniforms were worn at all times, and military instructors were always shown with their class." He circled back to the beginning of the row of images and called out each class by the year. "1938, 1939, 1940, '41, '42, '43, '44, '45. Now, look here." He pointed out the pin that the Class of 1945 wore, the crossed rifles with BMS. Then he moved to the picture of the Class of 1946. He examined it closely. "This pin changed after the end of WWII. The crossed rifles changed to the torch. So, the wearer of your pin would have to have been at Benedictine before 1946." Then, he circled back to the beginning pictures one last time. "1938, 1939. Look at the officers. The Army pin changed in 1939 to the eagle and flags. So, you must be looking for an officer at Benedictine between 1939 and 1945."

"That's incredible," Stephanie blurted out. "Thank you."

Father Gerald gave a satisfied nod, shook Keith and Stephanie's hands, then turned and walked back to his office with his hands grasped behind his back.

Stephanie looked at Keith in confusion. "Is that it?"

"Yes, that's it; he's off to the next problem. Now, let's write down the officers' names from the bottom of the pictures."

They scribbled down the names of four men who had remained in the same position for six years. Stephanie recognized the last name of one of the men, Elders. She graduated with Suzanne Elders from SVA and remembered that her father had been military. She made a mental note to contact her. There was one additional officer from the 1940 to 1942 photos. His face showed he didn't want to have his picture taken. His name was Sergeant Albert Muller.

"Before we leave, would you like to see if the historian is in today?" Keith asked.

"No, I've got a hearing this afternoon for the castle."

"The castle on Wassaw Sound?"

Stephanie smiled; Keith's description rolled right off the tongue like the formal name of an actual castle. "That's the one," she answered her brother, suddenly proud to be a part of the project. "And I can't wait to see what the castle's future holds."

———

Stephanie sat down at the large table in the conference room. She spread her paperwork across the table, looking over her recommendations one last time, then carefully placed them in the business folder for her company presentations.

Philip was the first to arrive. His face lit up as soon as his eyes made contact with Stephanie's. "Good afternoon, Ms. Normand."

"Good afternoon," she replied and then repeated herself when Mr. Henry entered the room.

"Shall we begin?" Mr. Lane responded immediately as he set his briefcase beside his chair and took a seat.

"Of course," Stephanie answered. "As you know, this is a tricky case because the building in question is almost 250 years old, unprecedented in our country. However, I performed all the normal examinations. I found it to be . . ." Her sentence trailed off as Tommy Morgan entered the room. Turning to Mr. Lane, she asked, "Do you find it appropriate to have someone present who has an active bid against this case?"

He waved off her request. "Please continue, Ms.

Normand."

She glanced at Mr. Morgan, "As I said before our intrusion, I performed all the required preliminary examinations. The foundation is sound, the walls can hold sustainable weight, and the property is adequate for further building projects." She slid the folder to Mr. Henry, whose face grew redder by the minute. "All of my initial findings are included in my report. The next step will be lab and mortar reports."

Mr. Morgan began to rise, but Mr. Lane held up his hand for him to stay put and said, "As you indicated, we are on unprecedented grounds here, with a 250-year-old building. I'm shocked that you believe we must go to the next step. This building is without modern footings, hurricane rods, and all the safety measures that should be in place. I thought you would spot that immediately, Ms. Normand."

"So did I," she agreed. "But somehow, it stands strong."

"May I interrupt?" Philip asked.

Mr. Lane shook his head, but Philip began talking anyway. "You have no reason to squelch this project; you just don't have any comparisons. Castles in Scotland last for hundreds of years without repair."

"We are not in Scotland, Mr. McLaughlin. There are ordinates in place in the United States."

"What if I can find proof?"

"And how would you do that?"

"Come to Scotland with me. You can see it with your own eyes."

Mr. Lane laughed at the very suggestion of going to Scotland. "There's not a chance of that."

Philip stood. "I have until the end of the year to prove,

without a doubt, this building is stable, and the land is prof-itable. Is that correct?"

Mr. Lane looked surprised. "Yes, as a matter of fact, that's correct."

"I'll tell you what. Let me take Ms. Normand to Scotland and show her the proof. She can write one of those handy-dandy reports you are talking about to explain everything in terms we all understand. If she can't find proof positive, I will walk away. It's all yours. However, you'll approve my case if she can find what she needs."

Mr. Lane held his head high, knowing there was no way a 250-year-old castle built upon marsh and sand could ever withstand the structural test. He also knew that Stephanie couldn't stand Philip; she told him that herself. Grinning, he reached out his hand to shake Philip's. "You drive a hard bargain. If Ms. Normand agrees, we've got ourselves a deal."

14

THE GOLFER

Philip walked out of the courthouse. He had just made a deal with the devil when he shook hands with Mr. Lane. He hated that his castle, hell, his whole livelihood depended on Stephanie. She was so strong-minded; he knew he must tread lightly.

He must convince her to go to Scotland with him, which would be a considerable feat. But he also had to find evidence to convince her that his castle would stand firm. How should he proceed? If she were like most girls, he would charm her and try to sweep her away on a fun trip for two. But she was intelligent and no-nonsense. It confused him. *I'll just do everything opposite what I usually do*, he thought. So, instead of waiting for her outside the courthouse, he walked straight to his truck and drove away. Instead of calling and asking her for dinner, he turned his phone off. It was killing him, but the ball was in her court. He couldn't scare her off.

Stephanie had pretended to discuss further business with Mr. Lane, allowing Philip time to leave the hearing. She didn't want to leave with him, knowing he would begin pressuring her to travel to Scotland. When she finally left, she searched faces when passing through the courthouse's front doors, thankful he wasn't one of them.

She crossed Bull Street and walked on the path into Wright Square. A lone bench in the shade called to her, so she walked over and sat. *This project isn't going as planned*, she thought. *A trip to Scotland? I can't just up and go to Scotland.* She worried about what would happen to the castle. She appreciated its beauty and didn't want to see it destroyed.

She watched the people coming and going in the square. A group of ladies strolled through its center, holding a map. A man played with his dog, and young parents sat beside Tomochichi's Boulder, watching their children run around it. She smiled as the children stopped running and began talking to their parents, then stomped off with arms crossed.

Stephanie knew the family must be locals. She made eye contact with the young mother and nodded. They both had undoubtedly had the wool pulled over their eyes by their parents in an attempt to teach them Savannah's history. Tomochichi was the leader of the Yamacraw Indians. In the early 1700s, he helped General Oglethorpe secure the land that became Savannah. Upon his death, he was brought back to Savannah to be buried among his English friends.

Savannahians still remember him by bringing their children to his memorial. The parents kneel beside the children and, speaking in their best mysterious voice, say, "Legend says, if you run around the boulder three times, saying Tomochichi's name, you'll hear him say...what?" They, in turn, run as fast as they can. When they have finished, they look at their parents questioningly, who answers, "If you run around the boulder three times, saying Tomochichi's name, you'll hear him say...NOTHING."

Stephanie smiled, thinking about her childhood. Even though her mother hadn't been a part of it, she had grown up surrounded by love. She was happy in Savannah and loved its history and traditions. Her thoughts drifted to Philip. *I'm sure he loves his traditions, too. And he's trying to share them with our city.* She pondered the situation a bit further. Her big project was on hold, and no one except her was hurrying to reopen it. She had always wanted to see Scotland, so why couldn't she go? She decided right then and there. When Philip asked her, she would accept.

She was sure Philip would be going crazy trying to contact her, so she checked her phone before leaving. No messages. *He's probably waiting at my office,* she thought. She left Wright Square and walked the three blocks. Still, when she arrived, there was no Philip. *I wonder what he's up to.*

She finished the few things she needed to do at work, then went home early. She wondered if he might have gone for a walk around the park, so she grabbed Cooper's leash and ran out the door. She was on high alert, watching everyone in her vicinity. After walking the entire perimeter of Daffin, she decided to venture off her regular route. She had looked up Philip's address on the permit, so she crossed Waters Ave and began walking down 45th Street. After crossing Reynolds, she looked for his truck but saw its driver first.

He was playing golf in the front yard of a red brick house. Its walkway cut directly down the center of the yard, from the front porch to the sidewalk. Using a chipper, he hit the ball from one side of the walkway to the other. Back and forth. He was so focused he didn't hear Stephanie come up behind him. Cooper barked when one of his shots landed short and bounced on the concrete, causing Philip to spin around. He smiled at first sight, then contained himself and simply said, "Hello."

"So, you're a golfer?"

"Well, obviously not a very good one," he answered and shrugged.

"I looked for you after the hearing," she said, knowing that she was looking to avoid him but looking just the same.

"Oh, I'm sorry. I had something I had to get to."

She looked at all the balls that sat high on the grass hills on each side of the sidewalk. "Yeah, I can see that." She felt like a teenager chasing boys and suddenly wanted to flee. "All right then, I'll let you get to it." Looking down at Cooper, she pulled at his leash to leave. "Come on, boy."

"Wait," Philip called out and walked towards her. "Would you like to come in?" She pursed her lips and hesitated, so he continued. "I'd like to talk with you.

"Okay, sure. Why not?" She followed him inside the front door to a wonderfully decorated room. A stuffed denim couch with colorful pillows and a matching chair made the space very welcoming. Linen curtains hung from the windows, and a large arrangement of sunflowers sat on the end table in a vase. "Wow. You have nice taste for a man."

He laughed, "I won't pretend to take credit for this. The place came furnished. It's not my taste, but it's comfortable enough." He motioned her to sit, and she chose the single chair while he sat on the couch. He rubbed his hands down his face. "I've tried to play it cool all day because I didn't want to scare you off. But I can't do this anymore. I need you. I hate to admit that and to put any pressure on you, but I do, lass."

She smiled in acknowledgment. "You don't scare me. How do you see this playing out?"

"I want you to come to Scotland with me. I have many castles to show you to compare them to mine. I realize we must act fast since the case is in three weeks, but if you agree, I'll pay for and handle everything."

Stephanie stood up, so he followed. Extending her hand, she said, "You have yourself a deal." As they shook, she added, "Just let me know when."

He walked her toward the door, opened it, and touched her back to usher her through. As she walked out, he leaned toward her.

"The flight leaves this Thursday at eleven a.m. I'll pick you up at eight. Good day, lassie," and he shut the door behind her.

Stephanie retraced her steps back home, but this time her mind was busy making lists of things she needed to do before leaving the country. *Thank heavens I kept my passport up to date*, she thought. It was Tuesday afternoon, and they were leaving first thing Thursday; the next thirty-six hours would be busy. Like she always did, she would start by talking to her dad.

She found him still at work, laid out underneath an old Buick working on its brakes. He had run the only garage on Wilmington Island practically his whole life. It was situated on what was once the only route from town to Tybee Beach. The traffic always kept the gasoline flowing and the car repairs in demand. Her dad was honest and kind and could fix almost anything, so he always had people waiting for his services.

Stephanie knocked on the car's hood like knocking on a door. "Anyone home?" she yelled out like she usually did when she found him under a car.

Her dad rolled out from under the car and smiled when he locked eyes with his youngest daughter. Stephanie held up a bottle of Coke and a pack of peanuts for him to pour inside.

"Well, this must be my lucky day," he announced.

"Is that for me or for the Coke and peanuts?"

"Definitely for my baby girl," he chided but embraced the Coke like the best gift anyone had ever brought him.

"Long day, Dad?"

"No longer than yesterday," he answered. "And no longer than tomorrow will be, God willing." He motioned her to the long bench on the side of the garage. "To what do I owe this pleasure?"

"I just wanted to let you know I'll be out of town for a few weeks."

"Where are you off to this time?"

Stephanie smiled. He knew her so well. She was slightly addicted to traveling and tried to save her money so she could travel at least once a year. There were many destinations on her bucket list. "I'm going to Scotland."

Her father whistled, "Whoa, I bet that set you back a pretty penny."

"Well, actually, this one is paid for. It's for work."

"Good girl," he said proudly. "Want me to watch out for the house while you're gone?"

"No, but I'd love for you to take Cooper."

"No problem. Just bring him down when you're ready."

Stephanie whistled, and Cooper came running around the corner. "I'm ready. I'm leaving on Thursday."

Her dad greeted the dog as it rolled over to let him rub its belly. "Have you talked to your mom?" he asked.

"I haven't, but she wouldn't know if I was here or there."

"No, have you spoken to your mom about Scotland?"

"No, why?"

"Because she was born there. Don't you remember your Gran telling you about Scotland and moving to the States when your mom was three?"

"No, I don't remember that at all. Oh my gosh, I'm Scottish? Where are we from?"

"Half-Scottish. I don't remember from where but reach out to your mom before you go."

Stephanie hugged him goodbye and patted Cooper's head; he was already curled up under her dad, taking a nap. On the ride home, she replayed their conversation. *I'm Scottish*, she thought. Then laughing out loud, she said, "I'm Scottish. My mom is from Scotland. This is huge." Still, the more she thought about it, she became angry. *Why didn't I know? What kind of mother doesn't share those things with their child?* And just like that, the image of her mom driving off and leaving her standing with her siblings on the porch resurfaced. The familiar clench in her stomach answered her question; that's the kind of mother that doesn't share those things with their child.

15

RUNNING THE STREETS

The cab clipped through traffic from the airport into Edinburgh. It had been a long flight through the night. She longed for a hot shower and bed, but when she looked at her watch, it read eleven a.m.

Philip caught her checking the time. "We've got to push through today and then go to bed early. If not, we'll be off kilter all week."

"Okay," Stephanie answered as she yawned loudly, letting her arm stretch across the cab. "You mentioned we were staying two nights in Edinburgh before driving to the Highlands, but I never asked where we were staying."

"My home is in Edinburgh."

"I thought you said you lived in a country estate outside of Inverness."

"Yes, I did. But my family home, where I grew up, is in Edinburgh. My mom passed away when I was a baby, and my father raised me in Edinburgh. We always enjoyed holidays in Inverness, but that definitely wasn't home. After university, I began working in the city. And my father moved to Inverness to begin renovations on the country estate. That's when he got sick." Philip looked out the front window of the cab. "It is right around the corner."

The car pulled down a small lane and stopped. Phillip pointed to the three-story townhome. "Come on," he said excitedly, and Stephanie followed with her suitcase dragging behind. The blocklike front of the house was encased by what appeared to be a continuous building. Still, on further inspection, each house had a slightly different stone size. The front doors and drainpipes that ran from the roof to the ground were the only way to determine how many houses were on the block.

Upon entering, Stephanie felt a connection to the historic homes in downtown Savannah. The brick floor of the first level brought in the cold from the outside, while the original dark wood tried to counteract it with a feeling of warmth. But her attention was drawn immediately to the back windows and door.

She pulled her bag over to the window and looked out onto a large piazza filled with people going about their day. Clapping her hands like a little girl, she asked if she could go outside.

The sound of Philip's laughter filled the room. "That's exactly how I felt as a boy. Let me throw my bags down, and I'll show you around Edinburgh."

"I'll wait for you outside," Stephanie answered as she opened the door that spilled into the large courtyard. Like the lanes in downtown Savannah, the courtyards showed the uniqueness of the families living in the surrounding buildings. Some homes had small gardens to their side, while others had children's toys scattered about. This was the heartbeat of the family, where they played and enjoyed time with each other. Stephanie was lost in another world. She spun around to take in each angle. Closing her eyes, she envisioned the gardens and children who had enjoyed that space for hundreds of years. Her senses heightened as she drowned out the sounds of the city and focused on the sound of someone approaching. When she opened her eyes, Phillip stood directly before her.

"Are you ready to see the city?"

"If it's anything like this courtyard, I can't wait."

"Do you have another jacket you would like to change into?"

She looked into the sky and answered, "It's just a light drizzle. I'm sure I'll be fine."

Smiling, Philip said, "Suit yourself." He motioned to a small gate in the rear of the courtyard that opened to an alleyway. "Shall we?" he asked, and Stephanie followed behind. With each step, the sounds of the city drew nearer. When they reached the end, they exited directly onto Main Street. "This is known as the Royal Mile. It runs between Edinburgh Castle and Holyrood Palace."

Philip moved along the streets with great ease, pulling up the collar of his Barbour jacket to protect him from the weather. The unending drizzle kept her hair wet, and her trendy cotton jacket had now become soaked. Stephanie asked if they could pop inside a shop that she noticed was selling coats and came out with a thick waterproof jacket and a ball cap. When she walked back outside, she was both warm and dry.

"I'm now ready to see Edinburgh. Not the one on the tourist map, but the Edinburgh where you grew up."

"I was a little ruffian growing up. Are you sure you can handle it?" he teased.

"I'll try my best."

For the next several hours, she followed Philip down every back alley. They jumped fences and squeezed between buildings. At each turn, he shared a piece of his life with her. As she followed closely behind, she thought of her mother. She didn't know where her mom had been born, but she could picture a three-year-old girl running these alleys. She was so deep in thought that she almost missed her turn. When Philip cut through a cafe to get from one street to another, Stephanie pulled him to a stop. She was cold, and her jet lag was beginning to pull her down. "Can we please break for coffee?"

"Sure, grab a table, and I'll fetch us both a cup." As he walked off, he called back over his shoulder. "Latte, okay?" She nodded, then plopped in a small booth beside the fireplace. Scooting her chair closer to the roaring fire, she held her hands open to the heat.

"Find your passion and let it guide you." The voice came from somewhere behind her. She was drawn to it and wanted to sneak a peek at the person who had made such a strong statement. But upon turning, she realized that the older lady, sitting on the opposite side of the fire, was directing the message to her.

Stephanie was unsure of how to respond to the unsolicited advice. People didn't say such intimate things to strangers in the States. She said, "Thank you," and returned to the fire. She wanted to get away or at least change tables.

Phillip turned the corner at the perfect time to save her. But when he noticed the two women's interaction, the happiness on his face defied all logic. He set the coffee on the table, walked straight to the older lady, and wrapped her in a hug. "Molly! It's so good to see you."

"Hello, my boy." She held his face between her hands with love. "I've missed you."

"And I've missed you. How are things in your world?"

"Just fine, just fine. The birds tell me to get ready for a cold winter. But heat begins in the soul, so I tell them not to worry about me."

Her toothy grin made Stephanie smile, and her uncertainty about the woman faded.

Philip moved the cups of coffee over to Molly's table, and Stephanie followed. "Molly, may I properly introduce you to Stephanie. Stephanie, this is my Auntie Molly."

"Nice to meet you, Molly," Stephanie replied softly.

Molly reached out her hand to Stephanie, not to shake but to hold. She then took Philip's hand into her other. "I knew that you would one day come. What took you so long?" She asked Philip, "What took you so long to find her?"

"You're so impatient," Philip responded. He glanced at Stephanie and seemed to notice the confusion on her face. He smiled and rolled his eyes, then nudged her with his elbow to ease her worry.

"Is Philip showing you his Edinburgh?" Molly asked.

"Yes, ma'am. It's such a unique city."

"How so?"

"It seems to have a heartbeat of its own, and everyone lives around it."

Molly nodded, "You have no idea how true those words are." Turning to Philip, she added, "This one, you keep."

Stephanie interrupted, "Oh, no, we're not a couple."

"Aye, not now. But you will be." With that, she rose and patted Philip one last time on the face before leaving the room.

16

EDINBURGH CASTLE

Stephanie woke to the sound of a flute drifting from outside her bedroom window. It was so faint she thought she might be imagining it, but after a while, she noticed the songs were changing. Following the music to the window, she searched for the lock to open, but in its place, she found a pulley mechanism with small cleats to tie off the ropes and hold the window open. "We are spoiled rotten with our new window systems," she muttered. However, as always, figuring out how something worked gave her joy, and she quickly opened the window.

The courtyard was covered with a thick layer of fog. Although it was the first light of day, the mist held the darkness and made it seem earlier than it was. The water molecules distorted the sound of the fife player camouflaged in the gloom. She thought of him playing to let people know that there was life in the thickness of nature. The sound of the flute drew louder as the song changed to a military sound. The new tune made her think of a fife and drum corps. She pictured a young man in a regiment, dressed in the traditional kilt and hat, calling out to his comrades with music, letting them know they weren't alone.

She left the window open as she threw on clothes, enjoying the serenade, then locked up to go find Philip. She found him drinking coffee beside the fire in the small living room.

"I only have coffee. Help yourself to a cup. We'll grab breakfast on our way out. Our train to Inverness leaves at three, and I wanted you to see Edinburgh Castle before leaving."

She poured a cup of coffee and settled into the matching armchair on the opposite side of the fire. Philip seemed lost in his thoughts as he watched the flames lick the top of the soot-faced bricks. "Are you happy to be home?"

"Aye, I've missed Scotland and enjoyed sharing Edinburgh with you yesterday. But, you know, all my memories aren't happy here. It was hard growing up without my mum. Women in the city, like Aunt Molly, raised me, but I was alone a lot."

"Nothing can replace a mother's love; I truly understand that."

He reached over and placed his hand over hers, acknowledging their mutual absence of a mother. "Edinburgh will always be my home, but I now understand, without a doubt, that my decision to leave is a good one."

Stephanie's face burned. Was it from the fire or Philip's hand still resting on hers? Suddenly, she felt trapped and wanted, more than anything, to escape their intimate moment. Taking her free hand, she gave his hand two quick pats. "Okay, then. We have lots to do."

He didn't budge as a mischievous grin played across his face. "Did you just tap out?"

"Uh, no."

"Yes, you did."

"I assure you; I never tap out." She gave a curt nod, thinking the conversation was over, but then she thought of playing with Keith as a child and regretfully added, "It drives my brother crazy."

Philip let his hand slowly slip away as he turned toward her. "Oh, I need to hear this. Please continue."

She was caught and now had to share an embarrassing story because she couldn't keep her mouth shut. "Okay. Keith would always put me in a headlock for any reason: to get the TV remote, to get the prize out of the cereal box, or just when he wanted to make sure I remembered he was my older brother. 'Tap Out,' he would yell. 'Tap Out, Stephanie. Once you do, I'll let you go.' I hate feeling trapped, but I never gave in. Sometimes he would lose interest, but most of the time, he would get angry and tighten. But one day, I had enough. I told my dad that neighborhood bullies were bothering me and I wanted to attend a self-defense class. The next time he put me in a headlock from behind, I stepped back towards him, bent over, and he went flying." She cleared her throat, "There were no more headlocks by him or anyone else after that."

Philip put his hands up in surrender. "Lesson learned. I'll NEVER put you in a headlock unless I want my arse thrown on the floor." He held her gaze, then nodded as if understanding her warning.

Stephanie felt her face flush under Philip's intense stare, but she had not looked away. Was he sizing her up? And when had holding someone's hand become more uncomfortable than a headlock?

They left their packed bags by the front door and walked towards Edinburgh Castle. The slow incline was so gradual Stephanie hadn't realized how high they had come. They came upon the esplanade outside the castle, which was covered with tourists. The wide tarmac was the perfect landing spot for a bird's-eye view of Edinburgh. She looked over the rows and rows of houses and businesses below and considered how many years people had lived there.

Philip explained, "Edinburgh Castle and its historical buildings date back to the eleventh century. It sits on top of dense granite left from a long-extinct volcano, now known as Castle Rock. This is the first of many castles we will visit. I will get out of your way and let you take your time researching. I'll be out here waiting for you."

Stephanie glanced at the enormous castle, then back to Philip. "I'm going to be a while."

"I hope you are."

She appreciated the time to herself. She had listed specific things she needed to see and didn't want to get sidetracked. She picked up the handheld audio device that accompanied the self-guided tour and began to walk around.

The castle was much larger than she anticipated, so she quickly jumped around, searching for the information she needed. She traveled through the great hall, past the Scottish Crown Jewels, through the Battery and David's Tower, but had yet to find any answers. When she glanced at her watch, she had been in the castle for nearly two hours. She was about to throw in the towel when she stumbled into Saint Margaret's Chapel.

A chill ran up her spine as she stood just inside the arched doorway. She shivered, then staggered to a long, primitive bench on the wall. Slowly, she let her eyes wander. The second they connected with a life-size stone statue, she knew. She had thought about it so often she could have drawn it from memory. But up until now, she had no idea who it was. "You're Saint Margaret," she said to the exact twin of the statue from Wassaw Sound.

The room was eerily empty, which was fascinating since tourists were everywhere. "You have my full attention," she said to the statue. "What can you tell me?" Closing her eyes, she waited for an answer that never came. However, when she opened them, she found the connection. The chapel inside the castle on Wassaw Sound was an exact replica of Saint Margaret's Chapel.

She wandered towards the statue but paused to read the monument sign beside it.

The Pearl of Scotland

Saint Margaret of Scotland was a devout Catholic Christian known for her kindness and good heart. She is admired the most for the love of her eight children and husband, Malcolm Canmore II, the King of Scotland. She taught others to model the holy family, a domestic church.

She was canonized as a saint in 1250 by Pope Innocent IV. In 1560, Mary Queen of Scots came into possession of Margaret's head. It was kept as a relic and said to have assisted her in prayer and childbirth. The head was said to be lost, but local tales said it was hidden in the small vault behind the saint's statue in Edinburgh Castle.

In 1745, an attack was made on Edinburgh Castle by the Jacobites, who were fighting to restore a Catholic, Stuart monarch, to their throne. Although they didn't have the necessary firepower to mount a serious assault on the castle, several Jacobite rebels succeeded in entering the castle and escaping with priceless treasures. One of them was rumored to be the head of Saint Margaret.

Stephanie unhooked the red rope dangling between waist-high poles to keep guests out of unwanted areas. She found a deep, empty alcove set into the wall behind the statue. Turning back to look around the room, she walked towards the altar. "This room would have been used for Catholic Mass and Adoration. Oh, my gosh, the Scots in Savannah were Catholic. I wonder if they agreed to settle in the colonies knowing they would be able to practice their faith?" She looked down her list. Her fourth question was, "Why would this clan go to such an effort to build a castle when they could have built simple houses?" She smiled. "You were settlers paving the way for your family's religious freedom. And you wouldn't have cut corners knowing many generations of your family would be living there. And Philip falls under that category." She continued to let her eyes scan the room, then added, "I'll do my best to help him."

Somewhere during her speech to herself, she had wandered directly under the statue and was staring at it as she spoke. She had been so focused she hadn't heard the throng of tourists enter the small chapel. But when she looked up, all eyes were on her. She quickly put her handheld audio machine to her ear and pretended to be talking into it as she exited. "Nice talking to you, too. Goodbye," she said into her fake phone as the recorder began blasting information about the next room.

Upon leaving the castle, Stephanie stepped into the gift shop. She went in to buy a book about the castle that she and Philip could refer to, but she was drawn to a children's book about Saint Margaret. The bright and colorful cover showed the young queen wearing braids under her crown and surrounded by several children. After purchasing it, she left, knowing their days ahead would be challenging as they searched for the perfect castle.

17

WHERE THE ROAD LEADS

"We're here." The words were out of place in her dream. Stephanie struggled to open her eyes, but only one responded; it was met by Philip's face. She smiled stupidly, causing him to laugh, and the sound made her bolt upright. Scanning her surroundings, she replayed their train ride from Edinburgh to Inverness. It had been five o'clock when they boarded for the almost four-hour trip. She was tired from walking around Edinburgh and still combatting the time difference from the States, so once night set in, the train's motion lulled her fast asleep.

She let her eyes wander around the compartment at all the seats that had slowly been emptied during the four-hour trip. Before falling asleep, she watched the other passengers as the train approached each stop. They would gather their things before the stop was announced, knowing what lay ahead. Walking like skilled tightrope artists, they seemed to anticipate the shimmy of the train as they gracefully made their way toward the door. Then, they exited in their allotted time before the train moved to the next stop. While watching, she worried about the scene she would cause when it was her turn, but now there would be practically no one to witness it.

As the train announced its stop, Stephanie hurriedly jumped up to gather her things. A still-seated Philip touched her arm. "The train ends in Inverness, so take your time."

Relief washed over her as she sat back down. She had once witnessed a lady get clipped by a closing door of the subway in New York while trying to jump on at the last second. The door had knocked the woman down while setting off sirens that delayed the train. She had been cautious of train doors ever since.

Once the train came to a stop, Stephanie grabbed her carry-on suitcase, placed the matching smaller bag on top, and pulled all her belongings through the train station to the waiting car.

They were met by an older gentleman who seemed to beam with pride when he saw Philip. He welcomed him with open arms. "So good to see you, Philip. I'm so happy you're home."

Philip closed his eyes as he embraced the older man. "It's great to see you too, Hugh." Turning to Stephanie, he added, "Let me introduce you. This is Hugh; he's my dad's," —he swiftly corrected himself— "my friend and property manager."

Stephanie extended her hand. "Hi, Hugh. It's nice to meet you."

He grasped her hand with both of his. "And you as well. Are you ready to see Beauly?"

Philip cut him off quickly. "It's late, so we'll go straight to the guest cottage."

Hugh nodded in agreement, but his eyes searched Philip for information Stephanie wasn't privy to.

They drove away from Inverness and down secluded roads until they came upon a town sign reading, "Beauly." The town was small but quaint, with old fashion streetlights illuminating the rustic buildings. Stephanie couldn't wait to explore it further during her stay.

Turning off the main road, they drove along a private drive for over a mile, then turned into the driveway of a stone cottage. Stepping out of the car, Stephanie was met by the woodsy smell of the forest and enveloped in the darkness. Her other senses tried to compensate while her eyes adjusted. A breeze swept through the trees. The sound of their movement, combined with the song of an owl in the distance, showed the depth of the forest. As the clouds shifted, she was thankful that the moonlight offered a touch of light on the empty cottage.

Philip walked ahead, turning on lights as he went through the cottage, while Hugh helped Stephanie gather her bags.

"He hasn't been back since his father's death. How is he?" Hugh whispered, causing Stephanie to move closer.

She now realized why the man had been watching Philip so intently; he was worried. Stephanie was glad to still be outside in the dark as she began to bite her lip, searching for an answer but falling short. "He's fine."

"Fine? Define 'fine.'"

Clearing her throat, she tried again. "I haven't known Philip very long, but he's strong and caring. He speaks of his father with great respect and shares happy memories. I'm sure he misses him terribly, but he seems to be moving forward and trying to get on with his life." When she finished, she waited for a reply that never came. The silence was killing her, and she wondered if Hugh was still beside her. Then she heard a sniffle.

"They were inseparable, ye know? You don't see many fathers and sons like them two. This town misses them both, but I'm glad they set things up so the town runs in their absence."

"This town?" Stephanie asked.

"Beauly belongs to the family. Well, now it belongs to Philip."

"Philip owns a town?"

"Philip owns the land where the town is built. He leases it to individuals. That's what I'm hired to do, manage their property."

Philip interrupted from the doorway. "Come inside out of the cold, you two," he called out.

Hugh picked up Stephanie's bags and carried them inside.

"Thank you, Hugh. Care for a dram?" Philip asked.

"No, no. We can catch up tomorrow. Are ye coming to the house?"

Philip nodded yes.

"Good. We'll catch up then. There's much to discuss." He looked at Stephanie and nodded curtly. "Goodnight," he called out as he closed the door behind himself.

"Let's get a nightcap, then we should be off to bed," Philip muttered in a tired voice. He walked to the cabinet and pulled out a bottle of whisky with two balloon glasses.

He knew where everything belonged in the small cottage, which told her he had lived there for quite some time.

"Did you live in the big house? Wait, that doesn't sound right. The estate house?" she asked.

"No, I've always stayed in the cottage when I was in Beauly." He looked around the rugged room. "Man, I love this place." He settled into a brown leather chair that seemed to have remembered where many backsides had sat. After propping his shoes up on what appeared to be an old trunk, he took a long sip of his drink.

She settled on a green velvet sofa and proceeded with a sip, which caused her eyes to water. The warm liquid burned all the way to her stomach, where it continued to spread its heat. She tried to hold back the cough, but it spilled out.

"Good stuff," he replied, standing with his empty glass. "Care for another?"

She looked at her glass, which was missing only one sip. "Oh, no, thank you," she replied while scanning the room, looking for a place to dispose of the rest.

He poured another one, then settled himself back into the hole in his chair. They drank in silence while Stephanie tried desperately to finish the contents of her glass since there was nowhere to hide it. She considered it sleeping medicine, which she was sure wasn't far from the truth. After her last sip, she couldn't stifle the loud yawn that escaped her.

"Why am I so tired? It's only nine."

"Not in the States. But also, we've had a busy day. Tomorrow will be the same. Probably a good idea to turn in for the night."

He pulled her luggage up the steps. She followed behind, listening to the protest of the primitive wood under the weight of the baggage and Philip's size twelve shoes. When they reached the top, Philip automatically ducked to walk under a low rafter.

"Good maneuver," Stephanie remarked, grateful he was walking in front of her.

"It only takes one time to make you always remember to duck on the last step, and that one time's a doozie."

Stephanie rubbed her forehead in response, praying she would remember without her "one time" but also acknowledging her clumsiness.

He dropped her bags in her room and said, "Get some sleep; we've got a big day tomorrow." Walking away, he let out a loud yawn that rivaled her previous one and called, "Goodnight," into the air.

18

FAMILY HISTORY

Philip adjusted his eyes to the morning sun coming through the tall windows. He had wrestled with the memory of his father all night but finally gave into it just before dawn and walked to the estate house.

His stomach clenched tight as he thought about the last time he had been in this room. His breath quickened as he fought the panic rushing over him. *Deep breaths*, he told himself. *Deep breaths*. Closing his eyes, he was transported back to that moment. The smell of sterility and the sound of that damn monitor surrounded him. He could go a whole lifetime without ever hearing the music of a heartbeat again and the terrifying silence of its absence.

He had laid his head on the edge of the bed, trying to be as close to his father as possible. His father had fought the disease with great fervor, but God had bigger plans for him. The heart monitor was the only way he knew his father was alive. Philip had been at his bedside all week, but why? He had no idea. He had barely recognized the small man lying on the hospital bed in this masculine-fashioned room.

His dad had been a person with such a strong character. Raised in the Highlands of Scotland, his loud voice and thick brogue made the average child run in fear. But they had no idea he had such a gentle soul. They had no idea that he loved with all his heart and gave with everything he had.

Philip had drifted off to sleep. During the night, Philip had stirred from an imagined touch but woke to find his father's hand sitting gently on his head. As a boy, his father had always placed his hand on Philip's head as he slept. Philip would often wake from the warmth of his father's broad Celtic hand. But today, the heat didn't wake him. When he reached for his father's hand, it was ice cold.

Philip had quickly turned to the silent monitor and tried to call out to the nurse on duty, but no sound had escaped his mouth. He had been paralyzed. Finally, he looked down at his father, closed his eyes, and made the Sign of the Cross. Then, taking four long strides across the room, he peered out the large arched window. The world had been just as it was the day before. And the day before that. The reality of that still confused him.

Philip opened his eyes and scanned the elegant room of deep mahogany and crimson. It looked exactly as it had before, minus the hospital bed. His father had planned so much for this building. He envisioned a vacation spot with hunting, tennis, and a world-renowned chef. But Philip had no desire to complete his father's dream. His only ties with this house; the Highlands; hell, with Scotland itself had left him standing alone in this room, just as he was now.

———

Stephanie woke at first light. She lay very still while letting her eyes scan the room. Her double bed was one of the many pieces of furniture in the sizeable wood-paneled room. The stone floor continued to the fireplace, the room's focal point. It sat with wood in place, just begging to be lit. Stephanie was surprised when she had first seen the bedroom. She was expecting dark plaids and wool comforters but was met by a rose-pink cotton comforter and a cream leather settee. Small female trinkets, such as an engraved mirror and brush, were scattered about, while the pictures were hand-painted florals.

As she sat up, she grabbed a worn quilt off the foot of her bed, wrapped it around her shoulders, and went searching for a cup of coffee. The small kitchen wasn't well-stocked, but it had the essentials. A gallon of milk and a white metal bowl full of eggs sat in the refrigerator, and a coffee maker sat on the counter. "Oh, thank heavens," Stephanie said under her breath, making a beeline to the coffee.

The sunrise summoned her to the back porch, so she pulled the quilt tighter around her shoulders and carried her coffee cup to an iron table and chairs outside. As she swallowed her first sip, she focused on the long drive past the cottage. She felt the familiar itch in her gut to put on her running shoes and find out where it led. Thankfully, she drank her coffee very hot, so she gulped down the cup, went upstairs, and changed into her running clothes. There was still no sign of Philip, so she wrote him a note and left.

Standing in the middle of the long drive, she looked both ways, pondering her path. She knew the town was in one direction, but her curiosity was drawn in the opposite way to the unknown. She began with a slow jog, connecting her breath with the rhythmic sounds of her shoes hitting the ground. The smell of damp leaves filled the air until the forest thinned and eventually leveled out to green pastures dotted with sheep and cows. There was a lake just over the ridge and rolling hills in the background, showing off their fall leaves.

The drive eventually forked down the middle, outlining a large circle in front of the house. She stopped to appreciate the scene. "I could live here," she said into the wind, then began to run around the drive. As she approached the house, a large fountain came into view. Swans ducked their heads in the water as they gracefully searched for breakfast. She became so focused on watching the birds that she ran right by the front of the building and hadn't noticed Philip standing on the front step. His shrieking whistle caused her to come to a halt. The gravel drive shifted under her shoes, and she fell to her knees.

Philip bounded down the stairs, apologizing until he was at her side. "I'm so sorry. I didn't mean to startle you. I was just trying to get your attention." Bending to help her, he asked, "Are you all right?"

She brushed the gravel from her knees. "Just my daily fall, no big deal," she said as she felt the scrape's blood trickle down the front of her leg. Embarrassed, she changed the subject. "You're out early."

"I could say the same for you." Smiling, he added, "I couldn't sleep."

She nodded, then looked past him towards the house.

"I'd love to show you the house. Want to come inside, or do you need to finish your run?"

"I'd love to come inside. Are you kidding me?"

"Great. I want to show you something I found."

The smell of mold filled the air as they walked into the three-story foyer. Stephanie quickly identified an active leak, mainly because of the bucket on the floor.

Philip watched Stephanie's face surveying the scene and began to explain. "My grandparents lived here most of their lives. But, towards the end, it had become too much upkeep for them. They finally moved to the guest house. After they passed away, it sat unoccupied for years. My father didn't want to pull me from the only home I knew in Edinburgh after my mum passed, so we came up a couple of times a year. The town ran smoothly without anyone living on the estate.

"A few years ago, my dad decided he was tired of the city, so he began to fix the place up. He wanted to restore the estate to its former beauty. Make it a lodge for hunting and vacationing. You know, to bring money to the city. Dad had completed the living quarters for himself and his property manager when he got sick." He motioned to a massive double door to the right and opened one side.

Stephanie was speechless at the beautiful drawing room she had now entered. Every detail was impeccable, from the crown molding to the original fireplace and hardwood floors. The end of the room morphed into an office surrounded by dark bookshelves and a heavy desk. But her eyes were drawn to the one thing that was out of place: a dark chest in the middle of the room.

Philip grabbed Stephanie's hand and pulled her toward

the chest. "Look what I found. This is what I've been doing this morning. My family history, all boxed up and ready for me to explore. Hugh brought it to me. I remember Dad telling me to go through everything, but I needed to escape after the funeral. I had just found out about the castle in Savannah, and Hugh had been managing the property for years, so I took off."

Stephanie kneeled on the hardwood floor, wincing on her scraped knee, and finally fell into a sitting position. There were file folders scattered about with Post-it notes sticking out at every angle. On the top of the stack sat a handwritten letter. She picked it up and read the greeting. Her eyes darted to Philip watching her, and he nodded with permission.

Philip, my boy,

It's easy to believe that our family history only goes back to individuals still alive. We can grasp the faces in front of us and understand if each individual had made other choices in life, we may never have been born. If you open your mind past that point, hundreds of thousands of choices were made in the many years before.

Some people are satisfied by what lies in front of them. Others know the names of the men and women who share the same DNA from hundreds of years in the past. Sooner or later, you must find a beginning point. For us, Philip, it began in 1701 with Robert Castell.

I want you to begin with his file and work your

way forward. You've come from a long line of archi-tects, builders, and artists. It's time for you to find your place among them.

I love you, son,

Dad

A tear escaped her eyes and trickled down Stephanie's face. She looked up at Philip, and their eyes locked. "Are you okay?" she asked.

His eyes wandered the room as he took a deep breath, then focused on the trunk. "Last night, when we arrived, I didn't know if I could handle being back here. But somehow, I can still feel him, almost like he's in the next room. His letter and all my family history put things in perspective." Shaking his head, a hint of a smile crossed his lips. "My biggest problem is when I'm going to be able to read all of this."

Stephanie thought for a moment, then came up with an idea. "You said we're driving all over Scotland to see different castles? Why don't I read while you drive?"

"You'd do that? For me?"

"I'd love to." Their eyes met, but she quickly looked to the floor and motioned toward all the scattered files. "Where do we begin?"

"Dad said to begin with Robert Castell." He picked up the file with the matching name and held it in the air. "Are you ready to read?"

She vigorously nodded.

"Then let's get to it."

19

———————

NESSIE

Philip drove away from the cottage and explained, "Since we're getting a later start, I thought we'd go up the road a bit today and visit just one castle. It's called Urquhart. It's only thirty kilometers away."

They came to the intersection at the end of the private drive, where they were forced to turn right or left. As Philip waited to make the turn, Stephanie's eyes focused on the magnificent park directly across the street. It stretched over the hill, with paths and beautiful greenery. She could even see a stone bridge that crossed over a small brook in the distance.

As they turned, Stephanie watched the locals going about their day in Beauly. Each was busy, carrying packages, small children, or both. The shops were all open with their doors ajar. Some had streetside items scattered about, luring their customers inside for more. She watched as they passed a hardware store, a pharmacy, a grocery, clothing stores, and a flower shop. There were a handful of restaurants and pubs dotted between.

Just as Stephanie always did, she looked past the people, past the stores, and focused on the guts of the city. It was laid out perfectly, divided into simple blocks and walkways that spilled into small gathering areas of green space. She could almost imagine an aerial view of the property. "This property was well thought out. The long drive ties Beauly Estate with the park and town. It's all situated to complement one another perfectly."

Philip glanced out his window and scanned the other side of the street. "It is, isn't it?" He looked at Stephanie curiously. "You got all that in the last thirty seconds of riding through town?"

"I know. Not your normal chitchat. But it really is something special."

"I've only felt this in one other city in the world. It's the perfect placement of blocks and green space."

"Where's that?"

"Savannah. Mainly downtown, but I found it in other areas, too. Like Washington Avenue and Daffin Park."

Stephanie smiled proudly at first but remembered how she always thought the greenspace around Savannah was wasteful. "You're right. Thank you for pointing that out."

The scenery changed as soon as they were out of town. Beauly was in the middle of the Highlands and surrounded by beautiful mountains, showing off their many colored trees as the leaves upon them embraced fall. The trip to Urquhart held many turns through the hills, and she quickly realized that every trip they took by car must travel through the surrounding mountains. She was happy she wasn't prone to being car sick and was grateful that Agnes wasn't with them.

Stephanie pulled the folder out of the tote bag. Philip glanced at her and nodded, so she unwound the twine that held it together and opened the front. She was surprised it contained only two books and a few sheets of paper. Opening the worn, red cover of the first book she read, "A Memoir of General James Oglethorpe, One of the earliest Reformers of Prison Discipline in England and the Founder of Georgia, In America. By Robert Wright, London 1867." She paused, deep in thought. "Now, why would this book be in this file?" she mumbled to herself, but loud enough for Philip to hear. She flipped through the book, noticing the many notes in place, and went straight to the end to find out how many pages the book held. "The book is 414 pages. Read from the beginning or just the marked pages?"

They turned to each other, locked eyes, and said in unison, "The marked pages."

She opened the first note and began to read but was interrupted when Philip reached out and touched the message, rubbed it between his fingers, and quickly turned back to the road. He chuckled to himself, "Always leaving me notes, weren't you?" he said quietly, then asked her to continue.

Stephanie glanced at the page in the book, which explained in detail the family of James Oglethorpe's descent. His parents were Jacobite sympathizers with a direct lineage to Scotland. It then went on to explain his youth and educa-tion. The note his father attached read, "James Oglethorpe studied at Oxford."

Stephanie excitedly flipped to the following note. "Please

read this marked page" was neatly written at the top, so she began.

"Mr. Robert Castell was a man of privilege. He was educated at Oxford and finished at Edinburgh University as a skilled architect and author. He published a costly book rejecting the flamboyant Baroque style in favor of symmetrical classical architecture. This book put him in debt, and he was arrested. The warden committed him to Corbett's, where smallpox raged. Poor Castell had never had that disease and begged the warden to be sent anywhere else, but he was rejected. He caught the disease and died just days later, leaving a widow and a large family." She paused. "At the bottom of the note, your father added, 'We are that family. This is where our story begins.'"

Philip parked the car and turned it off while Stephanie finished reading the last note in the book.

"I'm so enthralled with the story of James Oglethorpe and Robert Castell that I didn't feel the car stop. Sorry," she apologized. Glancing up, she was overwhelmed by the sight of Urquhart Castle in the distance and quickly put the book away.

It was a decent walk from the parking lot to the entrance, but her imagination ran wild once on the castle grounds. It was nothing like Edinburgh Castle, which stood tall and secure. Urquhart was in ruins. She couldn't see any of the things on her list but did see the depth of the walls with great accuracy, mainly because they had been demolished in most places, leaving many half walls which were easy to measure.

They walked through the castle. Although it was in ruins, it was built upon the most beautiful trek of land. They strolled along the castle's outskirts and down to a dock overlooking the water. "What waterway is this?" Stephanie asked.

"Loch Ness."

"Like the monster?"

Philip laughed, "A loch is a sea inlet. This one is Loch Ness. The beast that roams these waters is Nessie." He lowered his voice. "You'd better be keeping your eyes out for her." The sound of a fish jumping out of the water made Stephanie turn quickly. Philip took that opportunity to grab her playfully by the shoulders. "Watch out, lassie." She yelled out in response, making them both laugh.

On the way back to the car, they passed a trebuchet set up on the bank to demonstrate how a castle would be attacked. It was a catapult using a counterweight to sling rocks and boulders harder. She looked in the direction of the castle. She could almost imagine the feeling of watching a huge boulder falling down from the sky.

This castle taught her about the life of a Scotsman. After several raids over its lifetime, it illustrated that if you have something valuable, someone will always be trying to take it from you. She began to ponder the situation they were currently in and realized this statement still applied, even at another time in another country. It may not be done with swords and clans, but the viciousness was often the same. The castle on Wassaw Sound was very valuable in more ways than one, and someone was trying to take it from Philip. They had to find a way to stop them.

20

A LOCAL FROM BEAULY

The night began to set in as they moved into town. When she noticed the streetlights on, Stephanie realized they had missed dinner; her stomach responded with a growl. "Can we grab some dinner and a beer at that little pub on the corner?"

Philip checked his watch but didn't answer.

"I'm starving. Where do you usually eat in town?"

Philip quietly shrugged his shoulders, leaving his silence hanging in the air. He was very mysterious and held his cards close to his chest. Stephanie pressed her lips together to keep from asking further questions. She could respect his privacy. However, her hunger had no respect because it let out a low grumble that sounded like storm clouds were rolling inside the car. Philip smirked but kept his eyes on the road. She was pleasantly surprised when he turned into a parking place in front of the pub.

Stephanie smiled as she walked towards the building with a sign above the door that read, "The Glen." Its grey-stoned exterior rounded the corner unit to make it appear to run on for miles. Double windows ran across the front and were purposefully left open to let the music flow into the street.

They were greeted immediately by the bartender as they walked through the door. "Hello, folks, and welcome," he said, pulling them straight over to the man behind the long wood bar. "My name's Bobby. Wha can I git for yew?" Philip ordered them two beers as he and Stephanie plopped up on a barstool. "Are ye jist passing threw?"

Stephanie began to answer, "No, we are staying..." but she was interrupted by Philip tapping her hand. She looked up to find him shaking his head while the bartender poured the drafts. She tried to change the direction of her answer, "We are staying busy today. We just left Urquhart Castle and needed to get something on our stomachs."

"I'm sorry to tell you, lass, but our kitchen burnt down two months ago. I'm saving up for the repairs." He set a bowl in front of her. "Right now, all I can offer you are some bar nuts. But Pepe's is right across the street, and I'm happy for you to bring any food in that you'd like."

Philip left his credit card with the bartender to leave his tab open, then they picked up their pints and made their way to a table in front of the large fireplace. It was blazing with a roaring fire, probably to combat the cold from the open windows. Philip was surprised that Stephanie had brought the nut bowl and had almost finished its contents. "Let's finish the beer, then I'll grab us a pizza to bring back over."

Stephanie nodded in agreement as she looked around the pub. The front area around the bar was cozy, but it opened into a larger room with many full tables. Some people were just socializing, but some were playing cards. There was also a long, arched hallway where she could hear the familiar balls clack from a pool table. "I like this bar. Do you come here often?"

Philip smirked. "You sound like you're trying to pick me up, lass. Are you?"

Stephanie gave him a dead-eye stare. "You're avoiding my question once again."

"Okay, I know. I'm sorry." He took a deep breath, then answered. "I came into town occasionally with my dad, but he had built relationships with the people here. I've only been in The Glen once or twice, but I like it."

Stephanie nodded, "I do, too." She held up her beer, and they toasted, their eyes locking over above the rim of the glasses. She nodded slightly, then cleared her throat. "So, we learned a lot today from your family trunk of secrets, didn't we?"

"We sure did. I still can't believe James Oglethorpe and Robert Castell were such good friends. I guess that happens when you grow up with someone and attend university with them. I think it's fascinating that Oglethorpe had visited Robert when he was sick in jail, and after his passing, he worked to put an end to the treatment of those imprisoned because of debt. It really changed the course of his life. I can't wait to find out more tomorrow." Philip seemed to realize he had been rambling on and refocused on Stephanie. "Are you ready for pizza?"

She nodded her head vigorously.

"Okay, I'll be right back."

Philip was gone for less than fifteen minutes, but

Stephanie was nowhere in sight when he returned. He looked to the bartender, who motioned to the back. He walked through the arched hallway that emptied into a crowded pool room. Stephanie was in the middle of a game with many people watching for its outcome. She noticed Philip walk in and winked at him, then took her shot.

The loud "clack" awarded the burgundy number seven ball in the far pocket. She circled the table where only the scratch ball and the eight ball remained for her, but it was blocked by the green-striped number fourteen. All she could hope was to block her opponent, so she could finish. Her opponent wasn't happy about the position of her scratch ball and wanted to put her in her place, so he shot out of anger and cursed out loud as the black eight ball shot into the side pocket.

Stephanie noticed Philip standing in the doorway holding four pizzas. He watched the scene unfold, laughing when the crowd cheered as Stephanie won. She waved to him, which drew the crowd's attention in his direction. Once the group noticed he had pizza, they swarmed him. A robust woman "helped him" by placing the pizzas on a nearby table. Then, the box tops flew open, and everyone took a slice. Everyone thanked him and introduced themselves before walking off, and Philip seemed pleased with himself.

Stephanie made her way over to him. She watched as the robust woman leaned in to talk to him and patted him on the shoulder before walking off. Philip noticed her walk up and held up one of the pepperoni pizza boxes. She nodded her head and took a slice. "Looks like you're the new town hero."

"Who knew you had to share pizza at The Glen? I didn't

know what you wanted, so I bought four. Thank goodness. I assumed we would take the rest home, but there doesn't appear to be any leftovers. Everyone seems happy, though."

"Pizza and beer. Who could be unhappy with that lethal combination?" Stephanie quipped.

The neighboring tables began to call them over, each buying them a beer to repay them for the pizza. By the time they had visited with everyone, they were pulled into the front room as the band began to play. It was only a three-person band comprising a guitarist, an accordion player, and a drummer. Still, they had the crowd hooting and hollering by the third song. People began to sing, and some danced at random places around the room.

When the band slowed down and began to play "Will Ye Go, Lassie, Go," Philip held his hand to Stephanie. "Shall we?" he asked.

She nodded and placed her hand into his. The electricity of his touch made her heart quiver. He led her to an open spot before the fire and pulled her close, tucking their hands into his chest. The people around held their drinks in the air as they swayed back and forth, singing loudly, but Stephanie had closed her eyes and tuned out everyone around her. It was just she and Philip moving to the beat of the music. When the song ended, they didn't separate but continued to spin slowly until they felt the pings of the now-infamous bar nuts being pelted at their backs. Awakened from their trance, they jumped back from one another as their new pub friends welcomed them back to the group, and the band played their final song.

They decided to walk home from the pub. Once they were alone, walking down the quiet road, Philip admitted how much fun he had. "I've visited my dad several times in Beauly, but I've never had so much fun here. What is it with you?"

"It wasn't me. I think it was your pizza."

"No. It was more than that…" He trailed off as if he would add more but left it hanging in the air. They walked down the middle of the small drive, knowing no one else would drive to the estate house at that hour. What was left over from the full moon two nights prior lit the road but wasn't enough to see his face. They walked along quietly until he finally continued. "I've always felt separated from the people in town. I'm not really sure why, but I did. My dad had many friends, but he knew most of them from growing up here. I have always felt like an outsider, but it was never because I was treated that way. I've never really let myself be open to new friendships here. Tonight made me realize how much I missed out on."

"Coming to a town where everyone already has lifelong friends is hard. But judging from tonight, you fit right in."

"The great part of the night was that no one knew who I was or where I lived; they just accepted me as 'Philip.'"

Stephanie smiled to herself and was grateful to be masked by the darkness. She had seen the bartender showing Philip's credit card to a couple of men sitting at the bar. They all had stared over at him, surely recognizing his name. But what amazed her was that no one treated him differently. He was just one of them. And that was precisely what he now was, a local from Beauly.

21

ANCESTORS

S tephanie wasn't surprised to hear the distant ringing of church bells. Philip had asked her to be ready by 9:45 for church, and she was just putting on the final touches to her minimal makeup, applying lip gloss.

She always loved the toll of the bells in Savannah. Every hour during the day, they would ring across the city. She remembered racing against the chimes of the Cathedral of St. John the Baptist's bell. She would count them as she ran from her parked car down Lincoln Street while trying to make it inside the school before the eighth gong.

The church bell she heard today cried out excitedly, inviting people to come worship. She smiled while picturing the distance the music traveled, floating across the long fields and the surrounding forest before reaching her ears. It made her think of the quote: "If a tree falls in a forest and no one is around to hear it, does it make a sound?" She was grateful for her sense of hearing.

They drove into town, but when Philip came to the intersection across from the town park, he turned away from town.

"Where are we going?" she asked.

"The church in Beauly is The Church of England, and I'm Catholic. We go to St. Mary's in Inverness. Although, I haven't seen you at Mass at Blessed Sacrament Church."

"You're going to ol' BSC?"

"Aye, I've just been elected vice president of the church's Modernization Committee," he said proudly.

"Oh, have you now? I'm impressed," she said mockingly.

"Thank ya. They said they had been waiting for someone with knowledge like mine and felt extremely lucky."

Stephanie contained her smile, knowing how those committees worked, but then chided herself for being so jaded. Shame on her for being anything less than thrilled for Philip. She had sat on various committees with resentment, thinking she was doing some great service sharing her young, new ideas with a stale project. Shamefully, she felt the world would be much better off if we all served with such pride. "Please let me know if your committee ever needs help."

He nodded his thanks in response.

The road from Beauly to Inverness was peaceful, running along Beauly Firth, then driving slowly through the quaint town. They crossed the River Ness and walked along its river path towards the church.

As the priest welcomed parishioners standing outside the church door, he caught sight of Philip and excitedly shook his hand. "Philip McLaughlin, welcome home. How are you?" he asked with a thick Scottish brogue.

"I couldn't be better," Philip answered.

The priest nodded then to Stephanie. She was afraid she wouldn't be able to understand him. His accent sounded almost like another language.

"Good morning, lass. Welcome to Mass."

Relief washed over her.

"Thank you, Father. Good morning," she said, passing through the arched doorway. Philip talked with the priest a moment longer, then joined her inside.

She enjoyed the service. She had been pushing back from attending church in Savannah for so long. She had such animosity toward having to meet her family there. But today, it brought her such comfort. Knowing the parts of the Mass and that her dad was hearing the same readings in Savannah brought her happiness.

At the end of Mass, they had a parishioner step up to speak about their upcoming "Founding Day" celebration. "Each of us has a story of how our families kept their Catholic faith during the Reformation. Our church is proud of that. Even though they were forced to stay hidden for three hundred years, our ancestors kept their faith strong. They didn't have the Eucharist or the sacraments and everything we hold dear today; still, they persevered until 1829, when they were able to build this church. Let us honor the memory of our strong Scottish ancestors. The sign-up is at the rear of the church."

Stephanie scanned the room during the speech, watching each family sit up with pride. They were happy to be a part of such a wonderful church. After the final blessing, the priest said, "Go in peace, to love and serve the Lord." The congregation filed out, strengthened for their task on Earth.

After deciding to grab lunch, they walked along the river until hitting another crosswalk. As they approached the opposite shore, Philip pointed ahead. "That's the Old North Church. St. Columba brought Catholicism to the Highlands in that very spot."

Stephanie immediately noticed the large "For Sale" sign on the side of the building before her eyes fell on the old cemetery. Many people were walking around, looking at various markers and headstones. She referenced the historical marker that retold the story of Saint Columba and explained the different churches and monasteries the land had once held. The church that remained was once a Catholic church, but the British took it over, just as they did every other Catholic church in the 1500s.

She heard a passing tour guide explain that the bell tower had been used as a prison. Inverness was the closest city to the battle at Culloden. Many prisoners were brought to this makeshift prison and executed in this cemetery. "You can still see the bullet holes in the gravestones where they propped them up."

Stephanie was horrified. She turned to Philip, who nodded in agreement with what was being said. "I've heard of Culloden," she admitted.

"You have to see it to understand," Philip remarked.

"Can you take me there?"

"Yes. Let's grab a sandwich and go."

They drove the short distance from Inverness to the Culloden battlefield. The immense grassland with bog areas reminded her of the battlefield at Gettysburg. She had visited there on a high school trip. She could remember how uneasy it made her, knowing that so many people had died in that area. She was tempted to ask Philip if they could turn back when he held up two tickets he had purchased from the booth.

They walked into the Welcome Center and were met by many displays explaining the backdrop to this one battle. It described the key players, their hopes, and the dreaded outcome. When the guide called them for the tour, they followed him outside and down the path to the center of the field.

"Welcome," he called out in six different languages over chirping birds. "Where are you all from?" All thirty people yelled their place of origin while the guide acknowledged each. Then he asked, "Do we have any Scots with us?" Philip raised his hand like a schoolboy but was the only one. "Well, that's a nice change. Welcome."

He led them around the field, slowly explaining how this battle was the last hope for the Jacobites and the final straw for the British. This would be the battle that would end their civil war. Brothers were against brothers, and fathers against sons. Each one devoted to their cause, whether it was their economic security, property, or the faith of their ruler. In the end, the bloodshed that lasted just under an hour took the lives of thousands. It was also the beginning of many changes that ensued. The most significant was ending the clans, which had always been a constant in Scotland.

She was sad as they made their way around the fields, studying the many monuments, then stopping at the clan graves. Looking back on the whole day, Stephanie had developed overwhelming respect for the Scottish people. They had overcome so much adversity and grew stronger from it.

Stephanie and Philip drove back to Beauly in silence,

each deep in thought until the smell of Pepe's found a way into their passing car. "Pizza, again?" Philip asked.

"Heck yeah. And some beer from The Glen?"

"You've got yourself a date. And let's make sure to order enough to share."

22

THE GREAT CASTLE HUNT

The following day, they began The Great Castle Hunt. They would set out just after daybreak. The sound of the car's wipers set the rhythm for the day as they mopped away the daily dew from the morning air. The car, hugging the winding roads, would cause the fallen leaves to scatter as they passed. She would hold her warm mug of coffee close until its contents were drained entirely, leaving the cold porcelain behind. They would set off in many directions to locate a castle and often found it tucked inside breathtaking places. She began to wonder what came first, the castle or the stunning landscape. Feeling like she was on a treasure hunt, she tried to spot the castles before Philip announced their arrival.

While they were on the long stretches, she read from the many folders they had pulled from the trunk. Each one held the next piece of knowledge, which was beginning to develop into a fascinating family history.

They learned some interesting facts on the morning

drive to visit Eilean Donan and Pennyghael Castles. She had opened the folder to the spot where she had left off the previous day when a note fell in her lap. It said, "Castell had been at odds with his family for years. They disapproved of his marriage and didn't condone his spending all his money to publish a book. Oglethorpe made amends for his departed friend and had Robert's family welcomed back to Beauly." Under it was a photocopied correspondence from Robert Castell to James Oglethorpe explaining that his book, "The Villas of the Ancients Illustrated," had created alienation between him and his father and asking for James' advice. Stephanie turned a few pages more, looking for the response, but had to forego the hunt when they arrived at Eilean Donan.

They paid their admission at the visitor's welcome cottage and began to walk across the grey-stoned bridge which connected the castle to the mainland. Excitement rippled through her as she took notice of the bridge's detail. She could picture how it would look crossing the small inlet on Wassaw and made a mental note of how to draw it.

"I've got a good feeling about this one," she told Philip.

"Aye. She's a beauty. The family who owns the castle still uses it quite often. That often happens in Scotland. Families want to share their Scottish heritage with others."

Stephanie looked around at all the visitors wandering the property. "I'm sure they don't have privacy here, but I'm grateful for their hospitality."

They studied every inch of the castle, inside and out. While most of its visitors were looking at the displays, which showed how the castle would have appeared in the 1700s, Stephanie was measuring the arched doorways and window casings. She often had her back to the rest of the people touring the castle.

When the tour wound around to the Billeting Room, Stephanie once again wandered off on her own. But this time, she was approached by the tour guide.

"Do you have questions aboot these stoned walls, lass?"

She had been deep in thought and jumped when he spoke. Turning, she made eye contact with the Scot wearing green-tartan plaid from head to toe. She smiled and ran her hand along the wall. "As a matter of fact, I do. The engineering is remarkable. Are the architectural plans available for resale? I am interested in the footings and structural base leading to the outer thirteen-foot-deep walls."

The guide pulled back in surprise. "You had me at 'engineering,'" he said excitedly. "Let's walk a bit." He sent the group ahead and slowly led Stephanie around the castle. She eagerly wrote in a small notebook while the guide pointed out every architectural wonder of the large building. When they walked onto the terrace, he explained, "This would have been a lookout of sorts. Every castle had one. See the turret spaces for guns and cannons and the niches for shielding."

"What about this?" Stephanie pointed to a small sign that read, "Selkie."

"That is the sign to watch out for the selkies. That's the Scot's name for a seal. They are mythical creatures which take the form of a seal but can remove its skin to reveal a human underneath."

"Now, why would they do that?"

"Och, to get their way."

Stephanie pointed to another sign on the other side. "And what about this one?" The sign read, "Mermaids."

"Well, those are the things that keep every man alive: dreams and folklore. Without dreams, we would still live in caves, wouldn't we now?"

She acknowledged him with a nod.

"Now, I must be returning to my groups, but I have a question for you before I leave. What would an engineer from the States need with architectural plans for a castle?"

Stephanie and Philip shared their story of the castle on Wassaw Sound while the guide listened intently. When they finished, he commented. "There once was a story about a Scot who built a castle in the new world. Something about righting a wrong against the Jacobites." He paused, his face deep in thought. "Yes, it was an old pub song I heard as a lad. I only remember the chorus,

> *'The Jacobites' last stand*
> *Was found on unchartered land,*
> *As they brought the Pearl to safety*
> *To rest on foreign sand.'"*

Philip had excitedly joined in. "I would never have remembered, but my dad sang that."

The guide gave Philip two hearty pats on the shoulder, acknowledging their heritage. "It's the story of Scottish Highlanders sneaking treasures away from the British. It was everyone's dream at the time to pull something over on the Brits. Not sure why it just popped into my head."

Stephanie quickly scribbled the song lyrics in her notebook, then turned her attention back to the guide leading them toward the exit.

"I've got to return to the tour," the guide said. "Although we don't have architectural plans, you'll love looking around the final room. It has detailed drawings of the renovations." Turning to Stephanie, he said, "It was very nice to meet you. Speaking with people like you makes my job worth doing."

Philip snapped their picture together before the guide took his leave. Then, he and Stephanie slowly made their way around the many photos, plans, and models of the renovation. She thought they had taken the same skeleton of the castle and renovated it, but instead found out that the 1930s renovation had been a completely new project. That was why the electricity and plumbing had appeared to fit so neatly.

"Damn," she said to Philip. "I thought this was the one I could return to the board as a perfect comparison. Instead, I have all these pieces from various castles that I am trying to fit together."

"I know. It is quite beautiful, though," Philip added.

"Yes. It's a gorgeous 1930s castle built on an ancient site. And it does us zero good." She sulked back towards the car, but as she crossed the long stone bridge, she stopped and looked back one last time. "Shame on me. Look at her in all her glory. It is a work of art to have been built at any time. Let's keep this one in our pocket."

"Our pockets are getting quite full, aren't they?"

"Yes, I guess they are. How many more castles do we have?"

Philip took an exaggerated breath. "The next one is the

last one I had in mind. After that, I'll need to start digging a little more."

"Then I'm crossing my fingers for Pennyghael."

They drove such a short distance that Stephanie didn't have time to do any reading. Stephanie knew her crossed fingers didn't help their situation as they approached the castle. Pennyghael Castle, although not in complete ruins, remained just a shell of its former glory. Once out of the car, they were welcomed by the sound of happy visitors around the property. People walked through the castle and enjoyed the many trails and battlements on its outskirts and beside the sea.

They made their way around the property and began walking one of the trails leading to a hotel that resembled the castle. Beside the building sat a stable with horses roaming the field. In the distance sat many cottages that dotted the rolling hills and looked back across the field towards the castle.

Walking closer to the building, they noticed the sign, "The Pennyghael Hotel." The entrance was bustling with visitors and a line of cars of people checking in and out. As they walked through the giant castle door, they entered the grand reception area, which appeared authentic with all its modern charm. They stood gawking at their surroundings, marveling at the genius who decided to keep the castle open for tourists while utilizing the land around it so everyone could still enjoy it. When they both focused on a small café looking over the back garden, they found themselves inside and grabbed a seat beside the window. It was almost as if they had been walking around in a trance.

"Did you not know about this place?" she asked.

"I might have remembered my dad saying something about it when he was planning to renovate Beauly, but I must not have been listening completely. This is it, isn't it?"

She nodded her head happily as he began processing out loud.

"The castle on Wassaw Sound could be enjoyed just like Pennyghael. I would only do the necessary renovations to ensure it was sturdy for visitors, which you are already working on. The castle could be enjoyed without adding modern-day plumbing and electricity. Then, I could move my long-term plans up and go ahead and begin building on the land around it."

Stephanie couldn't hold in her excitement any longer. "Yes! That's exactly how I'm picturing it, too."

They laughed as Philip began running ideas by her on his new plan for the castle on Wassaw Sound.

23

OBAN

Hugh paced the cottage floor. *How long will they be gone today? I'm not equipped for this,* he thought. The call had come early that morning from Oban. Transport Scotland was reviewing their contracts and wanted to meet with Beauly Steel. It felt like yesterday when he and Mr. McLaughlin were racing to win those contracts. Had it really been five years?

Sean McLaughlin had trusted him completely. He had been handpicked years ago. Working at the mill himself, Hugh had become the town's representative to speak with the McLaughlins whenever there was a problem. The town had been in a downward spiral when old man McLaughlin passed away. Families were moving away in search of work, and the mill was producing marine parts that were barely in use anymore. But this time, Sean McLaughlin asked to speak to him.

He told Hugh his thoughts of revitalizing the city, and they devised a master plan with the growth of the mill in the center. It wasn't until they won the bid with Transport Scotland that things began to turn around, and now that contract was on the line. Sean had handled all of that. He was well-spoken and had a presence that commanded attention. Hugh had watched his presentation and was impressed by how he worked the room. The contract was given to them before they even left the meeting. Hugh had the knowledge and know-how but not that presence. He prayed that Philip could take over in his father's absence.

Hugh had asked to meet with Philip on his return from Eilean Donan but hadn't explained why. He arrived at the cottage early, too anxious to sit still. He began to walk around the outskirts of the house, mentally noting what needed to be done to winterize the building. The weather was changing quickly, and much must be done to prepare for the brutal Highland winter. The sound of gravel crunching drew his attention, so he walked to the front of the house.

"What's wrong?" Philip asked the moment he noticed the worry on Hugh's face.

"The plant. Transport Scotland is considering outsourcing the manufacturing of all harbor equipment, including the ferry parts."

Philip's heart dropped. Seventy percent of Beauly Steel's business came from Transport Scotland. "If they do, it will destroy our town. Most of the locals work there." He rubbed his neck, which had begun to stiffen. "What can we do?"

"I'm very good at what I do, but your dad always handled the large meetings. I think you need to represent Beauly Steel. We meet with them the day after tomorrow."

"I don't have the knowledge for this," Philip admitted.

"Neither did your dad. But he did have the Scottish presence, and that did the trick. However, I would suggest you speak with the foreman at the mill, Billy Galwick."

Philip went straight to the mill and was escorted to the foreman's office. "Hello, Mr. McLaughlin," he said, extending his hand.

Philip recognized the man as the bartender from the Glen. He grasped his hand, "Hello, Billy. You wear many hats, I see."

"This is my main one. My dad owns the bar and sometimes needs a little help."

Philip nodded, admiring anyone who helped family after working on their feet all day. He didn't want to cause worry but needed Billy to understand the importance of the situation. "I need you to educate me on the mill, from top to bottom. We have a big meeting with Transport Scotland, and I must be prepared. I also need to get a product and customer list printed to take with me."

The two men worked together well into the night. Finally, at two a.m., Billy pulled a bottle of Scotch from his drawer.

"I probably shouldn't let the head honcho know I keep good Scotch whisky in my work drawer, but I think we need a good luck toast." He filled each glass with a two-finger pour, and they slowly sipped the contents, praying for a good outcome at the meeting.

———

The landscape quickly changed as they drove out of the deeply wooded areas of the Highlands towards the coast of

Oban. Stephanie watched as they passed the many sailboats dotted along the shores of the Lochs, ready to make their way into the ocean. She felt the familiarity of being near the ocean and was looking forward to being in another seaside town.

As they arrived at the bed and breakfast, Stephanie walked over to get a better view of the harbor while Philip and Hugh went inside to see if their rooms were ready. Standing at the railed edge, she studied the waterway. The mountains protectively stretched their arms around the peninsula. However, its fingers didn't quite touch, leaving a small stretch of water for its occupants to stay connected with the rest of the world. She focused on that escape point and longed to know what was on the other side. So much so that she wondered if someone from her distant past was calling her to find out.

Hearing the drops of water on the pavement made her realize the rain was again chasing her. She should have expected it because Scotland's weather changes every five minutes. Still, she wanted to run for shelter. She wasn't like the Scots. After spending a week traveling through the Highlands, she learned much about the castles and the people who occupied them. They took each challenge headfirst, sometimes even running toward them. And they never ran from the rain.

Phillip called to her from the bed and breakfast. "Your room is ready. Want to take a look?" Turning towards him, she nodded, but something beckoned her back. It wasn't a voice, but a feeling, calling her. "I hear you," she said into the wind, then scurried across the street.

Phillip locked eyes with her. "I was hoping you heard me. I called you twice."

She nodded in acknowledgment but glanced back to the water. Why had she spoken to the breeze? *I'm sure it was nothing,* she thought. But deep in her heart, she knew it was much more.

Walking through the glass panel door, they were met by the manager. She welcomed Stephanie and showed them to their rooms. Phillip had booked the inn because it was known for its small but comfortable rooms. She knew the second she crossed the threshold that the inn was unique. It felt like walking into a friend's house, a friend with great taste.

"This place has a great feel," Philip said.

"I was thinking the same thing. People like you and me can design and construct a building, but we can't give something life." He studied her as if waiting for her to continue, but she was at a loss for words, focusing on the transomed doorways where small curtains hung inside. They drew your eye as you walked into the sitting room. "There's a difference, you know, between just living in a place and loving the place. There's passion. This place has character because its owners love it." At the castle in Savannah, she knew that there was passion behind every decision Philip was making. It wasn't just for profit; it was for fulfilling his dream.

"Aye. But this place is old. It would probably be better to go ahead and tear it down."

"Bite your tongue. It's unique and special. They should do whatever it takes to preserve it." She stopped and held Phillips' stare. "You got me, didn't you?"

"Aye, lass. This could be the castle on Wassaw Sound."

She nodded slowly. "It's not going to be easy."

"Nothing worth doing ever is."

"I officially think we've seen enough. I've kept a small journal since we began at Edinburgh Castle, detailing all the information from each site, referencing them every evening, and adding additional comments. I decided to tell you we had seen enough the minute I wrote on the last page, and this bed and breakfast will fill it. I'm ready to go home as soon as you finish your business in Oban. It's time to fight for your castle."

24

STEEL

The cries of seagulls pulled her from sleep. Grabbing the throw from the end of the bed, she snuggled into its soft wool that had been worn smooth over time and opened the window to find the source of her morning's alarm. Looking out over the harbor, she watched as a handful of fishing boats made their way out to sea for the day, just as they did every day. The gulls followed closely behind, watching from the skies in hopes the boats would stir up a meal for their bellies.

She focused on the small island and was surprised to notice a small light shining from its bank. It seemed out of place in the middle of the sea. Her thoughts went to Philip and his task ahead of saving Beauly. She prayed that he could smooth everything over.

Stephanie found Philip in the sitting room typing away on his laptop. He looked up when she entered the room, and a smile began forming on his face. Her pulse quickened from his response to her as she tried her best for everyday conversation. "Good morning. You're up early."

"Good morning. I was holding off breakfast until the last minute, hoping we could eat together before I left. Hugh said he was too nervous to eat, so it's just you and me. Hungry?"

"Always," she answered. They made their way to the cozy eating room. The galley-style kitchen was filled with luxury appliances, including an espresso machine that was calling out to Stephanie with its steaming milk voice. A chef stood cooking at the central stove on the island, welcoming them while he flipped a crepe in the air. Ten small tables sat across from the kitchen where everyone could watch the chef do his magic.

As soon as they ordered the brioche French toast, Stephanie turned her attention to Philip. "Are you nervous about this meeting?"

"People's livelihood, their families, all depend on these jobs. I'm worried I won't be able to represent the town as my dad did. He grew up in Beauly and knew the town well. I didn't. I just pray I can say the right thing."

Stephanie took a small sip of her espresso. "Your dad did know the town well. He hired well, too. He leaned on Hugh for a reason. If you get stumped, maybe you could lean on him, too."

Philip held his coffee cup midair, pondering what Stephanie had just said. Sometimes an outsider looking in could access a situation better. Hugh knew everything about Beauly. Who better to be standing shoulder to shoulder with going into battle?

Oban is known as the "Gateway to the Isles," with its harbor being the central hub for passenger and vehicle ferries. The Oban Ports Authority sat on the far side of the port, where the meeting was taking place.

Philip and Hugh walked into the large conference room with floor-to-ceiling windows running the expanse of the seaside. Philip was mesmerized by the view, the mountains touching the sea in the background with the constant movement of many watercraft in the front. He broke his gaze quickly, introduced himself to the board members, then took his seat.

The chairman began, "We asked to meet with you to review our contracts with Beauly Steel. Our business arrangement with your father is up for renewal next year. We have enjoyed a healthy and productive agreement and would love to continue doing business with you. However, with the cost of living going up five percent, we are trying to watch our overhead and save money. A rival company has approached us with better prices, so we are considering outsourcing our marine parts. We wanted to go over the possibility of you meeting these prices. I'll give you a few minutes to review."

Thankful that he had asked for a product list from Billy, Philip began to compare each item and was saddened that Beauly's prices were considerably higher than the outside source. He glanced at Hugh, who seemed amused as he circled specifics on each product, then shut the folder.

"You don't seem worried," Philip whispered.

"No, we are fine. Want me to take it from here?"

"Please do."

Hugh stood to address the group. "Thank you for your business over the last five years. Beauly Steel supplies you with quality components for all of your nautical transportation needs. With that in mind, quality cannot be skimped on. It keeps our waterways and our people safe. That's why Beauly only used stainless steel. Type 316, to be exact. It is the absolute best material against corrosion. Now I understand, on paper, this other quote might look better because it lists our same parts, in steel, for considerably less cost. But the steel they are quoting is carbon steel, which can pass saltwater tests but must be replaced every two years, causing you to replace it three times faster and hire more personnel for the maintenance.

Moreover, you are Scots supporting materials made one hundred percent by Scots. Doesn't that look good in ads?" Hugh paused for a breath, then added. "Our contracts hold firm if you re-sign with us. However, we will require a five percent cost of living increase."

Philip was about to burst with pride as he watched the board nod their heads, approving Hugh's remarks. When they asked for a small break to discuss the matter further, Philip leaned to Hugh. "Great job. How did you know to go straight to materials?"

"Your dad taught me to respect quality and never skimp. That's how we got the original contracts."

When the board reconvened, they offered Beauly Steel a new contract with a five percent increase. They also asked to meet with Hugh the following day to discuss expansion into storage vessels.

Hugh and Philip were beaming as they exited the building; they decided to walk along the seaside esplanade back to the hotel.

"You were amazing in there today, Hugh. Beauly is very blessed to have such a strong leader."

Hugh smiled up at Philip. "I've lived in Beauly all my life, and half my family works at the mill. It's more than a job, you know. It's the town. I was scared that I wasn't good enough to fight for them. It's been a hard year without your dad's guidance, but I have learned to stand on my own, and most of the time, it turns out great." They walked a bit further before Hugh added, "There are some things I want us to discuss before your leaving."

"Okay. Shoot."

"This problem with the mill made me realize the workers have nothing to fall back on. Would you be open to offering stock options where the workers could actually be owners of the mill? Where they have a vested interest and will receive dividends from our profits?"

"I think that's a great idea. Get me the proposal, and we'll make that happen. What else?"

"Something needs to be done with the estate house. Your dad was interested in opening it as a resort, but the town needs a hotel or, at the very least, a bed and breakfast. How would you feel about taking some of the savings and finishing it off?"

"I love that idea but don't see myself back at Beauly permanently. Are you asking for my help or just my approval?"

Hugh rubbed the back of his neck, hating to voice his opinion out loud, but his desire overcame his doubts. "Your approval would be just fine."

Philip's hearty laugh broke the sound of the waves hitting the walkway. "Hugh, you have my approval. Let's make arrangements for you to move into the cottage. I think it's high time we open Beauly to guests."

25

THE DINGHY

*S*tephanie jumped out of bed before daybreak, hoping to watch the sunrise from her third-story window. The hills surrounding the peninsula were dotted with lights from the houses on the bay's edge. But once again, her eyes were drawn to the small island between the stretch of water leading out of the peninsula. Closing her eyes, she slowly filled her lungs with sea air and held it as long as possible. Her exhale took form as it hit the cold air and floated off like smoke into the bay.

"Good morning," she said into the wind and wondered when she had begun to talk to herself. She continued to focus on the small island and was shocked when a tiny light began to illuminate on its border. She watched it change colors from orange to yellow, but it slowly disappeared into the darkness. None of the other lights speckling the bay had changed colors. They had popped on and off as their inhabitants needed. Her curiosity peaked, and she wanted answers.

After a hot shower, she threw on hiking pants and a shirt and met Philip downstairs for breakfast.

"Hugh will be in meetings all day today," he said. "What would you like to do? We can leave Oban and go somewhere else."

"No," she answered a little too quickly. "I'd like to spend some time around the islands and visit this cute little city. I don't know what it is, but there's just something about this island. I want to get out there and learn more."

He wiped his mouth and set the napkin on the table. "Hurry up, slowpoke, we're wasting daylight."

Stephanie picked up a tourist map from the inn and studied the layout of the bay. The small island was pictured but unnamed, so she asked the innkeeper for directions.

"Och. You don't want to go there. It's uninhabited."

"But I saw a light on it this morning."

"Not possible. No one's lived there for over fifty years."

Stephanie pursed her lips, deep in thought. "Okay, but let's say I still want to go there. How could I get to it?"

"None of the ferries run there, so you need a boat. Can either of you drive one?"

Stephanie looked to Phillip, who shook his head no. She knew she could do it because Maggie often had her run the boat when the group was together, but she was still unsure. Finally, her desire outweighed her doubt. "Yes, yes. I can drive a boat."

"Then you can borrow ours. It sits at the dock at the end of the street in slot seventeen. Keys are behind the desk on the ring with a miniature life vest. We only use it in the mornings to pick up things for the inn, so it should have plenty of gas." She patted Stephanie on the shoulder and added, "Watch out for the large ferries. They stop for no one," and just like that, she was given a boat. The owners had complete confidence that Stephanie would take care of the boat as well as they did. It's the Scottish way: trust others until given a reason not to. She hoped not to become one of those reasons.

A small dinghy with a drop-in outboard motor sat in slot seventeen. Philip stood on the dock assessing the situation. "Are you sure you know how to run this?"

Noticing the worry on Phillip's face, she mustered more confidence than she had and tried to answer with a steady voice. "Sure. It's a piece of cake." Her friend, Maggie, had a jon boat with a similar motor, and she had been Maggie's first mate often enough. But that had been years ago when Maggie's grandmother let them take it up and down Horsepen Creek.

Philip watched her check the lines and then fiddle with the motor. She appeared to know what she was doing. So, he climbed in and sat on the front bench facing the rear.

Stephanie dropped the engine in the water but then noticed its pull cord. I can do this, she thought, remembering how she started her dad's push lawn mower. She primed the motor, put one foot on the side of the boat, and pulled with all her might. She felt the handle slide from her wet hands. She cursed her clumsiness as she flew backward. Phillip had been watching her every move and jumped out of his seat, catching her before she hit her head on the side of the boat. His smug expression as he looked down on her was infuriating. "I've got this," she snapped.

"Aye. It's impressive to watch."

"My hands are just wet and slippery."

"Tell you what. I'll just give it a yank, and you can take it from there?"

She wanted to argue and give it another try, but then she looked out at the island. She was ready to be out there, so she nodded in agreement. Philip pulled the cord in one fluid motion, and the small engine began to purr. The dinghy was so small they had to maneuver around each other to reposition themselves back into their seats. Their knees touched when she settled on the back bench, causing her to stare down at the point of contact. She slowly ran her eyes up until they met Philip's and felt the sting of a flush in her cheeks. "Thank you," she said softly, "for starting the boat and breaking my fall."

"You're definitely worth catching, lass." He held her stare briefly, then looked past her to the lines. "Are we ready to shove off?"

"Yes, can you untie the lines and give us a little push?" Everything went smoothly once they were away from the dock. She drove the boat easily across the bay and then slid onto the shore of the small island. After jumping out, Stephanie stood frozen as she drank in her surroundings. "Let's go this way first," she announced. The island appeared to be around four acres in size, with a sandy shore on its bay side and a rocky surface on the ocean side. A square, stone structure, missing its whole front side, sat on its highest point. A matching shell of a building sat to its side. Other than that, the island was covered with rocks and vegetation. Stephanie walked quietly, absorbing the sight and smells of the island. Then, she stood facing out to sea. "What do you think?" she asked Philip.

"It looks like someone once lived here."

"That's what I think, too." She pointed to the tall walls. "I think this structure was a lighthouse of some kind, and this other building was where the keepers lived."

"Lighthouse keepers? Creepy."

"Creepy? They're not creepy. It's very romantic."

"Not in Scotland, it isn't." He changed to his best story-telling voice. "Not too far from here, north on the Flannan Isles, three light keepers vanished a cold night in December when there wasn't a storm in sight. It scared many a light-keeper, some up and leaving their posts."

"What was the date of this?"

"*Ah dinnae ken,*" he said, shaking his head. The story was told to many-a-wee'uns for years afterwards, trying to keep them away from the sea walls at night."

Stephanie shook her head, surprised at how easily tall tales get started. Still, she accepted there was usually a shred of truth at their core. They returned to the boat, and Stephanie climbed in while Philip pushed the dinghy deeper.

He jumped in and said, "I'm in. You can start the boat," but she sat still, staring into space. "Stephanie," he called, but she didn't budge. Raising his voice, he yelled, "Hey, Steph," and stunned her into looking at him.

She pointed back to the island. As the sun was directly overhead, it hit a thick glass pane on top of what she tagged as the lighthouse. "There's the light I saw this morning. It was a reflection from the sunrise."

"Problem solved," he teased.

"Or several ones now open. Who lived there? And why did they leave?"

Philip shook his head. "Are you really this curious all the time?"

"Yes, it's a blessing and a curse."

The glorious smell of fried seafood seemed to fill the air as they returned across the bay. Stephanie's stomach growled in response. She scanned the coastline for the smell's origin and noticed a small restaurant on the neighboring island called Kerrera. She wanted to ask Philip if he was interested, but the sound of the motor was too loud, so she nodded in that direction, and Philip agreed.

They walked up the path from the marina to a restaurant named Waypoint. Once they got closer, they found that the yummy fried fish smell was blown over the bay by a large kitchen fan in hopes of getting the heat out of the kitchen. Stephanie loved the restaurant immediately. The golden pine walls with nautical flags strung across the room made Stephanie feel like she had been at sea for the day, and actually, she had. Every table was packed with locals, a telltale sign that the food was good. Stephanie approached an elderly lady behind the counter to ask for a table. When the lady looked up, she took Stephanie's hands into her own.

"MacDonald, aye?"

Stephanie shook her head. "No, I'm sorry."

The old lady held onto her hands. "Oh, aye, yur a MacDonald."

Stephanie only smiled and changed the subject. "Do you have a table for two for lunch?"

"Oh, aye. Always for a MacDonald."

Once seated, Philip asked, "Who's your friend?"

"Just a sweet old lady who obviously thinks I'm someone

else." Still, she couldn't help but wonder who it was she resembled.

The restaurant's slogan was "From the farm, or the sea, to the fork," and the menu showed accordingly. They served local produce and meats from their farm on the island and seafood from the waters around them.

Stephanie and Philip enjoyed a wonderful meal that combined a lightly fried seafood appetizer with a mouthwatering pork chop for the main dish. They were too full for dessert but ordered a coffee to sip while looking out over the marina. When Philip finally asked for the check, the older lady reappeared. She pulled out a chair at their table and slowly slid into it.

"We'll never take money from a MacDonald," she said while taking Stephanie's hand. "You look just like her, you ken."

Looking into the woman's tired, green eyes, Stephanie asked softly, "Like who?"

"Your gran, that's who. You're the spit of her."

"So I've been told," Stephanie answered while patting the lady's hand in a slow rhythm. Smiling, she thanked her for the meal. When Stephanie stood to leave, the older woman struggled to stand, and Stephanie helped her to her feet.

"What's your name, my dear?"

"Stephanie."

"Stephanie MacDonald. Lovely."

"No. Stephanie Normand."

"Aye, that would be your father's name. But you're a MacDonald." She pulled Stephanie in for a hug, then turned and walked back to her desk.

Stephanie glanced over at Philip, who was watching her intently. "Poor thing. She's confused and thinks I'm someone else." But as quickly as she tried to dismiss it, something began to needle at her. Everyone always told her she was the spit of her grandmother. In fact, her grandfather told her it was like seeing his wife fifty years before. Could there be more to this story? Everywhere she had gone in Scotland, she had wondered if her family could have lived there. Now, she had someone verifying it. She turned to find the woman, but a younger woman was sitting at the desk.

Stephanie's curiosity got the better of her, so she approached the new cashier. "Hi. I wanted to thank you for the wonderful meal. It was hands down the best pork chop I've ever eaten."

"Thank you. We have happy animals that are spoiled rotten. They eat well, are loved well, and even get massages. They only have one bad day in their whole life. Just one."

Stephanie thought for a second, then remembered the pork chop she had eaten to the bone. "True, but that's a helluva bad day."

"Nourishment for the belly, nourishment for the soul," she answered.

"Just one last thing. We had a sweet elderly lady helping us."

"Yes. That's my gran."

"Is she well?"

"Oh yes. Her body has aged, and the cold Scottish winters don't help, but she's sharp as a tack. She doesn't forget a thing. In fact, she still handles our books. And she never misses a birthday, either. I only wish I had half of her brain power."

"She is amazing, thank you. And thank you for making us feel so welcome."

She turned to leave but paused. *I need to know more,* she thought. Turning back to the cashier, she asked to speak with her gran.

"She just walked back to the house for her afternoon nap. Can I leave her a message?"

Disappointment washed across Stephanie's face as she answered. "Actually, she told me she knew my grandmother, and I wanted to get more information."

"Oh, aye. Then why don't I give you the number at her cottage? You can ring her any time."

Stephanie smiled at the kind lady. "That would be perfect. Thank you."

Turning to leave, Stephanie held up one of the restaurant's brochures with a name and phone number written on the back.

"What did she give you?" Philip asked.

"They gave me the nice old lady's phone number."

"So you can call your new friend?"

She laughed, "No. Where I can reconnect with an old friend of the family. There may be more truth in what the lady said than I realized."

Philip smiled, "MacDonald, eh?"

Stephanie held her head high with pride. "Aye, MacDonald." And they both laughed as they made their way back to the boat.

26

THE CEILIDH

When Stephanie and Philip arrived that afternoon at the hotel, the innkeeper handed them flyers advertising an All Hollow's Eve *Ceilidh*. "A *ceilidh* would be the perfect way to end our trip to Scotland," Stephanie said excitedly.

"First off, it's pronounced kay-lee. And secondly, I'm not going."

"Why not?"

"When I was a wee lad in primary school, everyone was forced to learn the traditional dances. I won't be dancing them again by choice. Too many bad memories."

"Oh, please, won't you teach them to me? It would be fun together."

"No!"

"Oh, you're one of those guys who can't dance, huh?"

"I can dance just fine, lass. Might I remind you of the ball in Savannah?"

"Yeah, but that was different."

"I see what you're trying to do, and it won't work."

"Is there anything I could do to change your mind?" She regretted the question the second it hit the air.

He turned her to face him. In a low, sexy voice, he replied, "Can you not read my signals? Do ya really want to know what you could do to change my mind?"

His burning gaze gave her the answer to the question she had been asking herself a million times. Was something happening between them, and did he feel the same way? She now knew he did. She almost challenged him to answer but chickened out and sidestepped his question. "Okay. I won't push you," she replied. "I'll just have to go alone."

He looked her over, shaking his head. "I hope you have fun," he answered, almost daring her to go alone.

"I will," she said over her shoulder as she climbed the steps to her room.

"We are leaving early in the morning. Don't stay out too late," he called out to her, but she didn't bother to respond.

Once inside her room, she sat on the side of the bed, wondering what she had gotten herself into. She couldn't just go to a dance, not knowing anyone there. But then she thought about Philip's face with his sideways grin. He challenged her, and she couldn't back down. Besides, since she knew no one there, why should she care?

The dance was held on a tall ship that sat at the harbor. It had been restored to offer event space and was decorated with white lights that made the refinished wooden decks shine like glass.

The two-person band with an accordion and a bagpipe played strong as she climbed the narrow stairs below and followed the tunes. Tables had been set around the edges of the large dance floor, and a bar was set up in the back. Everyone seemed to know one another, and the lively chatter filled the air. Stephanie made her way back to the bar and scanned the room while she waited on a drink.

Everyone was in Halloween costumes, so it took a minute to get a vibe from the group. But she was able to focus on a table with two slightly older couples who seemed very pleasant, so she approached them and asked if she could join them. They welcomed her and explained that the *ceilidh* was an event the whole community could enjoy. Still, they were happy the one that evening was for adults only. They were in mid-conversation when the accordion player announced the first dance. Every table dumped onto the dance floor, leaving Stephanie sitting alone. She listened as the announcer briefly explained the run of the night. She watched as the couples began spinning each other, anticipating their partner's ducks and turns.

Glancing around the room, she realized she was the only single bystander. Sudden images of being at a middle school dance flooded her memory as she planned her escape. But as song number two began, her luck changed.

A woman dressed in an acorn costume slipped on a spilled drink, causing her to turn her ankle. As she hobbled to her table, she motioned to Stephanie to take her place with her partner, who was dressed as a squirrel. Stephanie waved her off, but before she knew it, the squirrel was helping her to her feet and pulling her onto the floor. The rest was a blur. She still couldn't get the steps down correctly despite her total concentration. The fast pace was confusing, and her heeled boots stomped on the squirrel's paws. In the middle of song five, the squirrel spun her into him to serenade, and her elbow jabbed right into his mouth. "Let's take a break," he growled and made his way over to the table where his partner sat. Surprisingly, the acorn was no longer alone.

Philip watched as Stephanie approached and stood to greet her with a deep bow. Her heart jumped. He wore his kilt with high socks and a white button-down and was the most handsome man she'd ever seen. That was until he opened his mouth.

"Thanks for leaving me sitting with the nut while you promenaded around the room with a rodent," he barked.

Stephanie started laughing and couldn't stop. Tears streamed down her cheeks while he replayed what he had said and started laughing, too. "I'm so happy you're here, Philip. Thank you for coming." Their eyes met, and he nodded.

When the sixth song was announced, "St. Bernard's Waltz," Philip offered Stephanie his arm, and they walked onto the floor. They stood face to face, neither one blinking. Stephanie hadn't realized she was holding her breath until they started moving. The dance was slow, and she followed his lead, moving in one fluid motion until the song ended, and they were left looking into each other's eyes. He leaned over and kissed her softly, then whispered, "Want to get some air?"

She agreed, and they went on deck. He walked her to the front of the ship, and they stood against the rail, overlooking the city. Standing behind her, he pulled her into his arms and whispered in her ear. "When all this is done, I'd like to take you on a proper date. No castles, no work talk, just me and you."

She wrapped his arms around her tightly and turned her head to look up into his eyes, "I'd like that," she whispered.

He spun her towards him into a crushing kiss. The longing they had been holding back finally came to the surface. His hands held onto her shoulders like he was scared of her slipping away, but slowly he brought them to rest on the side of her face, holding it adoringly. Pulling back, he let his fingers slide across her shoulder and down her arms until he laced them into hers.

"Let's go back to my room," he muttered, his hoarse voice craving more.

The hunger in his eyes matched the feeling in her heart. She kissed him, long and deep, shocked at how well their mouths fit together, before whispering, "Let's go."

27

HOME

Stephanie had traveled to many places in her life, both around the United States and abroad. Still, this was the first time she had returned to Savannah with a yearning in her heart. The feeling was so unfamiliar she questioned its existence. Once she came down Victory Drive, she pinpointed it. She missed her Savannah. She snuck a glance at Philip, driving her home from the airport. She wondered if he felt the same when they were in Edinburgh.

It had been a long flight, and she had no idea what time it was. Airports did that. Her brain was stuck between time zones, layovers, and airport bars. Her watch read midnight; she would have thought much later. Neither said a word; they were just too exhausted.

When he pulled into her driveway, he stepped out and grabbed her bag but left his truck running. She was only a little sad he wasn't coming inside; all she wanted to do was to curl up in bed alone. But first, she needed to thank him. "I know this was a 'business trip,'" she said, signaling with silent quotations in the air. "But it was so much more to me. You shared your world with me, and I'm most grateful."

He smiled down at her and slowly let his hand run along her face. "It is me who is most grateful for you." He leaned in slowly, their lips almost touching when a car's headlights pulled into the driveway behind him. Stephanie felt his body tense as he protectively moved in front of her. They squinted against the bright beams to better see the driver. Instead, they watched as Cooper jumped out of the car. He ran straight to Stephanie, who knelt down smiling and scooped him in her arms.

Her dad approached them both. He kissed Stephanie on the forehead, then turned his attention to Philip. "So, you're the one who dragged my daughter to Scotland?"

Stephanie cringed, but Philip answered without wavering. "Aye. I mean no disrespect. I swear to ye, I took very good care of her. Your daughter is quite wonderful. She alone can save my 250-year-old castle. I'm sorry if I caused you any trouble, sir."

Her dad stood a little taller from the respect that Philip had just offered him. He nodded in acknowledgment, then added, "She is quite wonderful. You're right about that." He turned and patted Cooper's head, then said to Stephanie, "Thank you for calling me when you got in safely. I thought you might be anxious to see Cooper, so I brought him over tonight instead of in the morning. I was going to leave him in the house, but you beat me here." He kissed her, once again, on her forehead. "You can tell me all about your trip later." He turned his attention to Philip, "The young lady needs to get some sleep. We should be going." He returned to his truck and sat down but didn't pull off.

Stephanie laughed. "You've gotta love my dad."

"Well, he sure loves you. But that's not hard to do." Realizing what he had just said, he quickly said goodnight. Once he shut his truck door, her dad pulled out of the driveway.

She barely remembered climbing into bed. When her eyes opened the following day, she was shocked at the amount of light coming through the blinds. Glancing at the clock, it read 1:45. "Oh shit!" she yelled, jumping out of bed and running to the shower. She was out so fast she barely remembered the water hitting her before she threw on her clothes and sprinted out the door to her office.

Stephanie and Philip were now racing against a clock. They only had a little over two weeks before the next hearing for the castle. Many things needed to be accomplished before then. They? When did she and Philip become "they?" Would they still be "they" if she found evidence that the foundation wasn't strong? She shook her head, trying to clear her thoughts. No matter, she jumped straight into work. She sent in orders for soil testing, drillers, and topographers. She had to find out what lay beneath the foundation.

———

Stephanie scheduled all her appointments for the following Monday morning. Then, she began sifting through all the emails since she had been away. "Project Reopened" was the subject that caught her eye. She was excited to see the police had now reopened the Daffin Park project. However, as she continued reading, her excitement dissipated.

The case record stated that the bones could have been

buried for hundreds of years because they didn't match any missing person in the system. Therefore, they were listed as "unidentifiable." She knew that wasn't the case. She showed the contents of the bag to the police. They knew the bones weren't that old. Still, they had listed it as a closed case.

Curiosity got the best of her. Stephanie went through the Saint Vincent Alumni directory. She found the number for Suzanne Elders, whose last name had changed after marriage. She loved this directory because it listed each woman by maiden name, which was vital since it was an all-girls school.

Stephanie made the call and was surprised when it was picked up on the first ring.

"This is Suzanne," she answered amid loud background noise.

Stephanie forced herself to speak loudly. She was bold when discussing her job but always struggled with casual chitchat. She decided to cut right to the chase. "Hi, Suzanne. It's Stephanie Normand from SVA. I was wondering if you might have some time when I could talk with you about something I came across." Suzanne didn't respond immediately, so Stephanie asked, "Suzanne. Are you still there?"

"Yes, I'm here," Suzanne answered. "Could you meet me after work, say, five-thirty, at the 17Hundred90 Bar?"

"Absolutely. That would be great. I'll see you then." But as Stephanie was in the middle of saying thank you, Suzanne disconnected. *That's so odd. What is her deal?* Stephanie decided to call the one person who knew the gossip about everyone: Kathleen.

"You're meeting with Suzanne Elders? Why?" Kathleen asked.

"I wanted to pick her brain about one of those pins I found buried at my jobsite."

"Why her? Do you think she killed the man?" Kathleen joked.

"Heavens, no. I'm not even sure who the man is. But the police have dropped the case, and for some reason, I feel responsible for those dead bones and want to find out the name of the man behind them. I know that sounds daft, but it's the truth."

"No, I get it completely. Well, here's the skinny. Suzanne Elders Shaw is in a neck-and-neck campaign to be Chatham County's school board representative. Last week, while you were out of town, there were heavy accusations against her, insinuating she was pretty cozy with the mayor if you know what I mean. Anyone with half a brain knows it was a dumb jab from her opponent. Still, she's probably just watching her back."

"Good gosh. I missed all that in the week I was gone. Thank you for always knowing what's going on around Savannah."

"I don't know whether to take that as an insult or a compliment, but you're welcome. Hey, I'm looking forward to lunch next Wednesday. I can't wait to hear all about your handsome, kilt-wearing Scot."

Stephanie hung up the phone and smiled, thankful for the many personalities and traits of her tribe.

28

CONFESSIONS

Stephanie left work at 5:25 and walked to the 17Hundred90 Bar in less than five minutes. Glancing up to the windows of the rooms above, she tripped on the curb and almost fell. "Slow down," she told herself, just like always, but then shivered at the thought of the ghost that might be looking out those same windows.

Entering the building, she looked appreciatively at the half-moon walkways and the brick walls. However, she immediately looked down to examine the mortar around the floor. One of the disadvantages of her job was she could never turn it off.

Suzanne Elders waved Stephanie over to the bar and stood to greet her. "Hi, Stephanie," she said as she hugged her. "It's been too long."

Stephanie was happy to see her old classmate. Although she didn't see Suzanne regularly, she always enjoyed her company. "Yes, it has. We missed you at the reunion."

Turning to the bartender, she ordered a pineapple upside-down martini, her favorite 17Hundred90 cocktail.

"I heard it got a little crazy, and someone fell in the Savannah River. You don't mess around River Street, do you?" Suzanne answered but shook her head regretfully. "I'll make it to one of those reunions soon, but I'm too busy now. So, tell me, what can I help you with?"

Stephanie decided to keep it simple. "I was at Benedictine a few weeks ago looking at old brigade photos. I noticed a Lawrence Elders and wondered if that would have been your grandfather?"

Suzanne eyed her cautiously. "As a matter of fact, it was. But what is this about?"

"I am trying to find one of the other men in the photo with your grandfather from Benedictine. You said, 'he was,' which makes me believe he passed."

"Yes, he passed away about ten years ago. But my grandfather was a sergeant over fifty years ago. What is it you're trying to find?"

Stephanie wavered but decided to be truthful. "I was working on a big project at Daffin Park, and we found bones under the pond."

"Nasty. Like, human bones?"

"Yes. The police said they were unidentifiable, but I had found military pins from the individual that placed him as a JROTC instructor from 1940-1946. I probably should just let it go, but for some reason, I feel obligated to find out who the person is and to let his family know."

Suzanne started waving her hands. "I don't want no part in this. I'm already in over my head. I don't want anything to do with a murder mystery. I think you should let the big boys handle this."

"I tried, but it hit a dead end." Stephanie slowly took a sip of her cocktail. She realized she was asking a lot from her classmate running in an election. She looked Suzanne in the eye and told her she understood.

Somehow, backing down made Suzanne begin to have second thoughts. "I tell you what, my dad might know something. Here's his number. Give him a call. He loves to have people visit him and adores Baker's Pride lemon meringue pie.

————

Mr. Elders was working in the small front garden of his house in Thunderbolt. He didn't hear her walk up but turned when she spoke.

"That's a beautiful patch of shrimp plants."

He smiled. "A young lady who knows her plants. Hello, Stephanie."

"Hi, Mr. Elders. I wasn't sure if you would remember me."

"How could I forget the graduate that fell down the granite altar steps at graduation so gracefully?" he teased.

"It's better to be remembered for something embarrassing than not be remembered at all," she teased back.

"And so it is," he replied. "I'm tying off my plants for this blasted hurricane heading our way. They say the big hurricane of 1898 was so ferocious that they found cows from fields on Tybee, right here on my property. That's fifteen miles away. Can you believe it?" He looked down at what she carried in her hands and quickly changed the subject, "Is that lemon meringue?" When Stephanie nodded, he said, "Let's go inside, and I'll make coffee."

As soon as they were both enjoying a slice of pie, Stephanie explained the situation and showed him pictures of Benedictine's pins and class photographs. He looked closely at the pins and then studied the pictures, one in particular. "I remember this man, the fifth officer," he said, pointing to the picture. "But none of the other ones. This man would always come to our house for dinner. But I was just a young boy. My brother and sister were older. She passed just last year. God rest her soul. But my brother would remember. He was a teenager and went to BC at that time."

Mr. Elders took a bite of pie and leaned back in his chair as if pondering something. He pointed to the picture. "You know, come to think about it, something big must have happened because suddenly he was gone. He used to throw the baseball around with me whenever he came to the house. But I saw my glove sitting high on the living room bookshelves one day. I called out to my mom, who was doing the dishes, 'Hey, Mom, where's Mr. Al?' She dropped a plate on the tile floor and just stared at me. My mom was never at a loss for words, so it scared me. But just like any other ten-year-old, I don't remember anything past then, and, to tell you the truth, I never asked again."

"I'm happy you remembered that much. I had the names of the other officers but not his. This really helps me. You don't remember more than 'Mr. Al,' do you?"

"I never knew him as anything other than Mr. Al. But, like I said before, my brother would." He scribbled the name

Buddy Elders with his phone number on a yellowed note-
card and asked her to call him. However, when Stephanie
was driving home that night, she decided that the time had
come to give up the search. If the police gave up, she should,
too. She had enough to do without chasing ghosts.

29

RIDING THE STORM

It had taken a whole week to get back all the reports from the castle. Stephanie was surprised they had been delivered one by one within an hour of the other. That sometimes happened on Friday, especially when a hurricane drew near. The weather stations assured people the strike zone would be between Jacksonville and Daytona, so everyone breathed a bit easier.

She slowly turned the pages of each report, then circled back and reread them. She let the last one slip from her hands onto the desk as her mind wandered to the property. "I don't know how you Scots pulled this off, but you did it," she mumbled as she dialed Philip's number.

He answered on the first ring. "Hello. Stephanie? I was hoping you would call."

She wondered if it was only because he wanted news about his project. Even if it was why, she drank in his words like a cold beer on a hot day. "I have some news about the castle. Could we ride out and take a look this afternoon? The weather will be a little crazy, but we shouldn't get the bad effects of the storm until tomorrow. Want to pick me up around four?"

"Aye. See you at four."

He showed up early, but she was ready. As she hopped up into his truck, he looked at the files. "I can't stand it. Can you tell me on the way?"

"I need to show you, but let's just say I think you'll be happy."

"I can go with that. Thank you for putting me out of my misery of worrying."

The rains of the outer bands of Hurricane Charlotte began to hit the windshield as they passed Skidaway State Park. "We don't have hurricanes in Scotland. Should we be worried about this one?"

"Nah," she said, waving him off. "They don't usually evacuate us unless it's a direct threat with a Category 4 or 5 hurricane. This is only a two, and its path is Daytona."

Philip looked at her questioningly. "Have you watched the news today? Hurricane Charlotte is now a Cat 3, and its path is Jacksonville."

Stephanie bit her lip and looked to the sky.

"Should we turn back?" he asked.

"I think we should be good. I want to show you something quickly, and then we'll head home."

He nodded and continued driving. They came to the private drive and then passed over the rickety bridge. Stephanie noticed the water was higher than expected and knew she needed to make haste. As soon as they parked, she walked him around the house. "I ordered three tests for this area." Pointing to the outlying land around the base of the castle, she said, "This land has a high sand and gravel content. This is excellent news because it will drain well." Then she walked him to the test site at the base. "This is the break we've been waiting for, and I still don't know how it is possible. Do you remember all of the castles we visited in Scotland and what their foundation was?"

Philip sighed, "Bedrock. The rock of Scotland."

"You got it. For stone-built castles, the foundations would be built directly onto the bedrock whenever possible. The builders would dig down to the rock before leveling it to create the strongest possible foundation. The stones for the walls would be laid directly onto the bedrock. So, imagine my surprise when the drilling produced bedrock near the surface. I confirmed it with the topographical images, and a band is running right across your little island. Somehow, your amazing ancestors found the one rare thing in Coastal Georgia, bedrock."

Philip let out a roaring yell, picked Stephanie up, and spun her in the air. "Are you saying my castle is stable?"

"I'm saying the castle is almost unshakable. You couldn't ask for a more stable foundation."

Philip set her down but continued to hold her against him. "Thank you, with all my heart. I'm eternally grateful to you."

The light drizzle became heavier, but he continued holding her. He pushed the never-ending water away from her face, leaned down, and kissed her. Oh, how she had missed his kiss. She didn't care if she was cold and wet; it was worth it. When they finally pulled back from one another, they realized it was pouring and ran to the truck.

"We better get going," she said, motioning him down the drive. But as they came to the bridge, it was one foot underwater. Philip continued slowly until Stephanie urged him to stop. "You don't mess around with storm surge," she announced, and he backed away from the bank. As the water continued to rise, they backed farther away. Finally, she said, "I think we should drive back to the bluff of the castle."

They sat in the truck listening to the local weather station. Hurricane Charlotte had made landfall, but it came in at Brunswick, Georgia, only seventy miles away. Savannah was in a dangerous spot with strong winds, torrential rains, and storm surges. Stephanie began to panic. What had she been thinking? She knew better than to leave the house with a hurricane making its way to land. Although the weather channel might predict where the storm will land, a hurricane is like a toddler and seldom listens to directions.

Philip could see the worry on Stephanie's face as the wind gently shook the truck. "I think we should go inside the castle to stay safe."

She stared at him in disbelief.

"Didn't you just say the castle was strong?" he asked.

"Well, yes. But you don't understand. We are sitting in the worse position of a hurricane, in the right top quadrant. Not only do we need to watch for strong winds, but we must also watch for tornadoes."

Philip jumped out of the truck, ran around, and opened Stephanie's door. "You don't have a choice. We can't stay in the truck. We are going inside."

She sat motionless, scared to proceed.

Instead of getting angry, he spoke to her gently. "Stephanie, I've got you. You're safe."

She held his stare, nodded, and followed him inside the castle on Wassaw Sound.

30

BINGO

"Hide me until I get to the table," Kathleen called out to the group as they walked up the steep stairs to the Knights of Columbus building on Liberty Street.

"I want no part of hiding your contraband," Jack responded, teasing his wife.

The annual Benedictine/Saint Vincent's bingo night only offered beer and wine, and the tribe had begged Jack to make a "drinkie drink," as they called it. The ladies had asked for hurricanes, celebrating Savannah not being directly hit by Charlotte. But Jack had made his famous Bahama Mamas instead. His only condition was he wanted nothing to do with sneaking the drinks into the event.

"I feel like a teenager sneaking candy and Coke into the movies," Kathleen whispered. She hid towards the back of the group, holding the most oversized tote bag she had in her closet.

"Is that your beach bag?" Maggie asked as they

approached the check-in table. Her voice must have been too loud for Kathleen's liking because she shushed her immediately.

"Yes, it is my beach bag, and it's killing my shoulder. I rinsed out three of my gallon milk jugs, which are now full of alcohol. Just get me through this check-in line and to a table," Kathleen whispered through clenched teeth.

"Welcome, everyone. You know the drill," the Grand Knight announced to the group. "Purchase your bingo cards here, and don't forget to write your name on the back of your entry ticket and place it in the bowl for the $250 raffle."

They each began to fill out the back of their tickets while Kathleen hung back from the group. The large hot-pink beach bag with "Life's a Beach" embroidered on the side got the attention of the Grand Knight. As he leaned around to see who was holding the bag, Stephanie lost her balance and bumped into the table. The bowl of raffle tickets flew in the air and scattered on the floor. While everyone stooped over to pick up the tickets, Kathleen made a beeline to one of the center tables and got lost in the crowd.

Once the group caught up with Kathleen, the men disappeared to the bar in the other room to watch the Braves on the big-screen television. The tribe poured their drinks and got their cards ready. Once the first number was called, there wasn't any messing around. Catholics take their bingo very seriously, and people are known to be thrown out for being too rambunctious.

The first few rounds went smoothly. Then, the fourth-card stretch was announced. Just like during baseball's seventh-inning stretch, the Knights played "Take Me Out to the Ballgame" first. Everyone stood and bent like they had just run a marathon. The second song played was always the DJ's pick. Tonight, it was "Brown Eyed Girl."

The commotion brought some men from the bar back into the group. One older gentleman gave his best Van Morrison impression as he made his rounds from table to table, followed by two of his friends. As the song ended, fake Van stood before the tribe's table.

"Hello, ladies," he said while unbuttoning one of his shirt buttons. "Would any of you be my brown-eyed girl?"

They looked at each other laughing, knowing Agnes and Latrice had brown eyes but dared not to point it out.

He narrowed in on the closest pair of brown eyes belonging to Agnes and knelt in front of her. Taking her hand into his, he said, "Do you remember when we used to sing?"

As Agnes said, "Hell No," the rest of their table sang the chorus. "Sha-la-la-la-la-la-la-la-la-la-la-tee-da."

The room erupted in applause. Fake Van began to get up to bow to the crowd, but his legs couldn't get him back to a standing position. He laughed it off and struggled again, but his elderly legs wouldn't work. Kathleen stood to help him, but he swatted her away. Yet, not before noticing her SVA ring. When he called his friends, they each grabbed an arm and pulled him to a standing position. Turning to the table, he said, "You must be Saints, right?"

Jan answered, "We're all Saints in the making now, aren't we?"

He bowed his head to the table and retreated without looking back.

"Who was that?" Latrice asked.

Kathleen answered, "That's Buddy Elders. He's one of Benedictine's baseball legends. He played for the Red Sox."

"Buddy Elders? Kathleen, are you sure?" Stephanie asked.

"Of course, she's sure," Jan snipped. "Kathleen knows everyone in Savannah."

Kathleen shook her head, "Yes, I'm sure. Why?"

"He's just the man I've been looking for. Excuse me, will ya?"

The ladies looked from one to the other until Agnes finally blurted out, "Just the man she's been looking for? No way!"

And, just like always, everyone answered in unison, "WAY!"

———

Stephanie walked up to the table of four men huddled together in the bar. Buddy saw her coming and threw up his hands in defeat. "I know, I know. I'm sorry. I get carried away. Forgive me."

Stephanie waved him off, "No, I'm not coming here to reprimand you."

"Oh, you interested?" he asked, wagging his eyebrows.

"No, I'm not coming in here for that, either. Can I speak with you in private?"

Buddy nudged his elbow into his friend's side. "She wants to speak with me in private. Excuse me, gentlemen. The girl of my dreams just walked into my life."

Stephanie stood motionless, wondering if the embarrassment she felt inside was shown across her face. Still, she followed him onto the porch once he got up from the table. He leaned on the side that looked down over Bull Street, and she did the same. When he looked over at her, his speech did not have a bit of flirtiness. "What can I help you with?"

She wasn't sure how much she needed to tell him but realized this was her last chance to get answers. So, she started at the beginning, telling him about finding the bones at her project in Daffin. She told him about the bag with the Benedictine pins, then about meeting the headmaster and looking at the pictures. She told him she had met with his niece and brother and admitted that he was the last chance for answers.

"This isn't the right place for this conversation," he said quietly. "Could you come by my house tomorrow? I'll be home all day."

He knows, Stephanie thought as she agreed to meet him. She could hardly wait for answers.

31

THE FAMOUS BUDDY BOMB

"Buddy Elders? Heck yeah, I'll go with you to talk to him. Did you know he pitched for the Red Sox?" Keith asked.

Of course, Stephanie had known. How could she forget? The man had told her three times during their very short conversation. She was happy that her brother, Keith, was going with her.

Buddy Elders lived in Thunderbolt, like his brother, but he lived on the water. His condo overlooked the Intercoastal Waterway. They were invited inside and escorted through the house. "I was watching the line of sailboats taking the ICW down to Miami for the winter. Come on back."

Stephanie and Keith followed him past the dining room and cut across the living room. She had been expecting more of a college-dorm decor, with posters and sports pictures of himself. However, she was pleasantly surprised at the classic coastal appearance surrounding her.

"Nick," he called out towards the kitchen as they

passed through the living room. "They're here." Then he opened the French doors and stepped out onto the back porch.

"Wow. Look at them," Stephanie commented, appreciating the beauty of a sailboat in motion.

"Yeah, we have a beautiful view this time of year. Then again in spring when they make their way back in."

Stephanie nodded and then introduced Keith, who was utterly starstruck. "It's so nice to finally meet the great Buddy Elders. I have watched you my whole life."

"And so have I," came a voice from the doorway. A sleek and stunning older lady stepped out onto the porch. "I've watched him since the day I met him in Boston. Hi, I'm Nichole."

"Yes, she has. My better half. She keeps me out of trouble." He took a tray of drinks and a small bowl of cheese straws out of her hands and set them on the outdoor dining set.

Stephanie smiled at the attractive woman. Her silver hair, cropped to her shoulder, showed off her tanned neck. Stephanie knew her comment about keeping him out of trouble was truthful; she'd seen that firsthand. "Very nice to meet you, Nichole."

"Shall we sit?" Nichole asked the group, and they followed her. She passed out glasses to each of them and began pouring, "It's Moscow Mule Monday," she announced. "My favorite day of the week."

Buddy teased, "You say that every day as you stir up your daily special."

"Aw, pooh." She kissed him on his temple and sat beside him. Looking across the table, she addressed Stephanie and

Keith, "Buddy has told me everything, so you can speak freely."

Stephanie relaxed. "Just so we're all on the same page, I found bones at my jobsite in Daffin Park, and for some unknown reason, I feel responsible for finding out more about them. I believe Buddy might be able to enlighten me."

Buddy took a large swig of his mule and began. "When I was a freshman at Benedictine, my dad was the Master Sergeant. In the midst of WWII, the world was different. Cadets close to my age were going to war. Some of them never coming back." He stopped and shook his head before continuing. "Since it was wartime, they petitioned to have five sergeants in commission at BC. Four of them were local, but the fifth was a newcomer. His name was Al Muller. There are several Mullers in Savannah, so everyone assumed he was one of them. However, he was new to the city.

"It was the Master Sergeant's job to care for those he commanded. So, my dad rented him our small house next door. He would come over several times weekly for dinner or to hang out. We loved him being around. He was a little bit older than my older sister, and he was strong. He would throw the baseball with us in the yard; he had a good arm. In fact, he's the one that taught me how to throw a sinker."

"Wait," Keith interrupted. "That man is the one that taught you how to throw the famous Buddy Bomb?"

Buddy grinned, took another sip of his drink, and set it down slowly. "Yes, he did. Honestly, I probably wouldn't have stuck with pitching if he hadn't spent so much time with me. That's crazy, isn't it?" He shook his head, took a deep breath, and let it out slowly. "One night, I came in late from a date to find my dad kneeling beside him on the living room floor. Al was bloody and appeared to be dying. I asked my dad what had happened, and he said someone had stabbed him. Then he yelled for me to lock the house, make sure the curtains were all closed, and go to bed. When I awoke the next morning, it was as if it never happened."

Nichole could see how shaken her husband was as he told the story. She walked around the table and refilled Buddy's glass. After setting it back in front of him, she stood protectively at his side.

"I tried asking my father about it later that night, but he told me never to tell another soul. Other than Nick, I haven't, until now. That was fifty years ago, and I have always wondered what happened that night." He sat back, deep in his thoughts. No one dared to interrupt. "When my father was dying, he asked for two people: the priest and Sergeant Bill Nettles. The priest couldn't tell us anything, but I wonder if Sergeant Bill could?"

"Is he still alive?" Stephanie asked.

"Oh yes, he's a spitfire. He lives over in Cohen's Old Man's Home. I see him at some of the Benedictine events. His body has aged, and he's on a walker, but his mind is sharp as a tack." Stephanie nodded in acknowledgment. "If you get any answers, please come back and let me know," he added.

"Of course, I will." She tried not to let disappointment fill her voice. Turning to Keith, she sighed, "Another trail to follow."

"How the hell do you keep getting yourself in these situations?" Keith asked.

Stephanie nodded. "My annoyingly curious mind. Still, I can't help but wonder, how many people in Savannah have buried this story, and why?"

32

BEDROCK

Stephanie opened the door to Hearing Room 341 at eight a.m. and waited in the doorway. *Surely, they are hearing many cases today,* she thought. *I'll stand in the back and wait my turn.* But as soon as she leaned against the wall, she heard her name being called, and the room fell silent.

Mr. Lane called to her, "Ms. Normand? Will you please find your seat? We're ready to begin." All twelve seats around the large oval conference table were occupied except for one.

Walking towards it, she noticed reporters, lawyers, and many executives lining the walls. Then she locked eyes with Philip. Easing into the seat next to him, she leaned over, "What's going on?"

"From what I can tell, this private hearing just went public."

The chairwoman called the meeting to order. She introduced herself as Mrs. Holmes then turned the meeting over to Mr. Lane. "We are here to discuss the property owned by

Mr. Philip McLaughlin and the safety of the building that sits upon it. This project has many uncertainties, mainly because no other buildings in the United States compare. With that being said, that may be proof alone that this building should be torn down."

Stephanie looked around the room at the many nods, and her stomach tightened. They were all against the castle before they even heard anything about it. Philip had been set up. The knowledge of that fueled her to help him. She sat and listened intently, biding her time for her chance to speak.

"We have with us a top-notch structural engineer. She graduated at the top of her class at Georgia Tech and has spent weeks investigating this project. She even made a trip to Scotland to run comparisons. Ms. Normand, can you say, without a doubt, that this building is stable? Is the foundation firm and unwavering, and can the proposed building plan be accomplished?"

Stephanie pulled four presentation folders from her bag. Inside each was a copy of the proposal. It included the original plans, the comparisons with pictures and data, the test results of the property, and finally, her suggestions. She walked around the table, spacing them where everyone could follow along.

"What is this, Ms. Normand? I didn't ask for paperwork; I asked you a simple question."

"Yes, I understand that. And my simple answer is on page sixty-eight. The information on pages one through sixty-seven helped me draw this final answer. The building is, without a doubt, strong and unwavering. It will likely be around another 250 years if maintained properly."

The people at the table began to shuffle through the pages, nodding each time they turned to the next page. Mr. Lane jumped to his feet. "As I said in our first hearing, the building doesn't have modern footings, has no safety precautions, and sits on sand and clay. There is absolutely no way that you could rectify those problems."

Stephanie smiled. "You're right. I can't rectify those kinds of problems. However, the original builders addressed those issues. The castle is built on bedrock."

Mr. Lane looked as if he'd been slapped across the face. "That's not possible."

"That's what I thought, too. But, somehow, the original builders discovered a band of bedrock running under the bluff on the island, and they built the castle upon it."

Mr. Lane snatched one of the presentation folders from the man beside him. He quickly flipped through the pages, then raised the page to his face and read. Flabbergasted, he sat down but swiftly regrouped. "How wonderful to find out there is bedrock that runs beneath one of our barrier islands. However, just because the foundation is intact, it doesn't change the fact that the castle is not secure. I bet stones fall off when we get a good nor'easter blow."

"That's not true. The castle is very secure in the wind."

"And how would you possibly know that?"

"I was wrapping up my final tests when Hurricane Charlotte came through last week with her seventy-five miles per hour winds. The storm surge closed the bridge, and we got stuck on the island. The castle held strong and never wavered."

Mr. Lane never missed a beat. He had noticed how Stephanie seemed different with Mr. MacLaughlin, as if they were a couple. Then she slipped and said "we." He went with his gut instincts and proceeded. "Were you out on the island by yourself, my dear?" Stephanie didn't answer, so he asked again. "I'm sure that was quite scary for a young woman to weather that ugly storm all alone. Did you have anyone with you?"

Philip rose to his feet. "Stop badgering her. She will not answer your question."

Mr. Lane turned to the chairwoman at the end of the table. "I have reason to believe that our evidence may be compromised. I will personally take on this project and have all the tests rerun. I make a motion to reschedule this hearing for the first of next year. Will anyone second that motion?"

"I'll second it," said a voice across the table from a man Stephanie didn't recognize. The two men then stood and walked out of the hearing together.

———

Philip leaned his head into his hands, murmuring, "What just happened?"

"I'm so sorry, Philip," Stephanie whispered back in reply.

"The first of next year? It will take them months to finish what you did in two weeks?"

"He wants your property and will do whatever it takes to get it. But we can fight this. We have actual reports and facts. It shouldn't be hard."

Philip let out a long sigh. "Let him have it."

Stephanie's head whipped around in surprise.

"I'm serious. I keep trying to make something work that

obviously isn't meant to be. I don't know what I thought when I moved to the States. I was looking forward to making this city my home, but I think it's time to return to Scotland. Savannah doesn't want me here." He reached out and slowly ran his hand down the side of her arm. Standing up, he leaned and kissed her cheek. "Goodbye, Stephanie."

She felt the air leave the room when he left. Just like the oxygen being pulled out, she struggled to breathe. *I should go after him,* she thought. But she had nothing left to give him. He was leaving. *Suck it up, buttercup. You knew better.* She glanced around the now-empty room and shook her head in disbelief. Why had she let him in? She had always tried to keep her heart safe. If someone got too close, she would find a reason to leave. She must have known the day would come when someone left her. Still, that didn't take away the hurt. She loved him, dammit. Now, what was she going to do?

Stephanie ranted the whole way back to the office. She had worked herself into a mess and needed to process everything that had happened in the last hour. She threw her bags in one of the armchairs and opened her bottom desk drawer, where she kept an extra running outfit and her older shoes.

The minute her shoes hit the pavement, she reviewed the meeting step by step, from the beginning to the unfortunate end. Philip told her goodbye. Did he really tell her goodbye in a board room? Was she that easy to walk away from when things didn't go his way? She didn't need that. No! She didn't deserve that. After all she had done trying to help him. The hours and hours she had spent on this project and the days spent with him in Scotland. He had to have known it could end up like this. Hadn't she told him that from the very beginning?

She cut over two blocks and ran down Barnard Street. Her dad had told her about the old street cars that once ran from north to south in Savannah. She loved to try to run their old lines. After passing through Pulaski Square, she enjoyed the four-block stretch, pondering how often the old oak tree branches must have fallen on the live wires. She passed through Chatham Square, then after another two blocks, she jumped off the pretend rail line and cut down Gaston until she hit Forsyth Park.

Each step took her further away from the meeting, from Philip, from feeling abandoned. Just like always, the sound of her shoes on the pavement calmed her mind.

She ran along the one-mile path on the outskirts of Forsyth Park, studying each of the historic houses as she passed. It always surprised her how the different areas of town had such different architecture, and the Victorian District stood out distinctly. She was thankful for the cold weather keeping most people inside, so she had the walkways to herself. She completed the first lap, then snaked her way on one of the many paths toward the fountain. She stopped when she arrived at the center and began to walk. This was her home. It was quirky and sometimes slower paced than she once wanted, but she was married to its history. And part of its history was the castle. She couldn't just walk away; it deserved more.

Her brain was calmer now, and she began to process things differently. That's when it hit her. Philip. He didn't have these ties in Scotland since his dad died. He was hoping to lay them in Savannah but was shunned. She tried taking the emotion out of the situation so she could pull everything apart. He wasn't tossing her aside; he was running off rejected. He had moved to this city, offering it a tremendous gift: a piece of Savannah's past. And what had we done? Tossed him aside.

She began to walk, unsure where she was heading, as she thought of Philip. Before she knew it, she crossed Lafayette Square and entered the Cathedral of Saint John the Baptist. She felt the pull towards the altar and settled herself in a pew facing the tabernacle. She couldn't do this alone.

Scotland had shown her how people had fought and died for their faith. Some families had even held onto their faith for hundreds of years, hoping they could have the freedom to worship one day. She could no longer be lukewarm. She was either in or out. She looked at the crucifix and bowed towards the tabernacle. As a tear slid down her cheek, she said, "I'm all in."

33

THE STAKEOUT

She approached her office and noticed a man lingering outside, peering into the front window. She slowed, watching as he nervously looked up and down the sidewalk. When he made eye contact with her, he turned in the opposite direction and quickly walked away.

What was that all about? Was he trying to break in? She remembered locking the front door and double-checked to make sure she had. Then she walked to the lane and entered through the back. Safely inside, she began to search for her purse. *Where did I set it? Could the man out front have taken it?* She searched around the chair where she had thrown the pile from the meeting, but only her tote bag with files was there. Had she left it in the courthouse? She grunted out loud, knowing she had. She had left it behind in her rush to vacate the meeting room quickly. But what should she do?

It was bad enough she had wandered into the cathedral in her running outfit, smelling like a wildebeest. Now she would have to return to the meeting room stinking to high heavens. Her car keys were in that purse, and her shower was twenty minutes away. Surely, there was something in her office that could take the smell of sweat away.

She put back on the clothes she had worn earlier, trying to pull her dress over her still-sticky body, then noticed the CVS bag on her desk from the day before. Her car had smelled moldy, so she had purchased one of those air fresheners to hang from her rear-view mirror. It was in the shape of a Christmas tree. It was red, and the scent read "Cherry Tree." She unwrapped the small freshener and smelled it, but her nose was always stuffed up after her runs. Still, it would have to smell better than her sweat. She rubbed the red tree along her dress, then stashed it in her coat pocket. That would help the situation.

When she returned to the meeting room, she saw her purse sitting on the table. She made a beeline towards it, hoping she could make a fast exit. She had yet to notice she was not alone. The chairwoman from her hearing was sitting at the long end of the table and had yet to look up from her writing. Stephanie pondered if she should quietly retreat, but then the lady's face scrunched, and she began to fan a smell away from her nose. She glanced up with disgust and seemed surprised to see Stephanie standing at the other end of the table.

"What in the hell is that smell? I expected to see a cheap hooker standing in front of me."

"Uh." Stephanie had no idea how to answer. "I think that might be me."

"Good gosh. Where have you been to smell like that in the last two hours?" She then held her hand up. "You know what, it's better that I don't know." She ruffled through some papers on the table. "What are you doing about the castle project?"

"There's nothing to do. I've been taken off of it."

The lady gave her a look that Stephanie's dad earmarked as the "stank eye," then asked, "Are you giving up that easily? I thought you had more grit than that."

"I've run out of options," Stephanie answered.

"We only run out of options once we're six feet under. Now lick your wounds; you've got some work to do. You can begin by reading Robert's Rules of Order. Then, look back over the conditions of the land grant and possibly change your course."

Stephanie looked at the older lady and smiled. She recognized something familiar about her but couldn't place her. Then she saw the royal blue stone from her SVA ring. Stephanie nodded and said, "I'm on it!"

The lady fanned her face harder and added an uncomfortable cough. "Whatcha waiting on? You should start immediately."

"Yes, ma'am. Thank you. I'll go right away," Stephanie called out as she retreated. Once she was back outside, her sinuses opened, and she smelled the cherry tree scent. For once, she was happy for the cold wind that seemed to whisk it away.

After driving home and showering, she made a cup of hot tea. She was chilled to the bone and hoped to pull from its warmth. Savannahians are known to have thin blood, so they feel like they are freezing when the temperature dips below fifty.

She held the cup with both hands while pondering what to do next. She had time to make things right with Philip. He had rented the house in Ardsley Park, so he most likely wasn't hopping on a plane immediately to travel back to Scotland. But what could she do?

The motion had been passed to postpone the hearing, but the SVA alumna told her she needed to do some research. She began by looking under the Chatham County website. She found the list of eight board members appointed by the City Council and slowly started scanning the list. She recognized three members' names, but they hadn't been present at the meeting. Who were the faces around the large table?

As she continued to read, she saw where the Zoning Board of Appeals met twice a month, the second and fourth Wednesday, but today was Thursday. A sinking feeling formed in her gut. She had been handpicked because she was young and naive, and her inexperience had ruined Philip. Standing from the computer, she began to pace, only to find herself digging in her candy drawer and eating Hershey's Kisses. Chocolate always made her brain think better, or so she told herself. *Who can educate me on how things work with the city?* Her smile spread across her face: Latrice.

Latrice came to her office later that afternoon. "Okay. Tell me how I can help you?"

Stephanie explained the first meeting and how the castle's land grant ran out at the end of the year. She then told her about why they had gone to Scotland, the test results, and finding the bedrock. Finally, she explained the second meeting with a room full of people and the motion to re-evaluate next year.

Latrice threw her hands in the air and wagged her finger.

"I smell a rotten apple here. First, the ZBA meetings are always on Wednesdays. Second, the postponement is null and void if they don't reach a quorum. Finally, members can be personally liable if they voted on a motion without a quorum."

Stephanie sat up excitedly. "Then we can fight this?"

"Possibly. But remember, that rotten scoundrel who orchestrated this is working just as hard as you to bring it home. You're going to have to outsmart the fox."

"Can you help me figure this out?"

"Wild hogs couldn't keep me away. There's nothing I despise more than a dirty city employee."

Stephanie hugged her, and they devised a plan to begin that evening.

"Okay, so what are we looking for?"

"We have to follow Mr. Lane. It helps that he leaves every afternoon at 5:30 on the dot. We just need to see what he does from there on. This might take several nights, so we must be patient."

Stephanie nodded as they both watched the doorway to the city building, then yelled excitedly, "There he is!"

When he passed the entrance to the parking garage, they threw on their coats, jumped out, and followed on foot.

"Where in the world is he headed?" Latrice asked as they struggled to keep pace as he cut through Madison Square and then Monterey, staying on Bull Street. "Is he going for a walk around Forsyth? If so, I'll have to bench it and let him lap us. I'm not a runner like you."

Stephanie enjoyed running; it had been her saving grace in dealing with the stress of living in Atlanta. Since she had been home, she had even joined the Savannah Striders and loved running as a team. But at present, her "team" was pooping out. "Come on," Stephanie urged, pulling Latrice's arm.

Mr. Lane made a left on the sidewalk as he approached Gaston Street. He then entered the door under the extended green canopy of the Oglethorpe Club, a prestigious private club in Savannah.

"Thank the Lord above!" Latrice exclaimed between deep gulps of air. "Now what?"

"Now, I guess we wait."

Latrice plopped onto the edge of the long concrete planter that ran the length of the club, and Stephanie jumped up beside her. As the sun began to set, it got colder and colder until they snuggled into each other for warmth. Finally, Latrice pulled away.

"I can't stand it any longer. What in the hell is that smell?"

Stephanie was stunned. She thought the smell must have stayed inside her nose and had no idea how Latrice would smell anything. Then she remembered dropping the air freshener inside her coat pocket. She held it up for Latrice.

"That smells like..."

"I know, a cheap hooker."

Latrice nodded as she fanned her face. They were so deep in conversation that they almost missed Mr. Lane walking out. It could have been because he didn't seem like the same man who had gone in. His tie had been shoved in the pocket of his jacket, which was now flung over his shoulder, and he whistled as he slowly made his way across town. Stephanie and Latrice giggled at him the whole way to Bay Street as he petted dogs being walked and took the time to pause in front of the monuments.

"He seems almost . . . hmmm . . . almost likable," Stephanie said when he had jumped out of the way of a little boy on a scooter.

"Don't lose sight that he's the bad guy," Latrice answered. They followed him until he walked in the front door of Savannah Steak House. They overheard him joking with the hostess. Hiding behind one of the planters with tall bamboo palms, they watched through the glass windowpane as she led him to a seated table of five men.

"That's them. All five of those men were around the table this morning at the hearing. Do you recognize them?" Stephanie asked Latrice.

"I sure don't. But they are just now ordering drinks for their meal. I think they'll be there awhile, and I'm starving." She glanced around and homed in on Moon River Brewing's outdoor seating across Whitaker. She pointed over. "You're gonna buy me a burger. Hell, I might splurge and order a beer, too. We can keep an eye out across the street."

Combating the chill in the air, they sat beside an outdoor fireplace while keeping a constant eye on the front door at Savannah Steak House. They ordered moon burgers with fries and enjoyed the small fire's warmth. However, as the night passed, they decided to sneak back to Savannah Steak House to see what course Mr. Lane was eating. When they came to the first window of the restaurant, they realized the staff was cleaning for the night, and all the tables were empty.

Stephanie hurried to the door, knocking to get the hostess' attention, who shook her head and mouthed, "We're closed."

"Can I just ask you one quick question?" she yelled through the glass. The hostess rolled her eyes and unlocked the door. *How can I get information from this young woman who only wants to go home for the night?* Thinking fast, she said, "My boss is gonna kill me. I was supposed to bring the credit card to pay for our client's meal, but I couldn't find it. Is there any way to get a copy of the receipt so I can turn it in for his expenses? Can you please help another working gal out? You know how they are."

The hostess looked at Stephanie from head to toe. "Yeah, I know exactly how they are. Those men have been pawing at us all night. Laughing it up. What's your name?"

"Stephanie," she blurted out before considering the consequences.

The hostess nodded, "Well, Stephanie, I am sorry you have to work for Tommy."

"Oh. No, I work for Mr. Lane. Did he pay the tab?"

"Nope. Mr. Morgan picked up the whole bill."

"Oh. Well, thank you." Stephanie paused for a second, then asked. "Hey, did Mr. Lane seem okay?"

Leaning in, the hostess answered, "Between you and me, I've never seen him like this. He's been coming here for years, usually with working men who I assume work with the city or with his family. But recently, he's been coming with Mr. Morgan, and his whole demeanor has changed. The poor guy looks almost ill. I was thinking earlier they must have something over his head to be hanging out with a bunch of jerks like that. But hell, what do I know?" She looked back at the restaurant. "I gotta go. Take care of your boss, okay?"

Stephanie met up with Latrice and explained her conversation with the hostess. "This Tommy guy is up to no good, and he's pulling our Mr. Lane in with him. We've got some research to do, but I'm ready for my warm, cozy bed right now."

34

HOLDING ON

Philip dropped the last bag in the center of the main hall, the loud thud echoing through the bare room. *What am I doing? This is insane. I should hop on a plane and head home.* But for whatever reason, he felt pulled back to the castle. It was almost as if he could feel his father there, although he had never been to Savannah. Letting his eyes scan the room, he smiled. He could imagine his father in this massive room with ten-foot-high fireplaces on each end. His father would feel right at home. A wave of sorrow hit him hard, knocking him down under the water. However, this time, as it retreated back into the sea, one image remained. Stephanie.

How can I leave her? But how can I stay? After the castle is gone, I have absolutely nothing here. He shook his head. Being with the person you love isn't absolutely nothing; his father taught him that. However, he had nothing to offer her in Savannah. All his dreams had been tied with this castle. He was wanted in Beauly. He had told Hugh to begin planning to finish the estate; he definitely would need help. But where did that leave him and Stephanie? Nowhere.

He began to wander the castle. But this time, it felt different. He was no longer picturing the modern lighting and the sounds of happy visitors but seeing it for how it really was. It was built in the 1700s. The fact that it was still standing at all was a mystery. Only a few places in the United States could compare. It was a treasure. How could they just throw away this history? His thoughts jumped to him and Stephanie tromping through all the castles in Scotland. Not one compared to this one. He wished he could have conveyed that to the board. If only he had more time.

It had been less than twenty-four hours since the meeting. A lot had changed in the short time since he said goodbye to Stephanie. Since he still owned the castle, he decided to enjoy its last weeks of life before they tore it down. So, he packed all his belongings, cleared out of his rental, and dropped by Bass Pro Shop to purchase camping gear. He wondered if he had made a mistake. No running water. No electricity and no heat. Was he crazy? Och, it wasn't the first time people thought he was crazy.

He started a fire in the large fireplace and listened as the birds, or bats most likely, flew out the top of the chimney in protest. Opening up a foldable camping chair, he pulled it closer to the fire, waiting for the heat to warm him. He looked down at his belongings piled in the middle of the room and focused on the large suitcase. Hugh had found it for him in the attic at Beauly. He had been able to fit most of the contents from his dad's trunk inside. He only had to leave a few of the more oversized items he and Stephanie had already read. Stephanie had laughed when he checked it in at the airport. Since it was full of books and files, it weighed eighty-nine pounds, and he had to pay over two hundred dollars. But in his heart, he believed that Savannah would be his new home, and he didn't want to leave anything of value behind.

He began to spread the contents of his dad's trunk across the floor, grateful he had already cleared most of the two hundred years' worth of debris that had covered it. The large windows offered him plenty of morning sunlight, so he placed the twenty-two files in order, beginning with number four, where he and Stephanie had left off. He settled in and began to read.

Eventually, the room began to darken. When he checked the clock, it was 6:30, and he had read all day, only stopping to add wood to the fire. Once he realized he had read through lunch, his stomach growled with reproach. He opened a container of sardines and Beanie Weenies, the dinner of champions, and turned on his new, large camping lamp. Reopening folder eight, he read until he could no longer hold his eyes open, then settled into his sleeping bag for the night.

The sound of birds woke him at first light. He noticed the steam from his breath and quickly zipped the bag around him until he was completely awake. His first thoughts were of Stephanie, but then his mind recalled some exciting facts he had read. He began to ponder each of them. General Oglethorpe had submitted a land grant for a fort to protect Savannah from the Spanish in Florida. However, he listed the grant under the name of Mrs. Robert Castell. Why would he have done that for his dead friend's wife, and why would she want to build a fort? The questions swirled in his head while pondering how a woman could have lived in this same castle. Then he wondered if she had been as cold as he was right now.

He felt his body tremble and knew he must make a plan if he was going to stay here for the next few weeks. He jumped up, added another layer of clothes, threw some logs on the fire, and hightailed it to his truck. He drove to the nearby Skidaway Island Campground, bought a camping permit for the month, then went directly to their showers. The cold had kept most campers snuggled into their tents, so he thankfully had the showers all to himself and used every drop of hot water.

When he left the campground, he stopped at the local breakfast joint. After finishing his Bubba's Big Breakfast and the second cup of coffee, he finally felt human again. He thought about Stephanie and decided to call her. He was disappointed when she didn't pick up and contemplated hanging up, but she deserved to know how he felt. Clearing his voice, he left his message, "I woke with you on my mind. I'm sorry I left the meeting so upset. I feel like we have much to discuss. Would you like to come to my place for dinner? Let's say seven. Call me, okay?"

Looking up from his phone, he noticed a table full of suits watching him. He nodded in their direction, then turned his attention to the hanging TV for the sports highlights.

"You McLaughlin?" he was asked by a balding, middle-aged man.

"That's right," Philip answered, giving him a good once over. Although the man was dressed borderline grunge, he had money. You could always tell by a man's shoes, and this one was wearing a Hermes loafer.

"I hear you're trying to save the castle."

"Was trying is more like it."

"Maybe I can help."

"Why would you do that?"

"Because I don't want some bloody casino bringing all kind of riffraff out near the Landings. May I sit?"

Philip nodded, and the man sat directly across from him.

Looking him square in the eye, the man explained. "The Morgan boys used to run this island when it was unincorporated. They somehow got wind of the castle's land trust and found the right person to bribe to make the time run out. There are a lot of people on your side."

"On my side or against the Morgans."

"It doesn't matter. Anyway, we may be able to help you. We have friends in high places, too. Tell your friend Stephanie to talk to Justin Baker. I'll be in touch."

Philip watched the man return to his table. The other three stood as he approached, then each one nodded at Philip as they walked out.

His phone had gone straight to voice mail during his strange meeting. He smiled when he saw it was from Stephanie. "I'm so happy to hear from you. I was scared you left. I'd love to have dinner. I'll see you at seven."

He smiled as he left breakfast, excited to share this news with the one person in the world who seemed to care, Stephanie.

35

SERGEANT BILL

Stephanie couldn't believe she had agreed to go to the castle that evening for dinner. She listened to Philip's message one more time. "I woke with you on my mind. I'm sorry I left the meeting so upset. I feel like we have much to discuss. Would you like to come to my place for dinner?"

Rolling her eyes, she thought, *I've tormented myself for the last twenty-four hours, and you're just gonna say sorry? Why are relationships so hard?* She tried to put her irritations aside. She was happy he hadn't left town, but what had he been doing for the last twenty-four hours? And why did he ask her to the castle? A million questions ran through her mind, but she would have to wait until that evening for answers.

Stephanie sat back at her desk. She had arrived at work early to catch up on several projects: a building in Pooler, a renovation for a bar at Tybee, and two private residences. Business was good. Since her work was done, she would have the whole day to worry about her evening. She decided to occupy her time by meeting Sergeant Bill and dragging Keith along with her.

The smell of rubbing alcohol and peppermint filled her nose the minute she opened the door to Cohens Men's Home. Some residents lived there out of necessity, but most were there by choice. Stephanie pictured the fraternity houses at UGA and multiplied the average age by four.

A perky red-haired receptionist welcomed them. Stephanie had to practically pull Keith from her desk.

"I'll be back to see you on my way out, babe," he told her as he walked down the hall.

"I can barely maintain my joy," the receptionist mumbled, making Stephanie giggle. Keith sometimes acted like a horse's ass, but he was always at her side when she needed him. She wished he would show that side of himself to more people than just her.

They followed the directions to Sergeant Bill's room, but their voyage went slowly. They were trapped behind a slow-moving gentleman wearing a hospital gown which left his buttocks in full view. He was creeping along, walking in the middle of the hall where no one could pass.

"Okay, Pops, pick a lane," Keith called out to him.

Glancing over his shoulder, he cried out, "Ah, go to hell, you whippersnapper."

Keith opened his mouth to respond, but Stephanie waved him off. "We can wait on him. Besides, I'm enjoying the view."

Keith glanced at the full moon on parade before him and yelled in disgust, "Gross. You're nasty!"

They began to laugh together, and Stephanie was happy her rude comment had disarmed him. When they finally reached Sergeant Bill's room, she was glad to see him sitting in a chair doing a crossword puzzle in the Savannah paper.

"Hello, Sergeant Bill. May we speak with you for a moment?"

Without looking up, he said, "T on both ends of this nine-letter word for a medieval engine of war with a sling?"

"Trebuchet," Stephanie answered, grateful she had just seen one in Scotland.

"T-R-E-B-U-C-H-E-T," he spelled as he filled in. "Cracker Jacks, I believe you're right." He looked at her with appreciation. "I have all the time in the world for you, my dear. What can I do for you?"

We are trying to find information about Sergeant Al Muller, who worked with you in the 1940s at Benedictine Military School."

He eyed them warily, so Stephanie told the story for what she hoped was the last time. She shared about finding the bones and speaking with Buddy Elders, who led her to him.

"After all this time," he replied. "It has weighed on my mind so much lately. Several things have been bothering me, if you must know the truth. It's funny when most of your friends are dead; you feel like you're in a hurry to tell people your stories. You know, to pass them on to keep them alive, so someone else in the world will know them before I die. That probably sounds odd to a young person, but if I die with my story, my story dies, too."

Stephanie found a seat in a chair across from Sergeant Bill while Keith plopped on the end of the made bed.

"I remember the day Sergeant Al came to BC. He spoke English but had such an odd accent I thought he had a speech impediment. Little did I know he was actually a German spy."

Stephanie and Keith locked eyes as the man went on.

"You see, during WWII, the port of Savannah had become a military cargo port sending goods to the Allied Nations. You know, things like paper, asphalt, naval ship parts, and more. Not to mention food and machines. The Germans wanted to squash these ports. Once they established their drop-off spot, they began to set up spies in major ports. Sergeant Al was one of those spies."

"Where did they find an open entryway?" Stephanie asked.

"He said it was on a nearby island with a fort of some kind. It was abandoned, so he could camp out there until he was ready."

Stephanie's stomach dropped. *Could he have been dropped at Wassaw?* she wondered. She thought back to the gun shells she had found on the lookout and was so deep in thought she barely heard Keith's question.

"What was his mission?"

The old man smiled, relishing the attention of someone eager to hear what he was saying. "His mission was to obtain the river pilots' route to bring the ships into port. With that route, the Germans could come into the city and destroy it from the water."

"Oh, wow!" Stephanie exclaimed as she pictured warships in the harbor destroying her hometown. "What happened?"

"What happened? He fell in love; that's what happened."

"With who?"

"Not who, what. He fell in love with Savannah. You see,

the Savannah River is very tricky. Its mud bottom is lined with sand bars and old ships that didn't know their way. Albert watched the ships and tried to label the turns of the river pilots who were trained to bring ships in and out. But between tides and ship sizes, it took much longer than expected. He was slowly keeping a chart over two years. He said he etched it in a minuscule form of dots into a cigar holder like the Germans had taught him to do. But, over those two long years, he fell in love with our city and especially the people in it.

"Albert became friends with me but closer friends with the Master Sergeant. Over time, Albert began to let his guard down. That's when the Master Sergeant figured everything out. At first, it was little slips: not knowing U.S. facts or food items. But it was finally pronunciations that got him caught. One day, in a casual conversation, Albert was forced to say the word 'squirrel.' The phonetic structure of the word is illogical, so foreigners cannot pronounce it. The Master Sergeant had heard they used this test to sniff out spies, but he had no idea that the young man he had come to love as a son would fall under that category.

"Albert confessed everything. He didn't have any family. So, when he graduated from the Naval Academy in Germany, they snatched him into their Navy. But he never knew what family felt like until he came to Savannah. Albert then told Master Sergeant about his mission to obtain the river pilots' route to bring the ships into port where the Germans could destroy the city from the water. Then he told him that he had no intention of giving them any information and explained how he intended to fight back."

Sergeant Bill gasped a little. Stephanie could see he was

getting tired. She brought him a glass of water, saying, "Why don't we come back tomorrow, and we can finish our conversation."

He grabbed her hand. "At my age, I've learned that no one is promised tomorrow. This story needs to be told."

She patted his hand like she had the older woman's hand in Oban. "Let's go slowly and take our time then, okay?"

Sergeant Bill nodded. "You can't just walk away from being a spy as much as you might want to. And you can't protect a whole city by yourself.

"Albert told Master Sergeant that the Germans had a specific place where they dropped their spies coming into the U.S., an abandoned fort or castle of some kind on the outskirts of town. He said they could only drop in the dark of night and could only get close enough with the tides of a full moon. Albert knew this, so he was able to fight back. Every month, he would take every gun he owned and camped out in this battlement, watching for the German ships. Whenever they got close, he would open fire. This went on for months and months until the Germans began to realize that it wasn't U.S. troops but only a single shooter. That's when they opened fire.

"They had no idea it would be one of their own. If so, they would have retrieved all of his information first. Instead, they shot Albert. He was able to make it back to his house, but barely. He pulled his car into the front yard of Master Sergeant's house and collapsed onto the horn. He knew he was dying and wanted to ensure Savannah was safe. When Master Sergeant came out, he explained that there was a hidden leather pouch in the back of the woodpile. He told him inside the bag was an address for his extended family and, after the war, to please write to them and tell them he was dead.

"But most importantly, he said to bury him with all the other items in the pouch. His last words were, 'No one must get their hands on its contents. You must protect Savannah.'"

36

BURGER WITH BACON

Stephanie and Keith walked out of the nursing home quietly. Keith didn't even think to stop and flirt with the receptionist, who was hiding behind a plant on her desk. They walked straight to Stephanie's car and stood stunned.

"That's crazy," Keith spit out. "What do we do now?"

"I don't know. Give me a little while to think about this. Albert was a hero. I don't want this to be spun any other way."

"Sure, sis." He side-arm hugged her. "This was pretty cool, finding out everything. You know, I might even come back and visit that old timer. He's a pretty smart tack." The thought of returning to visit must have reminded him about the pretty receptionist. "Hey, I've gotta run back in for something. I'll catch you later."

Stephanie kissed him on the cheek before he left. "Hey, don't forget about breakfast with Mom in the morning."

"How could I forget?" he answered as he hurried across the parking lot.

That plant doesn't stand a chance of camouflaging that receptionist from him, she laughed to herself.

Driving away, she replayed the story she had just been told. She could almost picture the young man defending a country he was ordered to destroy. He was a German U.S. hero buried anonymously to save a city. She thought of his friends, who watched him die and buried him without telling a soul. So much sadness but truly heroic moments. His story needed to be told. Her thoughts jumped to the drop-off spot Sergeant Bill had referenced. Could that have been the castle on Wassaw Sound? How cool would it be if Oglethorpe's castle had helped save Savannah in WWII? She couldn't wait to share this story with Philip.

When Stephanie arrived home, she checked the time and knew she must rush to get ready. But Cooper stood by the door, wagging his tail. She had been so busy she hadn't spent any time with him. They say a dog can't tell time, and you could be gone one day or twenty; he will love you just the same when you get home. But she questioned that. He had to be lonely. "Okay, boy. Let's go," she said, and they went to Daffin Park.

She glanced at her worksite as they made their way around the park. Beside it stood a man, looking down into the hole. She remembered falling into that hole and the struggle it was to climb out, so she walked toward him to warn him of the danger. As she approached, he looked up. She stopped. It was the same man she had seen looking in the front window of her office. Her defense mechanisms went off. Cooper must have felt them because he began barking as the man turned to flee. Stephanie didn't move as she watched him disappear down the park's center. Taking the fastest route home, she walked by her worksite. And as she looked down into the hole, there was a single red rose.

The whole incident creeped her out, but she was happy that the man knew she had a dog ready to attack him. She forced herself to put it out of her mind and rushed to get ready to meet Philip.

As she drove up to the castle, she realized that Philip had lined the path and entryway with candles. The light of the candles seemed to dance against the bricks. She felt silly knocking on the old wooden door to the shell of a house and was relieved when Philip opened it. She stood back awkwardly, not knowing where their relationship stood. Until Philip bound down the stairs and pulled her into his arms.

"I'm so happy you're here, lassie. Come in."

Her heart beat faster, anticipating the night ahead. He showed her to the great hall where both fireplaces were burning bright. The welcoming warmth pulled her further into the room, where he motioned toward a makeshift table made with scaffolding. More candles sat on top with a bottle of wine and to-go boxed meals. He motioned her to the table and settled her into one of the camping chairs.

"Wine?" he asked, and she nodded as he poured generously.

Pulling his chair closer to hers, he said, "I have so much to share with you, but first, I want to tell you again how sorry I am."

She only nodded.

"Surely, you must know how much I care for you."

"I believe I do," she said with a sheepish grin. "But I'm eager to see how much by what you prepared for dinner."

Her playfulness made Philip smile. "Well, by all means, lassie." He rose and took the lid off her dinner. "My feelings must be true. That's a one-pound burger WITH bacon."

"Oh my, I'm blushing. Did you have to be so bold as to add the bacon?"

He laughed, and they fell into casual conversation. "I've done a lot of reading in the quiet out here; I read all the way to file eight," he explained.

"Do tell. I've really missed the Oglethorpe/Castell saga."

"I learned that General Oglethorpe put the land grant into Mrs. Castell's name. First of all, let that sink in. Women didn't own land then; never mind, a castle. When my dad researched what happened to the Castells after they moved to the States, he found out Mrs. Castell had remarried. She and her children stayed in Georgia. Interestingly enough, the oldest boy moved back to Scotland. Following in his father's footsteps, he became an architect. And you'll never believe what he built." He sat on the edge of his seat, anxiously awaiting an answer.

"I have no idea. What?"

"Beauly."

Stephanie's mouth dropped in surprise.

"I know, it's unreal. Somehow, James Oglethorpe mended the wounds between Robert's children and his parents, who welcomed their grandson back to the estate. He improved the country house and basically revitalized the whole town. That's the reason we noticed the resemblance between Savannah and Beauly."

Stephanie stopped eating to take in all of this information. "That's unbelievable. James Oglethorpe changed so many lives." Her eyes moved around the room, taking in her surroundings. "And all these years later, Robert Castell's distant relative,"—she paused and pointed at Philip—"has been called back to where it all started, Savannah." Stephanie moved her fingers to the side of her temples and made a "this blows my mind" expression, making Philip laugh. The sound echoed around the large empty room.

"I've got one more really wonderful thing to tell you. I called you from the breakfast restaurant this morning. While I was there, I got into a conversation with a man about the castle. He said that most people wanted to see the castle succeed, and they had friends in high places. He asked me to tell you to contact Justin Baker, who works in the Zoning Department at the city."

Stephanie narrowed her gaze at him in thought, so he quickly asked, "Did I say something wrong? What's going through your mind?"

"You need me to contact this Justin person?" she asked.

"Yes. They want to help us."

When did it go back to "us?" she wondered. *He told me goodbye yesterday, and now it is "us" again?* She thought for a split second, then asked. "So, you tell me goodbye at the meeting yesterday, thinking the case was over, then you hear there is a chance you could still own the castle, and you pulled me back in by asking me to dinner?"

"No, it wasn't like that at all. First, I didn't mean goodbye for good when I said goodbye at the meeting."

"Could have fooled me. It sure felt like goodbye for good."

"Well, it wasn't. Then, I called you before I talked to that man at the breakfast spot."

She eyed him cautiously as the wall around her heart went up. "I can't do this," she announced.

"What?"

She motioned back and forth between them. "You. Me. This. I've been heartbroken for the last twenty-four hours, thinking you left. You didn't even have the decency to talk with me privately after the hearing." He began to talk, but she held up her hand. "I want this castle project to succeed. I think it's important, and I'll do whatever it takes to help, but I'm taking our relationship out of the equation."

He looked as if someone had just slapped his face. "I think you've got it all wrong."

"We'll see." She stood from her empty plate. "Thank you for the wonderful meal. I'll let you know what I find out from Justin." Making a swift exit, she attempted to get to her car before the tears slid down her cheek. Pulling out of the drive, she saw Philip's shadow in her rearview mirror. He was standing in the candle-lit doorway, watching her leave. The cry she had been holding burst through, making it difficult to see the makeshift bridge as she traveled to the other side. Through clenched teeth, she made a vow to herself. "I will never come back."

Philip sat in the middle of the floor. Paper upon paper encircled him like petals on a flower. He hadn't been able to sleep after Stephanie left two nights ago. How had she misinterpreted the situation so badly? He had told her how he felt. Why did she doubt him? He heard his father's voice, the one that always explained things patiently but sternly. "If someone doesn't know how you feel, then you did a poor job explaining it." He shook his head, wondering if she would ever give him another chance.

He had begun reading his father's files and became obsessed with finishing. He read and read, only stopping to eat and sleep. After the second night, he set the last piece of paper in the furthest pile. He stood and looked around at his history, spread out on the floor. It was quite a story. This castle had a direct tie to Beauly. After all this time, he finally understood his part in it. He had to find Stephanie.

37

THE FIRE OF REJECTION

The breakfast crowd began to thin out. Stephanie watched each customer leave, wishing she could go with them. Keith had visited several tables in Harry's, shooting the shit with the old timers who had been frequenting the establishment for as long as they could remember. He finally settled back at their table. "Big surprise. She's a no-show again."

Cathy checked her watch one last time. "I'm paying a sitter, something she never did in her life. She's forty-five minutes late. Let's call it quits."

Keith and Cathy rose from the table while Stephanie remained seated. She sloshed the coffee carafe that had been left on the table. "I'm gonna finish this up first. You guys go ahead."

They both sat back down. Cathy reached over and took her hand. "I know you want her to be different, but it's impossible. This is who she is. You don't remember her like we do. This was always who she was. It's probably better she left. At least we could get on with our lives without having to take care of her."

Keith chimed in. "You don't need this, sis. You've got us." Shrugging, he gestured to himself. "Could you really need more than this?"

Stephanie smiled back, acknowledging the hurt in her heart and how blessed she was to have such a wonderful father and siblings. Still, that one question lingered in her mind. That one thing that had been her gut punch for years. Taking a deep breath, she mustered up the courage and jumped right in. "Do y'all remember the day she left?"

Cathy held Stephanie's hand a little tighter. "Yes. We do remember." She shared a worried look with Keith and continued, "Do you?"

"Mom said, 'A foundation built on sand can never stand.' Was there more to her leaving?"

"Oh, please," clipped Cathy.

"Wait. You caught that, too? You were so young; how do you remember that?" Keith asked.

Cathy looked worriedly from Keith to Stephanie. "I have no idea what y'all are talking about."

"When Mom gathered us on the front porch, she said, 'A foundation built on sand can never stand.' It's been my motto ever since: to have a great foundation."

"Oh my gosh, I bet she was high. She was always so theatrical when she was high," Cathy exclaimed.

"You know, I thought so, too," Keith said. "I thought she must have been drunk or on drugs. When Mom burned rubber down the street, I ran straight to her room. I didn't want you to get into anything she left behind. Anyway, beside the bed was one of her tabloid magazines she got every week. On the cover was a picture of two actors who were getting a divorce. The headline was a quote from the actress, 'A foundation built on sand can never be built upon.'"

Stephanie dropped her fists on the table, "Are you kidding me? She couldn't even leave her family with her own genuine feeling. Didn't she owe us that, at least?"

"Like I said before, she's always been like this. That doesn't surprise me at all. Why didn't you say something sooner?" Keith asked.

"I don't know. I guess I felt like that was the one little secret she left with me. Dumb, I know. I've repeatedly played that moment in my mind and referenced that line for years, especially with my work."

"I hear what you're saying, but you were born to be an architect, with or without that silly line," Cathy added. "I remember you always drawing in the dirt in our front yard when you were little. I would ask you to show me what you drew, and it was always the layout of houses. 'This is the front door, this is the kitchen, and this is the living room,' you would tell me as you walked me through your house plan. Then you would draw us chairs to sit on. You were meant to create buildings. And look at you. You did it all on your own. We are so proud of you."

Stephanie smiled at the memory. "Thank you for always taking care of me. I love you guys." The three of them latched onto one another's hands and squeezed, as each looked at the door one last time. "Go," she said. "I'm finishing this coffee, then I'm right behind you."

Cathy kissed her cheek, Keith ruffled her hair, and they walked out together. Stephanie sipped the piping hot coffee from the stainless-steel carafe. She had come here so many times with her dad. She let her eyes wander the brown paneled room and focused on a booth by the window where they always sat. They talked so easily to one another about everything under the sun. She felt so blessed to have that happy memory while she felt so vulnerable inside. *I didn't need more growing up. I was well loved,* she thought.

She turned up her oversized coffee mug for the last sip. As she slowly brought it down from her face, her mother came into view. Stephanie watched her walk across the room. She appeared to throw a wake as she passed the few tables with patrons. Like the enormous ships that came into port and displaced the water around them as they passed, her mother did the same. Stephanie already felt both the pull and the push in her gut.

"Hey. Where is everyone?"

Stephanie sat speechless. She hadn't seen the woman in a year and greeted her like she had just stepped out for a minute. Stephanie shook her head, trying to regain her wits before answering. "You're an hour late. Keith and Cathy couldn't wait any longer."

"Well, how do you like that? Their mom is a little late, and they couldn't hang around." She loudly set her car keys on the table and picked up the now empty carafe. Swirling it back and forth, she noticed it was empty. "I guess we'll just have to reschedule."

"Sure, Mom. Whatever you say." Stephanie watched her mom stand and then raised her eyes to meet her mother's.

"Don't look at me with those puppy dog eyes. You could always get me to do what you wanted when you looked at me like that."

Not everything I wanted, that's for sure, Stephanie thought to herself.

"We can all do this again next week," her mom exclaimed, throwing her daughter the bone she thought she wanted.

Next week was next year, and Stephanie knew it in her heart. Yet, it wasn't worth the fight. "That would be fun," she said, bobbing her head like it was the best thing she had ever heard.

"Okay, then." Her mom looked down at her. "You doing all right? You look good."

Stephanie fought to keep the disdain from her voice. "I'm great. Just great."

"I knew you would be. I raised you to be strong." She grabbed her keys, saying, "I guess I'll see you next week."

Stephanie suddenly remembered the one question she had been trying to get an answer to for months. "Hey, Mom, where were you born in Scotland? Like, what city?"

Her mom's face scrunched in thought. "That's a strange question." She bit the inside of her lip and looked blankly at the ceiling. "O, O, . . . it was something that sounded like Open."

"Oban?"

"Yeah, maybe. I was only a couple of years old."

"And why did your family leave Scotland?"

"Geez, I don't know. It was something with lighthouses. It was a long time ago." Her hands became jittery. She plopped her massive purse on the table. Pulling out a cigarette and lighter, she rubbed them together in her hand for safekeeping. She turned to look at the door. "I gotta go. See ya."

Stephanie watched her walk out. The cigarette was lit as

soon as the glass door closed behind her. The fire of rejection was just as hot as the day her mom drove away. *Will I ever stop wanting this woman's love?* she wondered. But this time, something else came to mind: Oban. Stephanie smiled. Her mom verified something incredible that had touched Stephanie while she was in Scotland. Her family was from Oban. She wished her grandparents were still alive; she had hundreds of questions. But now she had the phone number of a sweet elderly lady sitting in a cottage on the outskirts of Oban. She couldn't wait to talk with her about everything. That knowledge somehow gave her power over the hole in her heart left by her mother. It gave her hope.

38

———

DANGEROUS WHITE POWDER

"Let's keep this snappy; I've got an appointment at two," Stephanie remarked as she sat down at the table for their Wednesday lunch.

Her friends looked at her with stunned expressions.

"I'm sorry, that was rude. Let me start over. Hey everyone, how are you guys?"

"Well, that's more like it," chided Jan. "What's wrong with you?"

"My annual Mom breakfast was this morning. And if that wasn't enough, the castle is killing me. Oh, and the Scot that goes with it. I have a big meeting with the permit man at two. I'm hoping it might help."

Stephanie was handed a menu as the other five ladies discussed what they were having. Huey's sat on the riverfront in an old cotton warehouse from the 1800s. It was known for its Cajun cooking with a Southern seafood flare. After placing their orders, they fell into comfortable conversation.

Maggie was traveling in Italy and had sent them all letters the prior week, so they each pulled them out to compare.

Agnes started the conversation. "I wonder if she'll ever come back. It would be a shame if we had to go get her."

"She's only been gone a few weeks," Kathleen quickly added. "She'll be back."

Their orders of everything from jambalaya and étouffée to fried green tomato muffuletta and catfish were brought to the table. As they ate, they continued their regular weekly catch-up until they got to Stephanie.

"How's your kilted companion?" Kathleen asked.

Stephanie rolled her eyes, "Not my companion, just a business associate."

"Yeah, right. Since when?"

"Since he made it perfectly clear that he only wanted me when I could help him." She glanced at her watch, which read 1:30, as the waiter brought a plate full of beignets to the table. They always finished with beignets. In fact, they sometimes started with beignets, too. She knew she must gulp her pastry before leaving and made the rookie mistake of inhaling the powdered sugar. She began to choke into the beignet she held in front of her mouth; powdered sugar sprayed the table and the front of her black dress.

"I'm so sorry," she said between chokes and gasps. The tribe all waved it off as they made her drink water. Finally, when she caught her breath, she told the group she had to get to that meeting and left. Her walk to the city building wasn't far. When she arrived, she was out of breath and still covered in powdered sugar. She stood outside Justin's office briefly, trying to regain her composure, then opened his office door. She was surprised she recognized the man from the previous meeting.

He welcomed her, eyed her warily, and walked over to inspect her. "I can't waste my time on anyone with bad habits."

Stephanie rubbed her fingertips from where she bit them to the nub, wondering what kind of fanatic she was dealing with. "We all have bad habits, but I try to work on mine daily. I'm sure we share some of the same ones."

"I assure you, I've never snorted cocaine."

She stepped back in question while he came towards her, then pinched some of the white residue from her nose and dabbed it on his tongue. She laughed out loud as they both said, "Powdered sugar."

She explained the beignet fiasco, and he explained his working assistant's addiction that almost put him in jail. After the very personal interview, Justin got right down to business.

"I was happy to sit on the board for the castle on Wassaw Sound. I have a business associate concerned about what might happen to the land if Philip's project falls apart."

"Hasn't it already fallen apart?"

"Not necessarily." He went to a cabinet and pulled out hundreds of files. "Please look over all these. See if you can find a consistent pattern."

Stephanie spread the papers across the desk and quickly noticed the similarities. They were all built by Morgan Builders and all signed off by only one of the seven inspectors, Henry Lane. "There is no way this is a coincidence, right?"

"One hundred and eight houses? I'd say that's no coincidence."

"So, what can we do?"

"You can file an appeal that would dig into Henry's past approvals, but that would take months. Henry Lane is a pretty nice guy; Tommy Morgan must have something over his head."

"We don't have months," Stephanie sighed. "Is there anything else we could do?"

"Possibly something to buy you time. What are the terms of the land grant?"

"It says that by the end of the grant's term, if the land is prosperous and residents dwell upon it, it is reevaluated, and the landowner begins paying taxes at the new level. If the land is not bringing in a profit or there is no building, then it will be auctioned for the highest bidder." Her brain turned that over again while Justin remained quiet. "The land is Philip's until the end of the year. Then, if he meets these conditions, he can pay taxes until we can figure out these other issues?"

"Yes."

"He's already using the castle as his residence."

Justin was surprised, "That's great news. Although I don't want any other appeals to pop up, so we might need to build a simple residence somewhere on the property. Let's get moving on a permit. I'll walk it through myself."

Stephanie nodded in acknowledgment.

"I also think Philip should withdraw his original application for the castle. Between you and me, it will never pass under current conditions," he said.

"We'll get right on it. And that just leaves us with the second part of the grant's term, to bring in a profit."

"It doesn't matter if you sell firewood or berries as long as you show a profit. You're a smart cookie; I'm sure you'll come up with something."

"I've got some ideas," Stephanie answered as she stood to leave. Before making it to the door, her curiosity took over her mouth. "Why would you help with this?"

Justin cleared his throat, "I have four kids that ride their bikes along that road every day. A casino is not what's best for our community. That's why there are laws in place on where they may be built. This 250-year-old trek of land has just slipped through the cracks."

She left his office and began to drive out to the castle. She was excited by the possibilities ahead and couldn't wait to share them with Philip. She got almost halfway there when she remembered her vow from the night before to never return to the castle. Her face flushed with anger, both at Philip and making dumb vows. Grumbling to herself, she turned around and went back to her office.

When she sat at her desk, she was flooded with e-mails and messages that required attention. By the time she finished, she called Philip only to be answered by an automatic message saying that his phone was out of service and to try back later. *Of course, it's out of service; he's in the boonies. Why didn't I swallow my pride and just drive on out there?* She peered out the window to the streetlights beaming and pondered driving to the castle. Her mind traveled back to the night of the hurricane. The two of them had huddled closely as the storm passed and then drifted off to sleep, wrapped in the safety of his arms. "No!" she said into the air, shaking her head in an attempt to also shake the memory. She would try to call him again in the morning, and if she still couldn't get him, she would then ride out to the castle.

39

THE WINTER SUN

"You can't hide from me," Agnes said, peering over the newspaper Stephanie held high over her face.

"I wasn't trying to."

Agnes gave her a knowing look. "I've seen that face before."

Stephanie framed her face with her fingers and plastered a smile that ran no deeper than the surface. "Rainbows and butterflies," she said mockingly.

"If that's what you want to call it, okay." Agnes reached under the table and rubbed behind Cooper's ear. "Keep him hidden under here. I don't want people to think I play favorites. The dog section is out front."

"You won't hear a peep out of him. We've been walking the park awhile; he's pooped."

Agnes looked down at one of her bowls sitting beside Cooper, almost empty of water, and then at Stephanie's empty coffee cup. "I see you both need a refill. Be right back." When she returned with the beverages, she had brought Cooper a dog biscuit she kept for the canine visitors and a sticky bun for Stephanie. "Okay, spill."

Stephanie glanced around the empty restaurant.

"It's barely seven o'clock, and no one is here yet. Tell me what's going on," Agnes said.

Stephanie set the paper aside and retold the story from the castle while Agnes listened without interrupting.

When she was done, Agnes asked, "Do you love him?"

"I don't really know him."

"Yes, you do. You know him. Even though it's only been a few months, you know him."

Stephanie nodded in agreement. "I thought I knew him, but what if he's just using me?"

"You've been cautious for a long time, never letting anyone get close enough where they can hurt you. Maybe it's time to jump."

"But what if I'm wrong?"

Agnes let the thought hang in the air before saying, "Don't let the fear of striking out keep you from playing the game."

"Babe Ruth? Really, Agnes?"

"I know it sounds dumb, but I always tell myself this. If I let my fears run my life, I would be paralyzed. You're scared to put yourself out there, but sometimes you must jump."

A tear slid down Stephanie's cheek, and she quickly wiped it away. "I really do have feelings for him, but . . ." She paused before continuing. "What if he leaves?" The tears began to tumble out as she quickly grabbed a napkin off the table and wiped them away.

Agnes didn't back away. "Okay. Let's go there. What if he leaves?"

"What do you mean?"

"What if he leaves? Then what? What will you do?"

"I don't know."

"Well, I know." She reached over and grabbed Stephanie's hand. Speaking more softly, she said, "You'll have no regrets. You might be sad for a while, but aren't you sad right now?"

Stephanie nodded.

"Then get to it."

Stephanie squeezed her hand in response. "All right, I will." Grinning, she added, "Just as soon as I finish this sticky ball of goodness."

She blew a kiss at Agnes as she left the restaurant, grateful for her friendship. What would she do if he goes? She played that over in her mind and came up with a different answer. She would be fine. She was surrounded by people who loved her, truly loved her. She was one blessed woman.

Now eager to see Philip, she quickly showered and drove to the castle. She walked in the front door, calling his name, but he was nowhere to be found. His truck was in the driveway, so she knew he couldn't be far. She searched, room by room, but she still couldn't find him. Wondering if he could be on the lookout, she climbed the stairs only to find it empty. But as she looked over the marsh, she spotted him sitting in an Adirondack chair. His legs were crossed, and he appeared deep in thought as he looked over the castle. His castle.

Philip's face seemed to change, and she wondered if he could see her, so she lifted her hand into a wave. The smile that spread across his face brought tears to her eyes, and she knew she had to get to him. She hurried down the turret stairs as he hurried across the lawn. She was almost in a full run as she dashed across the great room and onto the porch. They collided into a kiss, an earth-shaking, I-never-want-to-be-without-you kiss. All worries and all doubts were gone. She didn't realize she was crying until she felt the tears where their lips met.

Pulling back, he brushed her tears aside with his thumb and pushed her dark hair away from her face. "I love you, Stephanie. I should have told you before you left the other night, but I didn't know if you felt the same way."

"I've known for a long time now. I was just scared that you might leave and return to Scotland. I was scared you would break my heart." She ran her hands along his face, feeling the stubble that was quickly turning into an auburn beard.

"I'm not leaving. With or without the castle, I'm staying in Savannah. I'm staying with you if you'll have me."

The cry that had been sitting in her throat burst out in a yelp as he smiled down at her and kissed her once more, gently. He laced her fingers into his own, and they walked back towards the marsh.

"I want to show you something." He led her towards the Adirondack chairs, sat her down, then sat beside her in its match. "I haven't been able to sleep very well since you left the other night. I finished the last of my dad's folders before dawn this morning. I was wide awake and walked out here to see the sunrise. I watched it creep across the marsh and paint the sky. Afterward, I turned my chair towards the castle." He crouched closer to her and pointed towards the castle.

"What is that?" she asked.

"I don't know yet. It reminded me of your light in Oban."

Stephanie turned towards the water to see how the morning sun shone. The lady in Oban said she hadn't noticed the light from the island before, but maybe it only glowed a few days of the year when the sun was at a different angle. Growing up on the Wilmington River, she remembered how the winter sun always came in the windows stronger and wondered if it would have affected what was glowing.

They pinpointed that the glow was coming from what appeared to be a window behind the lookout, so they excitedly walked toward the house to try and find it. They climbed to the top of the turret and walked out to the lookout. Looking back at the castle, a window was on the rise behind the parapet. It was deeply encased into the structure.

"I wonder what that is, and how would you get to it?" Philip asked.

They went back to the stairway to see if there were further steps to that room, but the winding stairs ended at the lookout.

"Maybe there's another way," Stephanie added. "What would be on the other side of this wall?" she asked, pointing to the outer wall.

"The front bed chamber." They wound back down the steps, across the great hall, and up the main staircase. Entering the front room, they began looking for niches with a hidden staircase. "I don't see anything. It makes no sense. You know what? I'm going to get my big construction ladder from downstairs. We'll climb up from the lookout."

They struggled to get the ladder up the winding staircase, sometimes even knocking off pieces of rock and tabby that covered the walls. But they were on a mission and kept pushing forward until the ladder could go no further, then spent thirty minutes trying to back it out. When they were finally back on ground level, he said, "We're two educated architects; we can figure this out." He looked around the room and said, "I'll just build this scaffolding on the lookout."

Stephanie noticed a ladder leaning against the door jamb. "Or I could stand at the top of this smaller ladder and jump onto the roof."

"No," he said, letting his natural Scottish brogue come out strong. "I'll not let you do that. It's too dangerous."

She considered trying to convince him to change his mind, but she agreed with him. She wasn't sure what condition the roof would be in once she got to the top, and anything could happen. Looking at his face set stern, ready to put up a fight, she said, "Thank you for worrying about me. I think the scaffolding is a great idea."

As they began to build the platform, Stephanie told him about her meeting with Justin. He listened quietly, stopping his work during crucial moments to listen more intently.

"I think we should do as he suggested and withdraw the current application," she said.

Philip jumped down from the scaffolding. "I think we should do that sooner rather than later. Our glow can wait."

"Agreed. But in the meantime, we must consider the second part of the grant's term. It says we need to be showing a profit. I have a few ideas on that.

He smiled. "I'm sure you do, lassie. I'm sure you do."

40

THE BURDEN OF A BRIBE

Henry Lane propped his feet on his desk, relief washing over him. It was much easier making the call knowing his secret would remain buried, and his family was safe. "I've got great news, Tommy. The application for the castle has been withdrawn."

"Why would he do that?"

"I don't know. Maybe Mr. McLaughlin is leaving town and doesn't want to be bothered. Or maybe he's afraid they will try to pin the massive taxes due on his bill if the application is open. Nevertheless, you have five weeks, then you can bid on the land." The line was quiet. So quiet that Henry asked, "You still there, Tommy?"

"Yeah, I'm here. And I smell a rat."

Henry sat up at his desk and grabbed the bottle of Tums within his reach. Shaking out four and popping them in his mouth, he asked, "What do you want me to do?"

"I want you to get to the bottom of it."

This time, Henry was quiet.

"Elizabeth making good grades at Country Day?"

Henry's stomach tightened. "Yes. She does very well in school."

"How does she like that pretty blue Beamer you bought for her birthday?"

Bile rose in Henry's throat. No amount of Tums could make it go away. Five more weeks. He could hold on for five more weeks. Then he could have his life back. "Let me dig a little. I'll get back to you." The line went dead immediately. He let his head fall towards the desk. How had he let this go on for so long? They once were such good friends and had so much fun together. Sure, they raised hell some nights but didn't all twenty-five-year-olds? They were young, casually dating any skirt they could, and had a little money in the bank. They were living large. But it all ended that one night.

They had spent the evening at Malones on Bay Street, dancing and drinking into the wee hours of the morning. They couldn't find a ride, so Henry said he could drive them back home. They flew down Lincoln Street as fast as possible when Henry decided to relight his cigar. It only took that one moment. That one moment rewrote his entire future. The homeless man stumbled from a side alley in front of the car. Henry never even saw him; he only heard his skull bouncing like a bowling ball into his windshield.

It was three in the morning, and not a soul was in sight. He and Tommy looked at the mangled body whose head was turned at such an angle there was no way he survived.

"Should we call the police?" asked Tommy as he took the last swig of his beer, seeming unaffected by the scene before him.

Henry battled his conscience. This man was dead. There

was nothing he could do to bring him back. What sense was it to ruin his life over it? But then he knew he must pay the debt for his mistake. The man had a family somewhere. But wouldn't his family rather live with the picture of him wandering the streets into eternity than to know he had been plowed down by a car? He stood motionless, unable to decide, the blood from a cut dripping into his right eye. He was stunned by Tommy's voice.

"I know a place we can get rid of him." That statement alone should have thrown up a red flag. How did Tommy know a place to get rid of a dead body? But Henry could no longer think, so he simply nodded yes. They shoved the old man in the back of his Buick and drove across the old Talmadge Bridge. Turning onto Hutchinson Island, they drove until the road ended at the marsh, then carried his body as far as they could into the wooded area of the island.

Gasping for breath, Henry called out, "Wait. I can't do this!" He set the man's body on the ground as his eyes scanned the darkness surrounding him. His insides were churning, causing his body to respond. He turned and threw up in the opposite direction. When he spun back around, the body was no longer lying on the ground; Tommy had pushed it into the deep trench. Henry dropped to his knees and frantically began to dig, pushing the loose dirt down into the ditch in hopes of covering the body.

Tommy watched but eventually stopped him. "Henry, Come on, man. We gotta get outta here."

"Never mention this to a soul," Henry told Tommy.

"No worries, man. Not a chance," was his reply. But over time, it changed to, "Not a chance, as long as you take care of me for the rest of my life." And so began a twenty-five-year payback for his silence. The guilt over killing a man was a cross he carried daily, but the bribes added salt to that open wound. They didn't start right away. Tommy had given him time to get settled. Bribing a man with something to lose, like a great job and a beautiful family, was easier.

Looking back, he realized he should have called the police right away. Every lie and cheat he had performed for silence had sold his soul a little more to the devil. And now that he was getting older, he was beginning to have a much greater fear of hell. And now others were involved. Over time, Tommy's friends had become dirtier, and the stakes had become much higher. There was no way out.

Henry again looked at the application and homed in on the withdrawal date. It was stamped two weeks ago. How had he missed this? He flew out of his seat and into the chairwoman's office without knocking. "Mrs. Holmes, can you tell me why this application was withdrawn?"

"Good morning, Mr. Lane. How are you today?"

He straightened his coat and spoke more calmly. "Good morning, Mrs. Holmes. Could you please explain why this application was withdrawn?"

She smiled and nodded her head. "That's better. Let me take a look at what you're referring to," she said, knowing full well what he was holding and how hard it had been to keep it under wraps. "I don't recognize the address. I'll have to look it up."

"You know damn well the address," he snapped. "It's the castle on Wassaw Sound. Why was this application withdrawn?"

"Oh, yes. The beautiful castle. Mr. McLaughlin said he no longer intends on renovating."

Excitement fluttered in Henry's chest. "I see. Well, that's probably for the best."

"The best for whom?" Mrs. Holmes asked, holding his stare. A smile flickered across her face as Henry was the first to look away.

She knows, he thought, and knew he must escape quickly. "Good day," he said as he bolted out the door, leaving it wide open.

When he returned to his office, he called in the two college interns home for Christmas break. "I need you to review every new application in our system for Philip McLaughlin or Stephanie Normand. Let me know what turns up."

Less than an hour later, he had a permit dated two weeks prior on his desk. It was for a small cottage at the address he recognized and had been approved within days, which told him he wasn't the only one with interest in this project.

The only thing left to do was to tell Tommy.

41
____

THE GLOW

"We might actually pull this off," Philip told Stephanie as they walked around the cottage. It had been only two weeks, but the three crews, working around the clock, had promised they would be done before the end of the year.

Stephanie had reworked the original plans, taking the castle out of the equation. Pennyghael Castle had taught her how to use the surrounding land for people to come and enjoy the property. So, they were building the first of many cottages across the small bridge from the castle and a small overlook pass for people to walk across.

She was surprised how many people were adamant about a casino not being built near their neighborhoods. She happily benefitted from their desire for safety. They were well on their way to an approved dwelling, but she hadn't decided how to profit from the land.

She had made it a point to arrive at the castle early every morning to meet with the crew before they left at seven a.m.

and then speak with the arriving team. The sounds of hammering on the cottage and the thuds from the dock builders laying the pilings for the walkway bridge had given her a headache. She knew she couldn't leave, but Philip had things under control, and she needed a moment to herself.

What she really needed was to go to Adoration. She thought for a moment and decided to walk over to the castle. The middle room had once been used for a chapel; she could find a moment of peace there. When she walked into the room, she sat down on the floor. Leaning against the wall, she closed her eyes and began her prayers. She had started saying a morning offering the day she vowed not to be a lukewarm Catholic. This was one vow she wouldn't break.

She felt the familiar calm run through her once she reached the end. "Now I'm ready for my day," she said to herself. Opening her eyes, she found the room glowing. Chill bumps covered her arms and ran down her spine, but her logical mind kicked right in. I must find the source. She pinpointed it was coming from behind the statue she now knew to be Saint Margaret. She thought about the alcove she discovered behind the figure at Edinburgh Castle. Something inside that alcove was making the room glow.

She approached it with caution, still blinded by the light. Holding her hands up to the light, she tried to block what appeared to be a spotlight and wondered what in the world would have such strength in this 250-year-old castle. She was stunned when she heard her name. Spinning around so that her back was against the light, she watched Philip struggle to see into the room and find his way to her. But as he approached her, the light began to dim.

"Are you all right?"

"Yes. I'm fine." She reached for his hand as the last bit of glow left the room.

He exhaled with such force it blew her hair. "What in the bloody hell was that?"

She began to laugh. "I think we found our Oban glow." She motioned towards the statue. "Can you help me with her?"

They carefully slid the statue out of the way. Deep in the back of the alcove were several glass panels embedded into the mortar of the stones. "Where is the light coming from?" he asked.

"Give me a lift so I can see better."

Philip hoisted her up into the alcove, and she shimmied inside. She touched the different glass panels and was surprised at how sturdy they had been placed. She felt cold air on her back and shivered a little in response. But being with Philip made her brave this time, and she didn't want to flee. She turned to find its source.

"Wow! Philip. There's an open passage that runs probably twenty feet up. It must be open because I feel the outside air rushing down, and there appears to be something at the top."

"Like a room?"

"No, I don't think so." She spun her body and backed out of the alcove. "But where does that opening lead?"

"I'd say probably above the overlook. Let's go finish some scaffolding."

They worked for thirty minutes until one of the men on site called up to tell them they had a visitor. Philip noticed the disappointment in Stephanie's eyes.

"It's not going anywhere. We'll get back to the scaffolding after the next shift change."

She reluctantly agreed and made herself leave the lookout.

Mrs. Holmes was standing outside the front of the castle when they came out the door. "Oh my! It's remarkable. I had to see with my own two eyes. It's a piece of our city's history."

Philip replied, "In more ways than you know."

She studied Philip. "Explain, please."

He turned to Stephanie as if asking for her approval. He had shared all his findings from his dad's files with her, but they had been so busy trying to build the cottage that they hadn't had time to focus on the history. She nodded in agreement, and so he began.

"I'll tell you the story as I show you around." They walked through the main door and straight to the great hall. "Before General Oglethorpe settled in Savannah, he was good friends with my family ancestor. His name was Robert Castell. Robert was an architect that blended landscapes into grand building designs. However, Robert died young and left a wife and several children. Oglethorpe was a very kind man who cared for those who couldn't care for themselves. There are accounts of his kind acts from all over the world. At any rate, when Oglethorpe settled Savannah, he designed it using Robert's drawings with its squares and parks, among other things."

Mrs. Holmes seemed equally astonished with Philip's story as with the castle. They had toured everywhere except one place, the lookout. When they reached the stairway, Philip held one of her hands while she slowly ran her other hand along the stones for balance.

Once at the top, he continued his story. "General Oglethorpe obtained a land grant for this land in 1745 to help protect the city from the Spanish who were settled in places of Florida." Philip motioned across the marsh and out towards the Atlantic Ocean. "He then commissioned Robert's only brother, who was also an architect, to build Robert's plan, adding this lookout and parapet. But General Oglethorpe needed someone to help build and protect the city, so he returned to Scotland to get strong Highlanders. Scotland was under major oppression during that time from the English, so he brought back almost two hundred men. Upon completing the project, he returned to England one more time. He brought the widow Castell and her family to America. He failed to mention to anyone that the land grant was made in her name, Mrs. Robert Castell. Her oldest son moved back to Scotland, but most of her family stayed with her in America. There are even stories of her other sons in the Revolution."

The three of them stood at the edge of the lookout, but no one spoke a word. They stood like that for quite some time until Mrs. Holmes broke their trance.

"Have you ever heard of Big Joe's Gator Farm?"

They both shook their heads no.

"Big Joe, Uncle Joe to me, has a little strip of land just over the Houlihan Bridge. He once rented fishing boats. But the sun hit the bank on his property just right, and the gators love those sunning spots to warm their cold blood. So, there was always a full bank of alligators along the shore. Over time, people started coming to see the gators instead of renting his boats. So, he began charging them for something that was already there, just because it was his property. My thoughts about the castle are similar. You don't need a State of Georgia marker to have something wonderful here. However, that should definitely be your next step. But for now, I understand you need to show a profit, and what kid doesn't want to see a castle? And if you share your story with the adults, you'll have a genuine tourist site."

"Do you really think so?" asked Philip.

"Savannah cannot lose this building. It's too much a part of our history. I'll have news cameras out here first thing in the morning. Be ready." She turned to leave but hesitated at the top of the dangerous stairway. "Just one more thought. Section off these stairs; they're terrifying."

42

———

IRONY

Henry desperately tried to swallow the first bite of his $84 steak. He quickly grabbed his untouched glass of water and began to chug. He felt the beef move down and was happy to catch a small breath. The others hadn't noticed his distress, so he excused himself and walked to the bathroom.

Once out of sight, he began to cough. The force moved the steak, and his pain began to ease, although his eyes continued to water. *Maybe, it would have been better if I had just choked to death, right here and now,* he thought. *At least it would be an honest way to die.*

The bathroom door opened, and Tommy walked in. "You seem upset, Henry." It came out as an accusation rather than a concern.

"You're damn right; I'm upset. You force me to come to another of these dinners with people I would rather not be seen with while you smile and play nice with the scum of the Earth."

"You think you're better than us, Henry?"

Henry paused before responding. He *was* better than them. They were hoodlums who ran a gambling ring down the East Coast. They were dangerous men who never took no for an answer and never left a track. "No, Tommy. But I've done what you asked me to do. My hands are tied now. There's nothing more I can do for you. Can't I just be done?"

Tommy came closer to him, "You said you could handle this, did you not?"

"I did, but—"

"You told me to go ahead and start working with these guys, did you not?"

This time, Henry just nodded.

"Now we are both in over our heads. So, you see, neither of us will be done until we break ground for the new casino."

"It's not gonna happen, Tommy."

"Oh, it will. One way or the other. Now, come back to the table. You're making our friends uncomfortable."

"I don't feel well, Tommy. I think I'd better head home."

Tommy began to shake his head no. At the same time, the piece of steak decided to completely dislodge. Henry barely reached the toilet before the bile forced everything out.

"I'm going home, Tommy," he said over his shoulder.

"Okay, but don't go far. You still have work to do." The sound of the door closing finalized the conversation.

The hostess smiled at him as Henry approached the front door. "Mr. Lane. It was nice to meet your associate last week. She was very concerned about you."

He stopped at her window. "My associate?"

"Yes, she said her name was Stephanie. She came to try to help you, but you had already gone."

Henry picked up the pen from the counter and grabbed a Savannah Steak House business card. He wrote "Stephanie Normand" on the back and placed it in his coat pocket. Had she been following him last week? And what had she seen? He refocused on the conversation at hand. "Are you sure it was last week?"

"Yes, sir, I was out of town the week before." She stared at his paling face. "Are you okay, Mr. Lane?"

"Oh. Yes, yes, I'm fine." But he was far from fine. He was a dead man walking. He had complied for too long. He reached into his back pocket to grab his wallet for a tip but realized he no longer had it. He had misplaced it. Or worse, it had been swiped. Just another thing to worry about. Saying goodnight, he stumbled along Bay Street. For some reason, he turned onto Lincoln Street. He wasn't sure of his destination until he stopped. This was where it all began. He stared at the spot on the street and could still picture the man's mangled body. "I'm sorry," he mumbled. Then, looking into the night sky, he yelled, "I'm sorry!"

His nostrils flared, trying to intake the correct amount of oxygen. At the same time, he closed his eyes to try to erase the memory. But the strangest thing happened. The grip on his heart began to loosen, and his clenched stomach relaxed. Opening his eyes back to the sky, he felt at peace. Was he losing his mind? Probably. But things became very simple; he had to go to the police. He barely heard the car until it was upon him. As his body was flown in the air, his last thought was the irony of where he would land, right there, at the exact same spot, on Lincoln Street.

———

Stephanie patted the bedside table, feeling for the phone ringing. When she noticed it was 2:45, she sat straight up. She thought about how no one calls at this time of the morning unless someone was dead. Then cursed herself for thinking it. "Hello?"

"Is this Stephanie Normand?"

"It is."

"Ma'am, we need you to come to Memorial Hospital. There's been a hit-and-run; the only thing on the man was a card with your name."

"I'll be right there," she answered as she pulled on a pair of leggings and grabbed her jean jacket. She cursed herself for not asking questions as she drove the short distance. Who was this person? It could be anyone: her dad, Keith, or even Philip. And was he still alive? Her hands shook on the steering wheel as she flew down Waters Drive.

She was met at the door by the police, who asked for her identification and then ushered her into a private sitting room. She began rapidly firing the questions she had been mulling over in the car.

"The man had no identification on his person, but he was definitely targeted. We have an eyewitness who said the car didn't have its lights on and jumped the curb to hit him. They said the car scraped the building he had been standing in front of. It's a miracle he's still alive, although we're not sure for how long. He's in a coma from brain trauma."

She pushed them down the hall and into the ICU, anxious to find out which of her loved ones were fighting for their life. A cry broke out when she didn't recognize the man on the bed. "Thank heavens," she said under her breath, informing the officer she didn't know who it was. But then she walked around the bed and got closer to his face. Mr. Lane had been so bloodied and bruised she could barely recognize him. It wasn't until she noticed the old scar beside his right eye. "This is Mr. Henry Lane," she announced.

The officer scribbled the name onto a pad, then handed her the card found in his pocket. She rubbed her finger across the embossed printing of Savannah Steak House, then flipping it, she read out her name.

Stephanie told them everything she knew, from the very beginning of her getting hired to the end with her and Latrice's stakeout and the information they uncovered. She was exhausted when she finally walked out of the hospital, only to be greeted by the first morning light, time for her to take her shift at the castle.

43

THE PEARL

The early sun threw shadows from the forest onto her windshield. She squinted, focusing on the light at the end of the tunnel made from a canopy of oak limbs. When she finally reached it, she sighed in delight. She would never tire of driving upon the castle and watching its magic unfold.

Pulling toward the cottage, she noticed Philip had worked through the night. He had set out cones to mark a parking area and sectioned it off with yellow tape. He had also coned off the makeshift bridge where cars wouldn't attempt to drive over.

Turning her attention to the building project, she smiled at its appearance. It was the twin to the cottage at Beauly, right down to the front door's color. Although the stones used on the exterior weren't from Scotland, no one would ever know the difference. The only structural difference was that the large beam at the top of the stairs was missing.

Stephanie scanned for Philip and found him immediately. He was wearing his kilt. She hadn't seen him in his garb since the *ceilidh*. She felt the blush on her cheeks as her thoughts wandered to that night. Philip was speaking with the contractor, explaining what the next crew would be working on, and she walked up on the tail end of their conversation. She was surprised to hear they would be complete by the end of the week.

Philip turned to her. "Good morning. Would you like some coffee?"

"Yes, please. Can we sit for a minute?"

He poured from a giant stainless-steel dispenser into a disposable cup. "Here you go. Just like home."

They walked to the end of the porch overlooking the castle and sat, dangling their legs off the end. Stephanie filled him in on her evening. "Philip, the police said he was a target. Someone meant to kill Mr. Lane. I told them everything I knew and even the names I had heard, but I still have a bad feeling about this. You've got to be careful. I say that, and you're about to put your face all over the news."

"You're worried about me, are you, lass?"

"Of course, I am."

His knowing grin eased her worry a bit.

"I'll be careful. I promise," he said. "And we only have a week and a half left until the new year. Hey, I was thinking about that. Why don't we have a huge Hogmanay celebration to welcome people to our castle?"

"Hogmanay?"

"Yes, New Year's Eve. It's huge in Scotland. My dad said it's because Christmas wasn't celebrated for many years."

"Christmas wasn't celebrated?"

"No. During the Reformation, there was an extreme rejection of Catholicism. Christmas fell under its umbrella. So, in the mid-1600s, it was banned by Parliament."

"No way. How can you ban Christmas?"

Philip shrugged.

"Is it celebrated now?" she asked.

"Oh yeah, but Scotland did without it for over three hundred years, so it doesn't seem as important as it is here."

Stephanie stared over at the castle. "Hogmanay, huh?"

"That's right."

"I love the idea, but for right now, we should watch for the news reporters. They will be here at nine."

Philip jumped to his feet, then offered his hand to help her. "I've been busy. Besides the parking lot, the walking bridge is finished, and the areas around and inside the castle have been cleaned. I've even been working on my tour. Hey, by the way, should I mention your German spy yet?"

"No. Not yet. I'm working with a company to authenticate the cigar tube. Hopefully, that will give us the proof we need. We'll see."

The sound of tires on gravel stole their attention while one car after another parked in the new lot. Each of them exited their vehicle with their eyes focusing on the castle. Some were smiling while others scratched their heads in wonder. Then, and only then, did they look for Philip.

Philip met the group beside the newly finished walking bridge. With cameras rolling, he addressed the newscasters. "Welcome, everyone. I inherited this castle a few months ago and would like to share it with you. Would you like to come and take a look?"

He got yeses all around, so he led them across the bridge. Stephanie hadn't been across yet since they had finished late last night, so she paid close attention. The low tide kept the smell of marsh hanging in the air, and she could hear the clicking of fiddler crabs running from the movement above. The bridge itself was sturdy. It was built eight feet wide so people could pass one another, and it had safety rails so children wouldn't fall into the water as they crossed. The dock builders had done a fantastic job in the short time frame.

Once on the other side, Philip walked them to the back lawn. He then pointed out Wassaw Sound. "The purpose of this castle was to protect Savannah from the Spaniards who were occupying Florida. If the Scots saw enemy ships, they would have time to run a horse into town before the enemy could enter the city."

Stephanie loved how the reporters reacted to Philip's facts and watched the female reporters look him over. He didn't try to hide his Scottish accent and was so handsome as he told his story. Everyone was interested in what he had to say. How could they not be? They were standing in front of a genuine castle. She was lost in her thoughts when the group began asking questions but jumped at the boom of Philip's laugh. He was having a good time, and his happiness was contagious.

The cameras continued rolling as they walked into the great room. Philip explained the rooms as they moved from one to the next. But as he led them up the stairs, he stopped. Turning, he scanned the crowd until he locked eyes with Stephanie. "Can you come here, please?"

As she took each step, she realized the reason he had stopped. The chapel was glowing once again. Unconsciously, he grabbed her hand, and they walked to the top and entered the chapel. They stood just inside the doorway, watching intently as the glass panels captured the winter sun and flooded the small room. Only this time, the various rays shone on one spot.

"Why is it shining to the altar?" she asked.

"It looks like it's shining to a spot at the foot of the altar. Follow me."

They slowly walked closer and knelt beside the now glowing stone where the light seemed to absorb. Philip ran his fingers around the edges of this 18" round stone until he found a gripping spot on each side.

"Should I try to lift it?" he asked, weighing the consequences of what might lie beneath.

"I think you have to."

Philip struggled to get his fingers underneath while Stephanie added, "Go on the count of three. One. Two. Three."

Philip easily lifted the stone and sat it beside him on the floor. Inside was a cylinder-shaped wooden box that looked just like a small barrel of ale. He lifted it from the pit and noticed a latch on its side. Turning to Stephanie, he asked, "Will you please open it?"

She hesitated. "Are you sure, Philip?"

He nodded, so she slowly lifted the latch. When the cylinder opened, she and Philip were astonished to be looking down at a skull.

"It can't be her," Stephanie murmured.

"Can't be who?" he asked.

Stephanie noticed the large gap between the two front teeth of the skull. Taking a deep gulp of air, she whispered,

"Saint Margaret," then carefully closed the box and dropped the latch. Her hands began to shake, so she forced them into tight fists to calm herself. She then searched around the hole but found nothing. Her eyes focused on the stone Philip had moved. He had set it down where the underside faced up. Upon it was engraved, "Pearl of Scotland."

44

SOLSTICE

Philip and Stephanie heard the chatter over their shoulders. They turned to a sea of cameras and a room full of excited reporters throwing questions in the air, hoping for answers. Philip's stern voice quieted the room. "I am holding a holy relic in my hand. Please be respectful while I return it to where it lay." He carefully placed the box back into its original spot and returned the stone that covered it. The room was silent. The sound of distant hammering at the cottage was the only thing to be heard.

Philip turned to the group. Almost whispering, he said, "I respectfully ask everyone to leave. I promise to address everyone later, once we have researched these latest discoveries in depth. But if any of you press this issue, you will not be permitted back. Please leave this room and walk downstairs."

The group was reluctant to leave, each scanning their surroundings for answers to what they had just witnessed.

Philip didn't let anyone linger; he ushered the group out the door, following behind to ensure everyone stayed together. The group accumulated at the bottom of the stairs, waiting for further instruction. Philip escorted them to the front door.

"Thank you for respecting my privacy for the time being. You may wander the property if you'd like. I'll be in touch to set up an interview. Thank you for coming."

They had been too stunned or scared of being banned to ask questions before. However, as Philip opened the front door to the castle, the questions came. "What was that?" "What did we just witness?" "Do you know whose bones those were?" He forced a smile, nodded, and closed the massive wooden door.

He found Stephanie sitting on the bottom step, staring into space. She turned to him as he sat down beside her.

"Holy cow, Philip. You know who that is, don't you?"

"I believe I do, The Pearl of Scotland."

"How did I not put the pieces together? The strange feeling in the chapel, finding out the chapel was a replica of Edinburgh Castle, knowing that a group of Highlanders had broken into the Edinburgh castle, and then the old pub song. I must have been daft not to put the pieces together before now."

"No one would have believed it without the relic. But how did you know it was Saint Margaret before we saw the engraving on the cover stone?"

Stephanie looked sheepishly at Philip. "From a children's book. When I was at Edinburgh Castle, I bought a book for my niece. It had many drawn pictures of Saint Margaret, each showing her with a large gap between her front teeth. So, I knew the moment we opened the box."

"We knew from a children's book and a pub song. That's classic."

"The one thing I don't understand is the lights. I've been here many times, and the chapel had no lights. Why now?"

Philip grinned. "Oh. I think I can help you out with that, lassie. What date is it?"

"December 21."

He laughed. "It's winter solstice." He nudged her with his elbow, excited to share what he knew. "Now listen to this; you're gonna love it. There's a place in the Highlands called Clave Cairns. It's a Bronze Age site, over four thousand years old. And just like similar sites, such as Stonehenge, it marks the passage of the solar year.

"It's located outside of Inverness, very near Culloden battlefield. I almost took you there, but it was getting dark that day when we left Culloden. My father and I would go there at least once a year on December 21, the winter solstice.

"There are two main passage cairns at Clava. Both face the northeast and catch the midwinter rising sun. The sun continues to shine in that direction for several days leading up to solstice and following. Still, on the actual day, it lights up the inside of the cairns like they are on fire. I remembered Clava on the day I found you in the chapel alone, but I knew for sure today, on the winter solstice.

"The cool thing is that all Highlanders would know about the winter solstice, but not many others. It was the Scot's way of leading other Scots to their most treasured relic without leading others. Well, except you, a fellow Scot."

Stephanie sat up a little taller. Proud, for the first time in her life, to be related to her mother. She glanced at Philip, who was still smiling at their discovery. But a sudden onset of worry began to wash over her. As much as she didn't want to bring it upon Philip, she knew they must make a plan.

"Do you remember when they found bones at Daffin?"

Philip looked confused by her question, but only for a minute. "Oh no. They couldn't."

"Probably not, but I think we need to put some things in place so Saint Margaret lies undisturbed until it is decided where she will rest."

"Suddenly, it all seems creepy," Philip spit out.

"I think if we handle things properly, it won't. Let's go figure this out."

As they walked out the front door, they noticed the line of cars coming down the drive.

"Go back inside. Go upstairs and close the door to the chapel. See if there is any way to lock the door, even from the inside. I won't let anyone across the bridges." He must have noticed the fear in her eyes because he softened his voice. "Stay safe, and I'll be right back to you." He wrapped her in his arms and kissed her briefly, then dashed across the lawn like a Highlander running into battle.

She felt in her pocket and found the card the police had given her in the hospital hours before. She dialed the number. It only rang once before the lead officer answered.

"Hello. This is Stephanie Normand. We met this morning at the hospital. I think we need some help."

"We saw it on the news, Ms. Normand. In fact, everyone saw it on the news. We are out front and have already called in backup for crowd control. Oh, and a crazy man in a kilt is running our way. Is he with you?"

A cry escaped her mouth as relief passed over her knowing that Philip was not alone. "Yes. Well, really, I'm with him."

"Stay put in the castle. We'll get to you as soon as possible."

She went upstairs and into the chapel. The large doors to the room were warped and barely closed, but she heaved them one by one until they semi-met in the middle. She leaned on the crack, trying to keep them closed, then slid to the floor. Staring at the stone where the relic lay, her eyes were drawn to something beneath the altar. She vaguely remembered something falling when she picked up the box, but she thought it was probably a rock that had been misplaced. As she walked towards it, she reverently stepped around the cover stone of Saint Margaret, careful not to disturb anything. Crouching down, she picked up a brooch of some kind. It was shaped like an open ring with a long pin attached to its head. Its center was dotted with brownish-white gems. She turned it in her hands, held it tight, and walked back to be the human barricade to the chapel.

As she settled back in, she thought how the last hour had felt like a live-action scene from a treasure hunter show. Yet, this was real. It was both fantastic and terrifying. The rush of the crowd coming down the drive had frightened her. But why? Was she just being protective of Saint Margaret's relic, or was it something else?

All those people felt drawn enough by what they saw to jump in their cars and drive out to the castle? What had they seen exactly? She closed her eyes and replayed the whole scene. The glowing light in the room, finding the box under the stone, the skull, and returning the box to the floor. If the cameras caught all that, she could understand why people were coming. She thought of Philip and how protective he was and smiled as she pictured him racing toward the crowd. Somewhere in the stillness and quiet of the room, her mind relaxed. She was so tired from being up the night before, she settled into a numbing trance. She may have even fallen asleep. She pictured Philip running into the crowd, but he was joined by a throng of other kilts. Running, carrying something, being on a ship, building a castle, and protecting their families and treasures from Scotland.

She felt the nudge on her back but was too tired to acknowledge it. The next push made her roll to the side.

"Stephanie. Are you in here, lass?"

Stunned, she jumped up and threw her arms around Philip. But her eyes moved past him to the group standing in the doorway. "We have a lot to discuss," he said to her, then motioned for the others to enter the room.

She tensed at first, then noticed the familiar faces and relaxed. These people could be trusted and would help protect Philip and their discovery.

45

THE FIFE PLAYER

Henry tried desperately to open his eyes. The pain in his hand was excruciating. It had begun in his pinkie, then moved to his ring finger. He tried to move his other fingers, but something was around them. Was it someone else's hand? He wiggled the other three fingers as his middle finger snapped. The pain ran up his arm. Confused, he tried to take a deep breath, but something was around his neck. Was someone choking him? No, something was forcing air into his lungs. He tried to open his eyes again when he remembered getting hit by the car.

"Wakey, wakey, Henry," came a voice in his ear.

"That's enough, Mike. He can do us no good now," came a second voice. That one was one he knew well. Tommy.

He struggled again to open his eyes and was able to catch a glimpse from the sliver of one. He noticed Tommy standing back from his bed. Fear forced his eyes apart, and they darted from side to side. Worried eyes. No, scared eyes.

Another figure slid in front of him. "Henry, you sure have

caused me a lot of trouble. It would have been better if my driver had finished you off. I just came to see if you were going to make it. Between you and me, you're not."

Officer Monroe burst through the hospital door with guns drawn. "Put your hands in the air. You're under arrest," he yelled out.

Before Mike put his hands on his head, he smiled down at Henry and snapped his index finger, leaving him writing in pain.

Officer Monroe was glad he listened to that architect, Stephanie. After he and his partner controlled the crowd at the castle, he and about twenty VIPs demanded explanations. The crazy, kilt-wearing Scot had asked them to follow him to the chapel, where he explained everything.

Much of it had been boring history. He explained about General Oglethorpe; his good friend, Robert Castell; a family land grant and bringing Scots to help build and settle. Then he got into the exciting part of what they witnessed on television. Oglethorpe had returned to England and visited Scotland. He had gone to Edinburgh in search of warriors to help protect Savannah from nearby Spaniards. He was approached by a group of Jacobites in hiding, almost two hundred in all. They wanted to flee as a form of religious salvation. His parents were Jacobites, so he was always lenient toward them. Oglethorpe told them when to meet him at the docks in Inverness. The group was camped out two days prior, eagerly waiting. It wasn't until they were two days at sea that they shared their victory. They had snuck into Edinburgh castle. They were seen by the guards at their exit, but no blood had been shed. They had secretly taken the bones of Saint Margaret. For months, they had watched the British troops destroy their churches, trample on consecrated hosts, destroy relics, stained glass windows, and anything else that would remind Scots of their Catholic faith. They decided they would try to save the Pearl of Scotland and devised a plan. But the dream became plausible when General Oglethorpe came looking for volunteers to build a castle in the new settlement of Savannah.

Officer Monroe had never gotten into history much. He was the one that liked to make history, not read about it. But this story intrigued him. "Can you tell us about the glow in the room?"

Philip explained about the winter solstice sun and the use of glass to direct the sun's rays toward the stone. They all gathered around the rock, imagining what lay beneath.

"We're gonna need to see this skull," Officer Munroe continued, and everyone in the room agreed.

"Oh no, you're not," came a voice from the back of the room. Bishop Clark moved towards the front. No one had recognized him in street clothes and assumed he was with the other city and state representatives.

"Bishop Clark," Stephanie greeted him. "Welcome."

"Thank you," he answered with every bit of grace and poise he emanated wherever he went. He turned to Officer Munroe, "Forgive me for my outburst, Officer. Believe me, no one in this room wants to see the Pearl of Scotland as much as I do. Still, we must proceed cautiously. This is a 1,000-year-old skull that has been protected for the last 250 years. We must handle it carefully." He turned to Philip and put him on the spot, "Don't you agree, my son?"

"Yes, Father. I mean, yes, Bishop."

"Good. I have already put in a call to an assistant to the

pope. Since this is an international relic, we should be advised on how to continue." He opened his hands toward the group. "May God lead us on how to proceed."

Philip nervously cleared his throat. "I believe we're done here today. If anyone has further questions, please contact me before leaving."

As soon as everyone began to shuffle, Stephanie walked straight to Officer Monroe. "I'm worried about Mr. Lane." The officer nodded as he gave her his full attention. "You know how I told you that Tommy Morgan was bribing Mr. Lane with something; I'm not sure what. Tommy wanted this land to build a casino, but he's just the local thug. He's been working with someone bigger and better. Today's news report has sunk the casino idea, which will make some people very angry."

The officer added, "And angry people make bad decisions."

Stephanie nodded and walked with him down the stairs and out the door. Stephanie watched him walk quickly across the bridge, then noticed someone on the other side. It was just a shadow of the man, but she recognized him just the same. The strange man from her office and the park was just on the other side of the small bridge. She knew the police kept people from crossing, but he was here just the same. She had questioned whether seeing him a second time was a coincidence. Now, she knew it was no coincidence.

She walked back into the castle. It had finally grown quiet, with only a few people still talking with Philip. The chill of the cold stones cut through her top, and she wrapped her arms across her chest for warmth. She heard the faint sound of a flute playing softly in the distance and remembered her first morning in Edinburgh. The songs changed from one melancholy tune to another.

As Philip walked down the stairs, she noticed her friend Mrs. Holmes and the bishop were the last two guests. Philip felt for her hand and pulled her closer. The bishop thanked them and said goodbye. Mrs. Holmes wrapped Stephanie in a hug. "We really don't run out of options until we're six feet under, do we?" she whispered in her ear. Then, she reached out to Philip's hand. "We still need to do something to turn a profit in the next week. May I suggest charging for parking?" She air-kissed them both and left.

Stephanie looked over the bridge, but no one was on the other side. When Philip pulled Stephanie to sit on the stairs, she told him about the man who had been stalking about. Philip seemed to grow in size as he sat up protectively.

"I'll tell you if I see him again. But there's nothing we can do right now. Let's relax. It's been a long day," she said.

They settled into each other while listening to the fife player, and both began to unwind. Philip hummed along as the flute melodically began to play the next song. When the song got to the chorus, he chimed in,

"The Jacobite's last stand
Was found on unchartered land,
As they brought the Pearl to safety
To rest on foreign sand."

46

MAPS

"Did you guys notice my butt?" Stephanie asked the tribe. She had finally watched the news story and was mortified.

"No. We didn't notice anything," Kathleen answered, trying to keep a straight face.

"But we all want to know if you've taken on a new job as a plumber now?" Agnes teased.

"Yeah, got crack?" Maggie added, then snorted with a laugh. The snort made the table laugh.

"Oh my gosh. I just helped discover a missing treasure of sorts, and my very best friends are making fun of my outfit. Shame on all of you!"

Not knowing if she was serious, they each stifled their laugh until Stephanie burst out, "Wouldn't you know it? I finally get my moment of glory and expose myself in front of all of Savannah."

"All of Savannah? Try again," Kathleen said.

"The whole U.S.?" Stephanie asked.

"Bigger," Agnes replied.

Stephanie groaned, "I exposed myself to the world."

"That would be it," Kathleen agreed.

Another groan rolled out, "It's all your fault, Jan. You know that, don't you? You're the one who talked me into buying those jeans."

"My fault? I may have introduced you to midrise jeans, but I distinctly remember telling you to wear long shirts with them."

Latrice piped in, "Do you really think anyone was looking at your outfit when you opened the box to Saint Margaret's skull? None of us had noticed until you pointed it out to us." She shook her head in amazement, "The whole thing is mind-blowing. Really, Stephanie. I've watched it a hundred times. And the way you and Philip worked together was so sweet. We're really proud of you." The whole table agreed.

"Thank you. I love you guys." She squeezed her friends' hands on each side of her and smiled at the other three across the table.

"I love our Christmas lunch," Agnes said with a sigh as she pulled five small presents from her bright orange tote. "Don't y'all miss our holiday PJ spend the night?"

"It's probably my fault we no longer have those. It's just too hard with little ones at home," Kathleen explained. "Maybe, we're just growing up."

They looked at one another. Each shaking their heads, they agreed in unison, "NO! That's not it." They didn't think of themselves as adults. Especially when they were all together. They were still Saint Vincent's Academy high school seniors who would do anything in the world for each other.

Stephanie looked around the room. They had unanimously agreed to come to The Common Restaurant for their Christmas lunch. They had been a few times before, and the food and atmosphere were the best. None of the group had ever ordered a bad meal, and that was saying something for six picky women. The front glass windows offered a nice view of the Marshall House hotel. But today, they could watch Broughton Street's many last-minute Christmas shoppers.

Turning back to the group, she asked, "Who's coming to Hogmanay?"

"We all are. We wouldn't miss the party of the year. It's all over the news. You're gonna have hundreds to thousands of people there. Do you have room for everyone?"

"Yes. The island itself is huge, with large open fields to park in. The same people who built the walking bridge are securing the main bridge, so trucks can come across. We are setting up food trucks near the marsh, and Philip is opening the downstairs of the castle and lighting big fires in both fireplaces. Then, at midnight, there will be fireworks shot from Wassaw Sound. It should be a blast."

They all agreed to meet on New Year's Eve. Stephanie couldn't think of a better way to ring in the new year than with her sweet friends.

After lunch, Stephanie decided to stay on Broughton Street and join the throng of Christmas shoppers. She had been so busy at the castle that she was down to the wire buying Christmas gifts for her loved ones. Broughton Street cut right through the heart of town. It was one of the many streets that paralleled the Savannah River. It was filled with shops and restaurants and was always busy with people. At night, it was lit up with white lights and Christmas decorations. She hoped that she would be finished before they were turned on.

As she walked the shop-lined street, her thoughts drifted to the many shoppers like herself who had purchased gifts on Broughton Street. It had been the center of Savannah shopping for over one hundred years. Her dad even had an old black and white photo of Broughton Street with the street cars running and people scrambling about their day. The thought made her think of Scotland and the people in Beauly going about daily town life. Philip had mentioned how Savannah was laid out similarly, but she hadn't noticed it before.

In a very short amount of time, she purchased gifts for her family and Philip and also found a festive top for Christmas Mass. The added bonus was that she could walk off some of her lunch and all of the buzz from her lunch mojito.

She then ran by the grocery store to pick up the ingredients for her Christmas dish. Mrs. Wilmot had miraculously taken over the Christmas lunch menu and asked each of them to make a dish for the meal. Stephanie had volunteered for sweet potato casserole. She had found a recipe in Southern Living Magazine a few years back, and it always came out perfectly. It was the only side dish she made that everyone raved about.

While downtown, she swung by her office and was embarrassed to find her undecorated door. All the surrounding offices had decorated their buildings with swags or, at the very least, a wreath on the door. Some even had lights or other fun decorations. Her door was bare. She didn't even have a Christmas tree up at her house. Running back and forth from the castle had taken every bit of her energy. She had barely seen her family in the last several weeks but was looking forward to spending lots of time with them on Christmas.

She opened her door to a pile of mail. She had finished all her jobs, except her Daffin Park renovation, the week prior but still had bids and correspondence outstanding that required her attention. Carrying everything to her desk, she slowly began to go through all the mail. Job offers, proposals, and resumes flooded the space around her. It had only been a week since the news report. Still, so many people had reached out to her.

Amidst the letters was a small, padded 9 x 12 envelope. Opening it, she found the cigar tube from Daffin. She had sent it off for authentication after lunch with her family when Mrs. Wilmot said it looked like coordinates.

The letter thanked her for her discovery. It then said that the metal tube itself was made by a company in Germany in the 1930s. It was a thermidor used to keep cigars fresh. The etchings on the case were, indeed, coordinates. They had included two nautical maps. One was of the Savannah River channel, and the other was to Wassaw Sound.

47

THE WEDDING

Stephanie stood in the back of the church, staring down at her bouquet. So much had happened over the year. She could barely remember how it felt without Philip. She found it funny how her mind had erased all lonely memories before him.

She glanced over at Keith, fiddling with his tuxedo tie. He wouldn't be comfortable again until he was wearing only his undershirt. She moved her gaze to her sister in the classy bridesmaid's dress, bending to tie a ribbon in her daughter's hair. Stephanie smiled, knowing she would retie that same ribbon ten times over the course of the day.

The minute she saw her dad, a huge lump rose into her throat. She swallowed hard, trying to send it away. She even cleared her throat, hoping it would help, but finally accepted that the feeling was there to stay. Her dad had wanted this for so long. *Just look at him,* she thought. *Standing tall and proud, ready to show off.*

She tiptoed across the tile floor and quietly cracked the

church door to peek inside. Her friends were all sitting together towards the front, whispering to one another in their "not so quiet" way. They all had shown up for her. It was probably hard for some of them to arrange their schedules, but they figured it out for her. Because that's what they did for each other, show up.

She returned to her place, closed her eyes, and acknowledged the moment. At this specific time in her life, everything was perfect. She gripped her flowers tighter, almost scared to let the moment pass. She knew that things wouldn't always be perfect in her life, but thinking of everyone she had just viewed, she knew she could get through anything that lay ahead.

When the wedding march began to play, the main doors flew open. She watched her nieces slowly lead the way, pretending to throw petals. Keith escorted her sister, who followed directly behind, and then it was her turn. She took a deep breath, squared her shoulders, and prayed she wouldn't trip going down the aisle. As she approached the halfway mark, her friends began to wave at her, and she gave them a quick wink. When she got closer to the front, she locked eyes with Philip. Although she missed his kilt, he looked handsome in his new navy suit. A huge smile moved across his face, the kind of smile that said, "You have my heart."

She turned her attention back to the altar where her dad was waiting. He looked at Stephanie and winked as she passed and took her place beside her sister. She turned just in time to watch Mrs. Wilmot meet her father at the altar.

It was a simple wedding Mass, but the priest had known her dad and Mrs. Wilmot for years, so it was very personal.

During the exchange of vows, Stephanie subconsciously touched her engagement ring. She looked to Philip, who held her gaze. This would be them soon. They had only been engaged for a few weeks, yet she could hardly wait to be married. They had decided to call the church and pinpoint a day after the castle's ribbon-cutting ceremony in October. Still, now she began to worry if she could wait that long.

The August heat usually slowed everyone down in Savannah, but the work at the castle seemed to speed up. Over and above that, she had to turn away clients for the first time in her life. Every person in Savannah who purchased a historic house knew they had treasures inside and hoped she would find them in their renovations. It had become comical to hear the stories people concocted to entice her to take their job. Most houses were fascinating, with their history unfolding during every stage of construction. However, most of them would never find anything even close to a holy relic inside, though one might never know.

Stephanie was currently working on a renovation on 37th Street that was once the Little Sisters of the Poor Chapel in the late 1800s. She had noticed the familiar feeling when she walked into the chapel, the same feeling she had the first time she had walked into the chapel at the castle. It made her wonder if there could be more behind those walls, too. But she was sure of one thing. If so, it would reveal itself over time.

48

THE LOOKOUT

The colors in the sky set the perfect prelude for the sunrise that morning. Stephanie watched as it slowly crept into many shades of pink and blue. Until finally, she had to turn from its intensity. She stood on the lookout of the castle and let her eyes sweep across the marsh. The October gold of the sea grass seemed to glow in the morning sun. It swayed as the breeze off the Atlantic Ocean carried the scent of the marsh across the land. It was an acquired smell but a constant reminder to all Savannahians that they were part of this seaside city.

The silence of the morning was almost deafening compared to the day before. It had been the busiest day at the castle, with hundreds of people enjoying the ribbon-cutting celebration. Every dignitary and city employee had attended, along with Benedictine Military School, who brought their entire military brigade out to honor one of their past sergeants. It was a day full of recognizing many men and women who had made Savannah the beautiful city it is today.

During the service, they christened several historical markers. There was one for General Oglethorpe and the land grant he obtained from King George II to protect Savannah. Robert Castell also was given a marker to reward his brilliant architecture. And there was a separate marker near the marsh for Sergeant Albert Muller, a WWII war hero. With the signs now in place, the property surrounding the castle had quickly taken on the look of a state park with its many marked paths and signs. She was happy with the number of people who came to enjoy it.

Philip and Stephanie had taken the beauty of the castle itself and blended it with the property that sat on its outskirts. They had been approved for plans following the example of Pennyghael Castle, which they had visited in Scotland. Just like any state park, visitors could enjoy the property. They could walk the many trails around the castle and marshes and even lodge in the outlying cottages. They were currently up to five, with the original one used by the project manager, Philip. The long-term plan included an inn that would sit on the cove of Wassaw Sound.

Everyone had already begun to ask if they would be hosting another Hogmanay this year since last year had been such a success. She had never seen so many people at any New Year's Eve function. She smiled, thinking back to her and Philip collecting one dollar from each car for parking just to fulfill the terms of the land grant. They had stood at the end of the long entrance to the property, collected the dollar, and handed them a Xerox-copied map of the land and castle. Vehicles had been backed up for what seemed to be miles waiting to attend their first Hogmanay. Each car was shocked their New Year's Eve festivities were only costing them one dollar.

As the night progressed, she and Philip could hear the bagpipes and commotion from the end of the long drive. They eventually stopped collecting money and hopped on the tailgate of a slow-moving pickup truck. They were shocked at the sight of the castle lit up, the food trucks spaced out around the property, and the visitors dancing on the back lawn to the Scottish sounds of Savannah Pipe and Drums. The night ran way past the midnight fireworks show until she finally had to kick the last hoodlums, the tribe, out after three a.m.

She wondered how they would pull off Hogmanay this year since they no longer owned the castle. In the first week of January, Philip had donated the castle to the state of Georgia. At first, there had been much confusion since the holy relics were inside. However, the Pontifical Commissioner of Sacred Archaeology pointed out how to blend both elements. "The 'alleged' holy relic of Saint Margaret is actually part of the history of the Scots seeking religious freedom. The combined picture of the castle and relic should be celebrated. There is no reason why we should try to separate the two."

Still, much research was involved in verifying the remains of a 1000-year-old saint whose body had been moved by a group of Highland warriors over 250 years ago. A team of scientists had already reserved their cottages for December to watch for the winter solstice. The pin she found in the chapel helped aid the authentication process. The penannular brooch had been made from bronze material dated back to the ninth century. The brooch itself had an addition made to it at a later time. Pearls had been forged into its cross-section. And not just any pearls, Scottish pearls dating to the 11th century pulled from the River Tay outside of Edinburgh. That fact alone tied the relic to Scotland in the 11th century. No further research was needed for her to verify the remains of Saint Margaret. She knew in her heart it was true.

Stephanie looked out over the marsh again to mentally mark the sun's placement, then left the lookout. As she rounded the last few steps and walked through the great hall, she noticed someone walking in the back of the property. The gates were closed, and the scheduled open times for the day began at ten o'clock, so she wondered who it could be. She walked purposefully towards the back of the castle, peering into the open stretch behind.

Just like always, there he was. The mysterious man who kept appearing around her was standing on the back lawn of the castle. Fear rose inside of her. She could turn and run out the front and across the walking bridge to get Philip or hide inside the castle until he left. She was sure he hadn't seen her. And honestly, he didn't seem to be looking for her. He stood beside the marsh, looking away from the castle. She heard the fifer softly playing at that moment and knew she wasn't alone. Just like on the battlefield, the fifer gave her courage. This time, she trapped him in the back; there was nowhere to skirt off. So, she held her head up tall and walked out the back.

He didn't hear her approach. He was standing in front of the marker of the German soldier, Albert Muller. He was reading slowly and had swiped a tear from his eye. There was obviously more to this supposed stalker than she understood. She stopped walking and let him have his quiet moment. When he finished, he turned to leave, and they both jumped in surprise. He seemed embarrassed and looked around to see if other people had witnessed the scene.

"I'm sorry if I startled you," she began. "It's just that I've seen you several times in passing, and it seemed like you were intentionally seeking me out. But just now, I realized I might have been mistaken."

"Hello, Ms. Normand," he timidly answered. His eyes darted around the lawn, then to the ground before him. Then finally met hers. "My name's Harry Wilson. My uncle is Buddy Elders."

Stephanie nodded slowly. "Nice to meet you. Why haven't you introduced yourself before?"

"I didn't want to bother you. Well, that's not entirely true. Let's just say there's some family drama I didn't want to bother you with."

Stephanie took a deep breath and decided that honesty was always the best policy. "Mr. Wilson. You have scared me on several occasions. I have checked over my shoulder, worried you might be lurking, more than I care to admit. I think you at least owe me the courtesy of an explanation."

He looked mortified. "I scared you? What in the world could be scary about me?" Then he noticed the trace of fear in her eyes. "I'm so sorry I caused you any discomfort."

Stephanie's tension began to wane, but she simply said, "Thank you."

"Can you please be discreet with what I'm about to tell you?"

She nodded, looked to find the nearest bench, and motioned for them to sit down as he continued.

"First of all, thank you," he said. "You uncovered the body of a hero of Savannah. You could have let the police close the case, saying no record was found on the man. But you kept digging. Most of us would not."

Stephanie began to wonder how he knew all that he did while she anxiously waited for him to continue.

"As I said before, I'm Buddy Elder's nephew. My mother, Mary, was his sister."

Stephanie continued to nod while he explained.

"My mother passed away a few months ago. On her deathbed, she shared a secret with me. You see, I am the oldest of four children. And until then, I thought that was just how it was. But my mom told me that she had gotten pregnant out of wedlock when she was nineteen and married my father."

"That happened a lot back then," Stephanie said casually.

"Yes. But the person I thought was my father for my entire life turned out not to be my father at all. He was my dad, in every sense of the word, but he wasn't my birth father." He cleared his throat, swallowed hard, and went on. "My mom said she had fallen in love with a German spy. She said her family took him in when he worked at Benedictine Military School. He eventually moved next door into their rental unit. She said they had planned to marry until he disappeared. Her father told her that the Germans had found out he wanted to stay in the United States, so they killed him. She was devastated. She said she didn't get out of bed for a week. And then, she found out she was pregnant.

She married a longtime friend who had always loved her, and they had a wonderful life together. The story upset me, but it was a long time ago, and no one knew about it, so I let it pass. Then, last year, my uncle Buddy came to see me. He told me the rest of the story. And he told me how you had discovered the body and uncovered some of the story behind it. I've been following closely since then."

She stood and walked him back to the marker. At the top was a bronze etching of Albert's head that had been made from the old Benedictine photo. The marker read:

In gratitude to Sergeant Albert Muller, who single-handedly defended Savannah against a German U-boat attack on this site in 1943. He laid down his life for our country.

Stephanie looked at Al and asked, "What is your full name, Al?

"Albert," he answered. "She named me after my dad." A small laugh escaped his mouth as a tear passed down his cheek.

Stephanie touched his arm, "Would you like to visit his grave? We buried him in the castle's cemetery."

He looked surprised, "Yes! I'd like that very much. It's been haunting me how he has been under the lake all that time. I've walked by there hundreds of times and had no idea." He shook his head, closed his eyes, and added, "Thank you so much for finding him and giving him a proper burial." He looked at his shoes once again, then back to Stephanie. "I'd very much like to see where he was finally laid to rest."

As they walked toward the plot on the other side of the castle, Stephanie noticed Philip standing on the lookout, this time searching for her. She saw the concern in his eyes as he watched carefully until she threw a thumbs-up sign into the air. He nodded and smiled as he raised his hand into a small wave. She couldn't take her eyes off that spot on the lookout. She could imagine General Oglethorpe standing there, looking out over the Atlantic Ocean. Then, all the Scots who had stood watch to protect Savannah. She then thought of Albert standing at that spot, watching for the fellow countrymen he had deserted for the woman and city he loved.

That lookout had offered so much protection over the years. She narrowed her gaze onto Philip, who was watching her intently with a fierce gaze of protectiveness in his eyes. He was now the one standing watch over her. And for the first time in her life, she knew her foundation was strong. It consisted of her family, her faith, her friends, and most importantly, her soon-to-be Scottish husband, Philip.

The End

ACKNOWLEDGMENTS

I've thought about my mom numerous times while writing this book. She has shared so many of her wonderful traits with me; the love of architecture and house plans, the gift of writing, and the ability to cook good ole' Southern dishes, to name a few. But the best gift my mom has given me is her constant love and encouragement. Quite the opposite from the character of Stephanie's mom in this book, my mom is the best of the best, and I am thankful for her every day.

I'd also like to recognize my crazy and wonderful Scotland travel companions. Although they had already planned their trip far in advance, they let me join at the last minute. We took Scotland by storm and saw almost every inch of it in ten days. When I see our group text name, "Team Scotland," on my cell phone, I know I'll get a good laugh. Thank you for an unforgettable adventure.

God has blessed me with many talented individuals who help me bring this novel to fruition. Thank you to my editor, Patrice MacArthur; my cover designer, Sarah Hansen with Okay Creations; my fantastic marketing team at Cecilia Russo Marketing; and my sister for her many suggestions and constant love. I am most grateful for all of your hard work.

To all those who call me Mom (or Mayme), thank you for your unconditional love and support. You are the ones who witness me staring into space while I work out a scene in my head or typing away while dinner burns on the stove. Each of you loves me through the craziness of writing. My heart is full.

To my husband, John. Thank you for being my rock and letting me lean on you to complete this book. It is not until we read it aloud that I know it's ready to be released into the world. Thank you, also, for still taking me dancing. I truly am spoiled-ass rotten.

And finally, to my readers. You are the ones that keep me writing. Thank you for giving me the privilege to entertain you...if only for a little while.

ALSO IN THE SAINTS OF SAVANNAH SERIES

THE BLESSING OF THE CELTIC CURSE

Leaving behind her fiancé, Jack, just weeks before her wedding, Kathleen embarks on a six-week trip to Knock, County Mayo, Ireland. While Kathleen digs into the lives of her ancestors, her life and that of the townsfolk of Knock become intimately bound in unimaginable ways.

THE SAVANNAH GONDOLIER

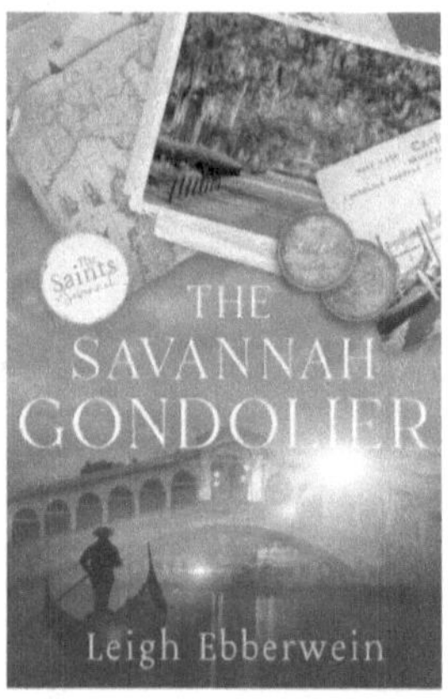

When Maggie reunites with her childhood friend, Leo, she realizes he is running from his life in Venice, Italy. After offering him a job at her haunted adventure kayak company, Leo plans a new future for himself. However, he needs Maggie's help. She jumps at the chance to travel to his hometown of Venice and quickly understands that she is also running from her life in Savannah, or at least from her broken heart.

STOP IN FOR A VISIT

If you love the beauty of Savannah and enjoy traveling the world through a novel, stop in for a visit to <u>Leighebberwein.com</u>. You'll find questions for your Book Club, live video scenes, up-to-date information on future books, and so much more!

www.ingramcontent.com/pod-product-compliance
Lightning Source LLC
Chambersburg PA
CBHW051135190726
48290CB00006B/1860